IMAGO

Eva-Marie Liffner

IMAGO

Translated from the Swedish by
Silvester Mazzarella

THE HARVILL PRESS
LONDON

Published by The Harvill Press 2005

2 4 6 8 10 9 7 5 3 1

Copyright © Eva-Marie Liffner 2003

English translation copyright © Silvester Mazzarella 2005

This book has been published with the financial assistance of the Swedish Institute

Originally published with the title *Imago* by Bokförlaget Natur och Kultur, Stockholm, 2003

Maps drawn by Reg Piggott

First published in Great Britain in 2005 by
The Harvill Press
Random House, 20 Vauxhall Bridge Road,
London SW1V 2SA

Random House Australia (Pty) Limited
20 Alfred Street, Milsons Point, Sydney,
New South Wales 2061, Australia

Random House New Zealand Limited
18 Poland Road, Glenfield,
Auckland 10, New Zealand

Random House South Africa (Pty): Limited
Endulini, 5A Jubilee Road, Parktown 2193, South Africa

The Random House Group Limited Reg. No. 954009
www.randomhouse.co.uk/harvill

A CIP catalogue record for this book is available from the British Library

ISBN 1 84343 146 7

Papers used by Random House are natural, recyclable products made from wood grown in
sustainable forests; the manufacturing processes conform to the environmental regulations of
the country of origin

Typeset by Palimpsest Book Production Limited,
Polmont, Stirlingshire

Printed and bound in Great Britain by
Mackays of Chatham plc, Chatham, Kent

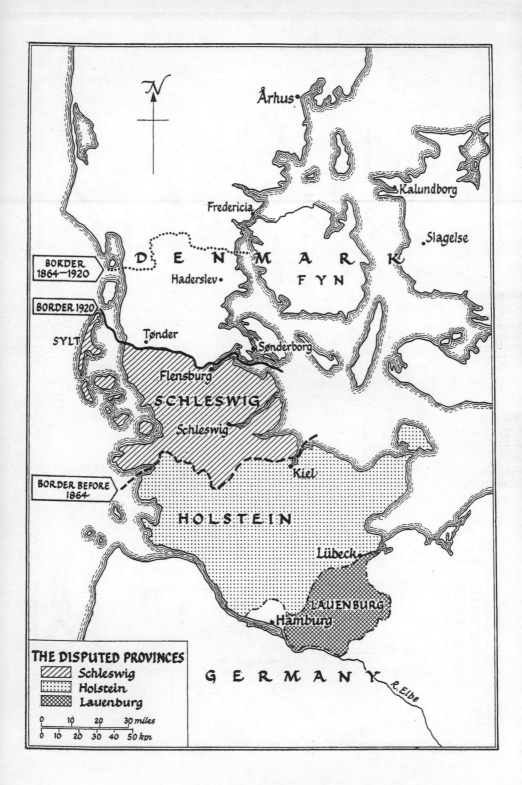

N

Århus •

• Kalundborg

Fredericia •

Slagelse •

D E N M A R K

BORDER
1864—1920

Haderslev •

F Y N

BORDER 1920

SYLT

Tønder •

Sønderborg •

Flensburg

SCHLESWIG

Schleswig •

BORDER BEFORE
1864

Kiel •

HOLSTEIN

Lübeck •

LAUENBURG

Hamburg •

THE DISPUTED PROVINCES

Schleswig
Holstein
Lauenburg

0   10   20   30 miles
0 10 20 30 40 50 km

G E R M A N Y   R. Elbe

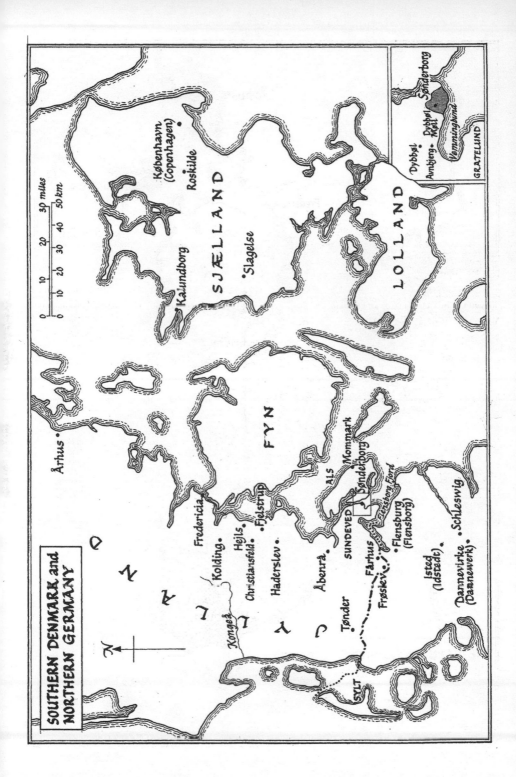

SOUTHERN DENMARK and
NORTHERN GERMANY

SJÆLLAND

LOLLAND

København
(Copenhagen)

Roskilde

Slagelse

Kalundborg

Århus

FYN

Fredericia

Kolding

Hejls

Christiansfeld

Felstrup

Haderslev

Åbenrå

Tønder

Kongeå

ALS

Mommark

Sønderborg

SUNDEVED

Fårhus

Frøslev

Flensburg
(Flensborg)

Isted
(Idstede)

Dannevirke
(Dannewerk)

Schleswig

SYLT

50 km
30 miles
40
20
30
10
20
10
0
0

Sønderborg

Dybbøl
Knit

Vemmingbund

Dybbøl

Annbjerg

GRATELUND

IMAGO -inis, f. (root IM, whence also imitor and sim -ilis). **I.** Objective, **A.** Lit., **1, a,** gen., *an image, representation, portrait, figure, bust, statue*; ficta, *a statue*, Cic.; picta, *painted bust*, Cic.; *a portrait engraved on a seal-ring*; est signum notum, imago avi tui, Cic.; **b,** esp., imagines (majorum), *waxen figures, portraits of ancestors* who had held curule offices, placed in the atria of Roman house, and carried in funeral processions, Cic.; **2,** *a likeness, counterfeit*; imago animi et corporis tui, filius tuus, Cic.; imagi animi vultus est, Cic.; **3, a,** *the shade or ghost of a dead man;* imagines mortuourum, Cic.; **b,** *a dream;* somni, noctis, *a dream*, Ov.; **c,** in the Epicurean philosophy, *the mental idea or representation of a real object*, Cic.; **4,** *an echo*; laus bonorum virtuti resonat tamquam imago, Cic.; **5,** in discourse, *a metaphor, simile, image;* hac ego si compellor imagine, Hor. **B.** Transf., *the appearance, pretence;* pacis, Tac.; decoris, Liv.; imaginem republicae nullam reliquerunt, *they left no shadow or trace of the republic*, Cic. **II.** Subjective, **1,** *the appearance*, imago venientis Turni, Verg.; **2,** *the image, idea, conception, mental representation of any object or event*; tantae caedis, Ov.; tantae pietatis, Verg.

IMAGO *(Entomology)* the final and fully developed adult stage of an insect, typically winged.

DYBBØL (German Düppel), parish or village on the Sundeved peninsula in northeast Schleswig. Between Als Sound and the village the land rises to a height of 72m to form the so-called "Dybbøl Ridge", which slopes down gently to the north and east, but quite steeply to the west and south. In 1861, when the relationship between Denmark and Prussia was becoming increasingly tense following disputes between the two countries over the exact location of the Prusso-Danish border within the duchies of Schleswig and Holstein and over the Danish annexation of Schleswig, Denmark built ten small redoubts or forts at Dybbøl to form a curve from Als Sound in the north over the ridge to Vemmingbund in the south. On February 5 and 6, 1864, the Danes abandoned their historic "Dannevirke" fortifications west of the town of Schleswig and retreated in good order to Dybbøl, which was then encircled by the Prussians between the 17th and 22nd of the same month. The siege which followed caused heavy losses, particularly to the Danes. Eventually the Prussians managed to extend their trenches almost up to the redoubts, which their infantry stormed on April 18, killing a further 4,800 Danes and capturing 3,400. In 1865 Prussia erected a victory monument on the ridge.

FRØSLEVS MOSE,
WEDNESDAY, AUGUST 30, 1938

WHEN YOU CRACK an old bone, it gives out a very particular sound. Not dull and juicy, like the marrow-filled bone in a fresh leg of pork or lamb, but sharp, dry and staccato like the sound of a twig snapping underfoot on a forest path.

The man was out in the middle of the bog when it happened, under a blue dome of late summer sky broken here and there by thin white strips of cloud frayed at the edges like worn canvas. Occasionally these clouds slipped in front of the sun, tinting the light with yellow. The only other sounds were of birds, marsh harriers and curlews flying low over the swampy land, which now, at the end of August, was almost completely silent. The man had been digging methodically, occasionally leaning for a moment on the handle of his spade, which after years of use was as smooth and soft as skin. His body was telling him that he had about another hour's work to do before he could take his midday break.

The man's flat turf-spade had cut right through what had once been a shinbone, though it now looked more like a thin branch than anything else since the body's tissues had absorbed so much of the bog's juices, of its dark, muddy, humus-rich water. He was cutting turf for Viberød Manor and had already dug out a good two square metres in fat, dark squares which he'd carefully stacked on his cart. Now he put down his spade and bent over the pit he'd dug. He could see more pieces of bone in the ground, and something that looked like coarse cloth stuck fast to the bone sticking up from the turf. He knelt down. Bog smells stung his nose: time, water, putrefaction and oblivion. Smells which almost had a taste, a physical presence on his tongue. From the vegetable life on the ground came the scent of heather, hot sun and heavy late summer. He closed his eyes, suddenly made dizzy by the heat and the clinging odours. Water was rising in the pit, running and babbling as if from an underground spring. A fat, oily film formed immediately on the surface, reflecting the summer sky as if clouds and sky were also down there in the ground, though in a different, duller range of colours than the clouds and sky overhead. He opened his eyes again and looked carefully around him, but nothing had changed in the landscape. A raptor swooped on its prey so fast that it almost seemed to fall through the air. That was all.

Carefully the man began to free the body. At first he used his spade but soon laid it aside to dig with his bare hands. This he did slowly, with a gentleness he himself didn't quite understand. The earth was cold and heavy under his fingers. Unyielding. Sweat ran into his eyes. It tired him to hold himself bent forward over the pit, and he could feel his shirt sticking to his body. His breathing became as heavy and laborious as if he'd been running. A fly crept over the sweat that streaked his face; irritated, he whisked it away. It flew off but came back, obstinately searching for somewhere else to land, and discovered the strange thing sticking out of the turf. And another face, this one dark brown, tanned to leather by the bog's resourceful juices.

*

The creature lay bent double with its legs drawn up to its chin as if in sleep. The lower part of one leg had come loose and stuck up at a sharp angle from the body. The man moved carefully in the pit, trying as far as possible not to touch skin, bone or leather. Soon the body was nearly free of the earth and seemed complete with torso, arms, legs and head. Locks of reddish hair clung to its scalp. The man thought the hair remarkably fine in colour. Resplendent. It seemed a wonder that a body could have lain at peace in this place, protected by turf and spring floods from ditch-digging and the underground burrowing of small animals. Beside it lay what looked like a backpack or knapsack with rough leather corners. Whether this had been fabric or leather was impossible to say, it was so saturated with mud and water. A piece of cloth, now half rotted, had been spread over the body. A coat or cloak? The rotten cloth clung to the legs and torso like an extra skin; it must have been pressed into its present shape by the weight of the soil. There was no trace of shoes or boots because both feet were missing. The bones of the lower parts of both legs had been cut off at one clean stroke, as if by a butcher's cleaver. Round the slender neck a rope had been looped and pulled tight in the sort of knot the man liked to use when hanging hares on his larder wall, where they remained for several days until they were ready for the pot. He was amazed at how familiar the knot looked and how much tension there still seemed to be in the rope, which had been cut off abruptly a foot or so from the neck. He touched the end of it cautiously. Whatever had been done here had been done long ago, that was clear. The body smelt of earth and water like the bog itself, and even when he came very near he couldn't tell their smells apart. When he bent forward his shadow fell over the dark face, and for a split second the dead man's expression seemed to change as if he was suddenly more fatigued or in greater pain, or as if now his peace had been disturbed he must again suffer agonies in sunlight. When a curlew cried out in shrill lamentation across the sky and the desolate wooden-bridged marshland, the turf-cutter could take no more. Something of a child's irrational fear of darkness and night came over him even though it was still broad daylight. He heaved himself out of the pit, crawling over its slippery edge as quickly as his strength would allow. Suddenly there was fear in the air, as though the dead man was sharing his last conscious emotion. The turf-cutter grabbed his spade and ran for his life as though someone was after him. The bog landscape remained as still and peaceful as before.

*

Frøslevs Mose lies near the small town of Grænsebyen in the far south of Jutland, right on the German border. If you look at a map you'll hardly be able to get your fingernail between Grænsebyen in Denmark and Flensburg in Germany. That's how close the two towns are to each other.

On the afternoon of August 30 information reached Grænsebyen police station in the form of a telephone call from Viberød manor reporting the discovery of a dead body out in the peat. The voice on the telephone was disturbed and breathless, a woman calling on behalf of her husband, who had gone to lie down straight after his dinner, having first unburdened himself of a garbled story. The woman found it difficult to stick to the point, repeating constantly and irrelevantly how unlike his usual self her husband had been when he'd come home, so that Police Constable Jens Madsen in Grænsebyen could get no clear idea of where the body was. The most precise information the woman could give was that it was in an area out on the bog "where we started cutting peat last spring", as if the doings of those at Viberød must be known to everybody. Madsen was not by nature an impatient man, but he was becoming irritated. He tried to get the woman to let him speak to her husband, but she refused. She was phoning from the gate lodge, some distance from where they lived. Her husband had had one drink and then another, and had finally pulled the blanket over himself and gone to sleep facing the wall, and she flatly refused to wake him.

So-called bog people had been found in the vicinity before so Police Constable Madsen didn't immediately think of murder. He had himself just eaten a substantial meal of beer, sausage and sauerkraut, so he could well understand the turf-cutter's decision to grab forty winks after his dinner. Nonetheless the matter had to be reported, and his boss, Police Chief Rav, was a man who attached great importance to the formalities. So Madsen started a report, forming each letter with care. *Place: Grænsebyen. Today's date: August 30, 1938. Time: Three in the afternoon.* The nib of his fountain pen caught in the paper and spattered, making an irritating inkblot. A fat bluebottle buzzed and bumped angrily against the frosted windowpane. The sound made him sleepy. An after-dinner lull had fallen over the little Danish town, and Jens Madsen felt a craving for something sweet, a jam-cake perhaps or a piece of nougat from the box on the hall table at home, the one left over from his wife's fortieth birthday. Both Madsen's palate and his eye had a weakness for sweet things. The police station was only a few hundred metres from his home, and his warm uniform was making him sweat. But Tomas Rav was bound to come in later, and Madsen would have to be ready to report. Which meant that every fact, however trivial, must be written down. He buttoned his collar and sat up straight. Once again his pen rasped over the paper. *Reporting the discovery of a body . . .*

T HERE ARE OF course many ways of starting out to make the Great Discovery. I'm not talking about splitting the nucleus of the quark or identifying the ingredients needed to create the drug that will give us eternal life, or perhaps eternal oblivion (one may be a prerequisite for the other). No, nothing like that. What I dream of is discovering a little piece of paper or a book no-one has noticed before. Or a box of papers. Documents. Let me be clear: I'm a historian. I search for the past. The only thing that has any real meaning for me is the hunt. Not the sort of hunting that goes on in forests or when you burst your lungs leaping over hedges and galloping across open fields – no, for me hunting means searching through dry-as-dust libraries, or private collections it's difficult to gain access to, or bundles of private letters I'm the first person to look at and find fascinating. That's my sort of prey. Call me Esmé.

*

It's not a common name in this country. My father, Kai, who died two or three years ago, admired the American writer J.D. Salinger and sent him a letter every year on their joint birthday. (Kai had been born on December 10, 1919, and had decided Salinger should share that day with him. In this Kai was not what you would call a serious researcher or historian.) But Jerome David Salinger was a shy man and never liked opening his front door to anyone far away over there in America.

I can imagine the postman wearily approaching that door and knocking on the frosted glass. Perhaps he tries to peep behind the dirty closed blinds even though he knows it's a waste of time. No sound can be heard from inside the house. It's wintry and cold in Cornish, New Hampshire. A thin white column of smoke rises straight up from the chimney and from somewhere comes the incessant hoarse barking of a dog. No-one shouts at the dog to shut up. The landscape seems to be holding its breath. By previous arrangement the postman leaves a bottle of bourbon on the doorstep, nothing more, and goes away again. It's the same this particular morning.

So the letters – all twenty of them – were returned to Kai unopened, and they became my first collection. He wrote "For Esmé" on the bundle, tied a piece of brown string round it and presented it to me as a memento of himself together with a water-damaged Parsifal-brand wristwatch which had stopped following a thoughtless swim some time in the 1960s. I haven't yet opened any of the letters. Kai had great plans that never came to fruition, and I've inherited those too. I suppose I'm afraid of being disappointed. His greatest interest – I forgot to say – apart from the hermit Salinger was the history of the American Civil War.

I live in the heart of the city, right behind the University, in a dark, narrow dead-end alley that reminds me of an intestine. I call it by a name I found on an old map, Lille Novicegade. Its real name isn't important. The fact is, long ago monks taught here. I can picture them singing in the Danish winter nights, loud and confident in their faith, at the same time striking a slightly false note as they break the ice on their water-barrel and dream in vain of institutions of higher learning in Paris or the comfortable warmth of Bologna. Probably some of them are still there now under the foundations of the present buildings, wedged fast for ever in cold and darkness. Part of their garden was near what is now the entrance to the building I live in. I can imagine narrow winding pathways and perfumed herb-beds, and allotments arranged as neatly as the beads on a rosary (and, presumably, the odd practical pigsty and vegetable patch).

*

My flat is small, not modern; one main room plus a littler one, a gas cooker, green doors and a loudly flushing toilet with a dark wooden seat. The cistern keeps up a constant soft babble like a little waterfall or spring. Over the washbasin hangs my only mirror, set rather high for my 152 centimetres, but at least I can see my straight brown hair, strong eyebrows and blue eyes (if I lowered the lid of the toilet and stood on it I'd be able to look at the rest of my body too, but I never do that).

Late in the evening or during the night I go over to the University and let myself into the Institute for Historical Studies, which it takes me exactly two hours to clean – I hoover the rooms and empty the waste baskets, and then, like an archaeologist with a sieve, I search meticulously through the material I find there. Mostly it's of no interest, but I have been known to make discoveries. I have access to a lot of junk but also a unique opportunity to make comparisons – the Middle Ages with the Renaissance, the Enlightenment with the Romantics, apples with pears. Something the other researchers daren't permit themselves for fear they'll be thought stupid. Interdisciplinary study in its noblest form. When I've finished cleaning I read.

I usually sit in Professor Rosen's room since it's the most spacious and also nearest to the main library. Besides, the window looks out on Frue Plads Square, so I can hear the clock strike on the cathedral of Vor Frue. It sounds muffled through glass, as if heard from afar. Maybe this has something to do with the shape of the room or the thickness of the old windowpanes. With time the glass has flowed down unevenly, distorting what you see through it. Maybe sound gets distorted in the same way. The striking of the clock plays over the surface, gliding like an instrument taking soundings at the bottom of the sea.

When I'm on my way home at dawn after a night's intensive study, I sometimes detect a whiff of cloves, cinnamon, aniseed or nutmeg, the kind of strong stuff people used in the Middle Ages to spice their not very fresh food. These smells come and go and are not specific to any place. No point in trying to trace them. Dawn's my favourite time of day.

It's always cold in Rosen's room in winter. The University lowered the central-heating setting after the oil crisis in the 1970s and hasn't changed it since then. Every bit of cold that wants to come in crackles in the radiators and taps at the windows. If you sit still it creeps slowly into your body. Which is why I take a thermos of strong, hot coffee with me and sit with my coat on – I have an ulster made of thick double-weave '50s wool. I found it in a flea-market one Sunday when I wasn't working. Under my ulster I wear a thick Norwegian sweater from which the lanolin hasn't been removed. I also wear woollen gloves from which I've cut the fingers. Even so the cold penetrates to my marrow.

I've developed a special interest in the Denmark of the 1860s and '70s, a period summed up in the word *Klunke*. Unfortunately Rosen's library doesn't have much to offer on this subject: three essential standard works and a few essays – none of them particularly outstanding – which I've secretly copied. *Klunke* actually means tassel or fringe, and refers to the obsession of the time with covering furniture legs right down to their feet, but to me what matters is the *sound* of the word, like water on its 10-kilometre route through the lead conduits of old Copenhagen, or bubbling in the shiny red round beer-vats in the New Carlsberg Brewery, or lapping as soft waves against the quays at Sortedams Sø. That sort of thing.

*

About three weeks ago I was sitting as usual fighting off fatigue in Rosen's room. I'd made a late start, because the first seminar that evening had run over, forcing me to wait for ages before I could start cleaning. The room was still filled with half-empty wine bottles, plastic mugs sticky with lipstick stains, and half-eaten cheese biscuits which looked as if they had been gnawed by a small rat, but I was able to identify the teeth confidently as belonging to Fräulein Ulrike Langer, a postgrad from Berlin and Rosen's latest sweetheart – Rosen is of course married and the father of five pimply adolescents, but he's incessantly randy. In one corner someone had organised an intimate picnic with wineglasses and camembert on the carpet. I didn't feel up to facing that miserable mess just yet. The stale smell of garlic, cigarillos and sour breath forced me to open one of the windows a crack despite the cold. Though to tell the truth, I wasn't feeling so much frozen as hot and overexcited by this invasion of my territory. I do understand that people have parties from time to time and eat and drink among the books, but I don't approve of it. Anyway, it was quiet now; there was no sound from the corridors, and despite everything I felt myself becoming increasingly calm. As usual I'd shrouded the reading lamp with a cloth to discourage prying eyes, and it spread a soft green light. It was like sitting in a nest. Soon the clock on the cathedral would loudly strike two, thus giving me an opportunity to close the window without making a sound.

*

But something was bothering me that night. Despite his weakness for cheap red wine and young postgrads with pony-tails – so long as they're female – Rosen is an original and conscientious researcher. He's also anxious to keep well ahead in the academic rat-race and is therefore constantly looking for worthwhile new fields for research. His predecessor as Professor at the Institute for Historical Studies was a legendary figure whose name is no longer mentioned, a *professor emeritus* considered to have lived up to his title since he has so clearly vanished from the world. I'd never managed to ferret out the name of this figure, but it is clearly hostility to his own immediate past that most stimulates Rosen's appetite for academic glory. He had recently sent to Berlin for some material once stamped SECRET, filed away in the German State Archive in the city's former Russian Zone and now accessible to the outside world for the first time. These documents were in an ugly brown cardboard box at the edge of the lighted area (someone had put a bundle of maps on top of the box, thus cleverly concealing it from curious eyes, but I saw it at once). Rosen – or more likely his bony secretary Dorthe W., so called to distinguish her from young Dorthe N. who works on the Middle Ages – hadn't yet cut through the mass of tough dark brown parcel tape that sealed the box, and the shadows in the room made it look larger than it really was. I had eyes for nothing else.

The box was a cube about 50 centimetres high with Rosen's name written in block capitals on the top. Nothing about it hinted at valuable or even personal contents. I knew from the bulky bags stored in the broom-cupboard that Rosen received packages of many different kinds. Junk mail usually comes neatly addressed these days, but bony Dorthe W. isn't easily taken in; she has a sharp eye when it comes to separating the wheat from the chaff. However, I knew this box had arrived late in the afternoon since I'd run into the carrier, a sweaty youth, down at the entrance as I was on my way to the library. That must have been why neither Dorthe W. nor Rosen had had a chance to explore this new and highly interesting *objet d'histoire*.

I approached the box cautiously with my ears pricked. It gave off a faint smell of old paper and archival cardboard, sour and damp but not at all unpleasant. Less predictably there was also another smell, of fire, but it was gone before I could fix it in my mind. The tape had rolled itself up into a string-like length that seemed intended for pulling. Enough said; the documents were an irresistible provocation to all my senses, and I gave in.

At the top was a packer's list. *Ordered from the National Archive in Berlin*, blah blah . . . I ran my eye down it quickly, and as I did so the cathedral clock struck two bronze blows. The papers Rosen had sent for dated from the late 1930s, a period just beginning to excite nervous interest at the Institute. Documents from the war years were no longer classified, so items from the late '30s had taken on a new significance, making it possible at last to fit the final piece into some puzzle or the final link into some chain in the way we historians love so much. In any case, most of the people our discoveries might embarrass were either dead or too old to be able to make a fuss. There was of course always the danger that inconvenient information might still put state grants and funds from big business at risk. But Rosen was ahead of the game as usual. I assume it had been at the most recent conference in Berlin that he'd made the contacts he needed. Getting special documents out of the German National Archive must have been like fishing for crabs in the Kyrillergraven moat – no doubt he'd had to use a tasty piece of bait. The first item listed was a copy of a Danish police report from August 1938. The light was too dim for me to be able to see the exact date it had been filed away by the Germans. During the Occupation? I put down the packer's list and concentrated on the contents of the report. Sprawling handwriting. *Reporting the discovery of a body*, I read. Suddenly someone flicked the main switch by the door, and the room was flooded with light.

*

Rosen's room is shaped like a large L. If you're by the door you can't see round the corner into the foot of the L – a circumstance Rosen makes the most of during his individual supervision sessions on Thursdays (don't ask me how I know . . .). So I was sure the night-watchman couldn't see me kneeling in front of Rosen's box. What I usually do once an hour while he's on his rounds is turn off the light and sit as quiet as a mouse, but this time I'd forgotten all about him. A simple case of cause and effect. *Causa sui*, the discovery caused itself, as Spinoza would have said. I'd been criminally careless.

I'd never stolen anything before, unless you count snipping off the odd rose in the Kongens Have gardens on lonely summer evenings, but now the situation was desperate. I decided to take one of Salinger's more down-to-earth pieces of advice, "Desperate times call for desperate measures." I shoved the police report and as many other documents as I could get hold of under my Norwegian sweater, shut the cardboard box and snatched up a wine bottle – all in less than a second.

It was the messy state of the room that worried me. But Mogensen the nightwatchman, always slow on his feet, as usual took plenty of time to make his way into the room. I could hear him breathing heavily through his short fleshy nose and could imagine his brown beard trembling. Presumably he was as scared as I was; his bunch of keys was jingling nervously against his fat thigh. He was preceded by a heavy smell of beer, which rapidly added itself to all the room's other smells, making the mixture even more unappetising. Professor Rosen's room now smelled like the bar at The Blue Grape in the small hours. Finally Mogensen rounded the corner, swaying slightly, and stared stupidly at me.

"Esmé," he brayed thickly. "Hell, you nearly scared me shitless."

He rocked backwards and forwards on his heels, struggling to keep his balance.

"What you doing here this time o' night, lass?" His eyes took in the irregular bulge under my sweater.

"Mus' be cold. Let me warm you up!" He took an unsteady step forward and knocked over an unfinished bottle of red wine. The contents ran out quickly, making a large kidney-shaped stain on the beige wall-to-wall carpet. A little reached the cardboard box.

"No thanks," I said, at the same time noisily dropping the empty bottle I was holding into a waste basket. Mogensen shifted his feet nervously. Rosen's pernickety about who has access to his room. He can't bear anyone prying into his research projects – except the raw young doctoral students (known as "food-gatherers") who gather information for him like diligent worker-bees serving their queen. Mogensen's job was to see but not touch. He gave me a pale smile; I was a witness. He got down and began nervously fumbling round the box and the carpet with a greasy handkerchief, mumbling about "wonderful lass" and "our secret".

By the time I locked the door to the Institute it was nearly 5 a.m. I'd cleaned and aired Rosen's room, and it looked no messier than usual. Mogensen had vanished into his cellar-hole down by the garage after helping me with the hoovering. He wasn't about to tell anyone what had happened, nor was I. I'd transferred the documents to my bag. *Tace lingua, dabo panem* as the Roman writer Petronius is supposed to have said – Hush, my tongue: I'll give thee bread – and *he* knew a good deal about hubris and tinpot dictators. I'd shoved the cardboard box under a table, where it lay hidden behind several piles of ageing copier paper. With a warm feeling of anticipation in my stomach I went home to Lille Novicegade and slept.

*

I didn't wake till the afternoon of the following day. It must have been after two, because the last rays of the sun were straggling in through the narrow windows. I lay still and watched them move across the old map of Copenhagen on the wall. The light seemed to wander up and down the streets, where noteworthy features like Christiansborg Castle, the Royal Theatre and the remains of the old city walls were drawn in light relief. In fact with the help of a magnifying glass you can walk about the map city. The light brushed against the Rosenborg Gardens, splintered by the old glass drop that hangs from a string in one of my windows. (It came from a chandelier that once belonged to a well-known actress called Frøken Jessen at the old Royal Theatre, the building pulled down in 1874. She's mentioned in one of Hans Christian Andersen's letters. Now all that's left is this single drop.) The sun's warmth carried the drop across the map. The spectrum settled at various points in 1860s Copenhagen. I took this as a good omen. Soon I too would have an opportunity to explore a bit of the past.

I'd hung my sweater over the back of a chair and set the documents carefully on my writing table. I always make sure I'm well rested before I tackle a new problem, and strong black coffee aids concentration and sharpens one's powers of perception. So I resisted the temptation to sit down at the table immediately and went into the kitchen to heat some water. Time's something I've got plenty of.

The back of the block I live in faces across an enclosed yard towards a tall building with greasy dark red brick walls which make a rugged, uneven line against the sky. Right at the bottom of the shaft formed by these buildings rattles and whirrs the ventilator of The Blue Grape, a pub where you can get virtually nothing but beer and a kind of unappetising small sausage. Sometimes the ventilator seizes up when some poor creature gets trapped in its mechanism and is ground to mincemeat, a mouse perhaps or a young bird that's tumbled down from the roof. When this happens the ventilator has to be taken apart and cleaned. There's also a row of elderly dustbins and what's supposed to be a garden area where all the plants died long ago from lack of light, except for one evergreen with a pale green trunk that has managed to survive in some miraculous way for years. My neighbour, an inquisitive old lady I usually avoid, says it's a Siberian larch. Maybe somewhere inside its dry bark it preserves a happy memory of Karelian gloom. Anyway, my kitchen window gives me an uninterrupted view of these familiar sights.

I looked down into the yard as I ground the coffee beans, but my thoughts were elsewhere. Before going into the kitchen I'd pulled on my sweater, which was full of the previous night's smells, especially stale smoke. For a moment I wondered what Mogensen's smell was like but banished the thought (washing clothes isn't something I attach much importance to; I avoid my building's own laundry room – a meeting place for residents obsessed with minding everybody's business but their own – preferring to take my dirty clothes to an anonymous coin-operated laundrette). Mogensen was too much of a coward to give anything away, I was sure of that. And Rosen wouldn't realise anything was missing from the box but the list of contents. I was the only one who knew everything, and knowledge is power, as Sir Francis Bacon might have said.

With the hot cup in my hand I settled down at the table. It was already 3.00, but I had no cleaning to do on Saturday evenings, so I was in no hurry. I carefully opened the first document, the police report, and began reading.

*

Place: Grænsebyen. Today's date: August 30, 1938. Time: Three in the afternoon.

FRØSLEVS MOSE,
THURSDAY, AUGUST 31, 1938

O N THURSDAY MORNING three men are ready to step out onto the bog. The dawn's damp and misty, a silent milk-white world that muffles their footsteps and restricts their field of vision to a few metres all round. The three are not at all alike. Dr Franz Aloysius Nagler has crossed the border from Flensburg in Germany, but he really belongs in Berlin, where he works as an assistant at the archaeological museum at Spree. He's a fat, rather stocky man, with a thick neck, like a caricature of one of those profiteers who prospered in the post-war world of the '20s. His friends call him F.A., which they pronounce in a clipped manner.

Police Chief Tomas Rav attaches a lot of importance to protocol but is so careless of his own appearance as to be almost shabby. He is tall and lanky, lean as a bloodhound in his long brownish coat. He's crushed his felt hat down on his head for the car trip out to the bog. His powerful jaws are clenched round a sour-smelling pipe, and no-one would ever dream of calling him anything other than "Police Chief". Not within his hearing, at least.

Young Gabriel Mayer stands a little apart from the others. He works as secretary to old Pastor Aronius of Grænsebyen. Mayer is responsible for making entries in the local parish register, and every death – even if it happened long ago – must be recorded. The damp has already penetrated his well-cut but thin jacket, and he's shaking with cold. Suffering from a bad hangover, too.

*

The three have come to the bog in Rav's car, a lacquered black 1927 Ford Model A, a faithful servant with no noticeable springs and a persistent oil leak. F.A. Nagler's in a bad mood because Rav has insisted on smoking his pipe in the chilly car; not only that, but the road through the plantation to the bog is hardly more than a convex sandy path, and so poorly maintained and full of holes that the three men have been thrown about in the car in an undignified manner. They've reached the end of the road at last, and the Ford has screeched to a halt. They're now right at the edge of the bog, in a round open space with a gravel surface. The heather has sent tenacious shoots out over the gravel in an attempt to reclaim this meagre bit of territory. A copse of spruce has been planted to the north-east, the trunks set at regular intervals and very close together as though holding a darkness between them, their small, sharp twigs forming a fine-meshed net. Despite its being man-made, the copse seems impenetrable. The idea is that one day spruce will completely surround the wetland, but to the south the plantation so far consists of nothing but sparsely planted seedlings. This uneven forest screen lends the place a sort of gravity, an atmosphere of alertness or concentration.

Nagler has moved a little to one side and is gingerly stretching his battered body. He takes out a pair of field-glasses and studies the marshy scene. The mist has temporarily lifted a little to reveal . . . nothing. Only a flat, disconsolate landscape with wooden planks here and there leading further out into unknown dullness. From where they are now they'll have to proceed on foot, balancing carefully on the narrow track, which must carry their specimen-bags as well as themselves. Police Chief Rav also has a field-stretcher made from thin poles and canvas. He avoids the doctor's eye and carefully locks the Ford, as if anyone would steal it. Nagler chuckles to himself. He has on long leather leggings and sand-coloured riding breeches. A sportsman. The leather creaks as he walks, even though he was careful to grease it with saddle-soap last evening.

*

So off they go out into the waterlogged russet-coloured landscape in brisk single file. Nagler has recovered to some extent and takes the opportunity to hold forth about similar finds on the German side of the border. *Moorleiche*. Both the others find his high, shrill voice affected and tiresome. His broken Danish is larded with German phrases, as if to give the language greater authority and weight. He snaps off the soft Danish words in an abrupt German manner as if annexing them. Rav bites the stem of his pipe angrily. Young Mayer stays silent, apparently not listening. He falls a little behind the others on the uneven path. Occasionally it becomes a bridge over black water of cracked grey boards that bend and creak under the weight of the three men. Sedge sticks up between the planks, sharp as a saw if you're careless enough to touch it.

They've been walking for nearly an hour. Now they can see the turf-cutter's abandoned cart in the distance. Suddenly the mist has gone, as if swallowed up by the ground. Slowly the sun mounts the sky, warming the earth and drawing from the bog a heavy stale smell that includes the odours of late-flowering marsh plants – bog myrtle and slender pink heather with its little oblong bells. Nagler falls silent at last when they near the open turf-cutting site, its surface grass stirred by the breeze into patches that look like wounds. A flock of crows rises and staggers a bit further off to settle in uneven rows on a tall slim birch on the very edge of the excavation, as if to observe the three men. They show no fear or timidity, just impudent curiosity, cheeky as street urchins.

Several paths run back from the marsh to the plantation like the spokes of a wheel, and Gabriel Mayer suddenly feels unsure which of these paths they came by. The landscape is confusingly monotonous. Perhaps they'll never identify the right path again – he quickly suppresses the thought: the methodical Nagler is bound to find the way back with his binoculars and field compass. Or Rav, who knows the bog like the back of his hand. The crows snap and clatter their beaks, jabbering dully in some secret language about things only they can understand. Mayer wishes they would shut up.

*

Oddly enough the dead man looks undisturbed, huddled as if asleep in the pit. His brown face gazes smoothly and timelessly out into the morning sun. It takes Mayer a moment to realise what the face reminds him of. It's like an old man in a storybook he had as a child who stepped out of an illustration and thus ended up outside time. In the story the old man tried in vain to find his way back into the picture. Outside its frame he eventually became invisible. Mayer has only a hazy memory of the story, but he can see the illustration clearly. Pale pastel shades outlined in black Indian ink. He can also remember the smell of the page. Acid with an undertone of damp. All totally clear, but then the memory slips away as capriciously as it came to him.

*

The stillness lying over the place is so deep that the men hesitate to break it. Rav unhurriedly extinguishes his pipe, knocks the dottle out against his heel and waits a moment till the smoke has dispersed before sniffing the air like a dog, an impression reinforced by his big powerful nose, pointed and slightly upturned. No, he can't detect the smell of death. Thoughts go round and round in his head. Well, it certainly looks like a crime committed long ago. He'll have Madsen put that in his final report. As far as Rav's concerned, the case can be filed away. But of course the German must do what he must . . . The police chief moves forward to the edge of the pit and looks down, curious. A few clumps of earth come loose and roll in, and Nagler clicks his tongue in irritation.

The body lies huddled as if asleep, just as the turf-cutter described it. Its arms are crossed over its chest and its narrow wrists held close together. The left shinbone, almost entirely separated from the body, lies bent at an unnatural angle where the spade fractured it. Fragments of skin remain, dark brown like scraps of tanned leather. The dead man's curly hair is the colour of dark copper, smeared down on his skull and preserved by the oxidising elements in the bog. Gabriel Mayer tastes gall in his mouth, or maybe it's sour coffee, and turns away abruptly. F.A. Nagler doesn't hesitate to jump heavily into the hole.

Muttering to himself, he struggles out of his rucksack, and the two Danes notice his shirt is drenched in sweat. His face is red and covered with small beads of perspiration. But he radiates a chill energy and fixity of purpose. He squats down by the corpse while some of the crows take off from the tree, glide low over the bog and come as near as they dare. Tomas Rav remains standing at the edge of the hole. Surprisingly sure-footed on the soft ground, he pulls a camera out of his rucksack and goes through the elaborate procedure of fitting a magnesium flash into its holder. Time, light, definition. Everything ready. One dry, hard click. When the shutter opens, it's as if time is standing still.

*

"Well," says Nagler, squatting clumsily over the body, "there can be no doubt that death resembles sleep." His plump lips pout as he glances round the pit, touches its sides and passes his eyes over the dead man. Over everything. Then he leans forward and pokes cautiously at the loose shinbone. "Well," he says again, "the tibia has been almost completely severed. A fresh break. Our friend the turf-cutter must have done that." He shakes his round head crossly. Then he treads carefully round the body, observing it from various angles and occasionally making notes in a little black English notebook. The wet earth seems to sigh softly as if from somewhere deep underground. After a while the German takes his rucksack by the straps and begins rooting about inside it for something without taking his eyes off the body for a second. Rav joins him in the pit and squats beside him. Eventually Nagler finds what he's looking for, a clasp knife with a narrow blade. The metal gleams coldly in the pit. He begins to manoeuvre the knife carefully into the dark layer that covers the body, working infinitely slowly on the black tarlike stratum, all the while moving his tongue backwards and forwards over his soft lips. His face, round and rosy as the Baroque features of the cherubs under the organ loft in Grænsebyen church, shines with sweat. Rav is content to look on. He begins to fumble for his pipe, but a look from the German stops him. Suddenly Nagler sits back on his heels. Small bubbles break plaintively from the ground round his feet. His eager expression has gone, and he looks thoughtful. He shoots out his lower lip like a discontented child and stands up.

"Not as old as I thought. Pity." He dries the clasp knife carefully with a handkerchief and closes it. The spring mechanism clicks loudly in the clear stillness.

"What we have here is a soldier. The body may have been lying here for sixty or seventy years for all I know. Outside my field of expertise. Could be a local peasant boy. Poor sod. Look, that's a uniform jacket." He brushes the edge of the dark material with the toe of his boot. "And it looks as if a rat's been nibbling at his ear. He's obviously been brought here from somewhere else." Nagler points at the soldier's head; all that's left of the ear is a little leathery circle round the ear canal.

The German moves away, leans against the side of the pit and lights a cigarette, tapping it first against a shiny cigarette-case. At last Rav can light his pipe, and soon the two are puffing away together, tall thin Dane and stout self-satisfied Berliner. Now that the other two seem to have lost interest, Gabriel Mayer steps down into the pit for the first time. As there's no longer any question of murder or a prehistoric find, just the discovery of an unknown body in unconsecrated ground, it'll be his job to provide the information for the entry in the parish register. Pastor Aronius will presumably hold a service and give the body a proper burial, even though the death was neither recent nor really ancient. Old Aronius loves to assemble the dead round him in Grænsebyen churchyard, as if forming a guard to protect his own life. Which is why he and all the other old people of Grænsebyen are always so eager to read the death announcements in the local paper *Avisen*. It's as if the names of the dead have been entered on an ancient roll.

Mayer stumbles and nearly falls over the bog man but at the last moment manages to save himself. Nonetheless he slightly dislodges the body. When he glances at Nagler, the German merely shrugs and inhales cigarette smoke deep into his lungs, making the tobacco glow. The look he gives Mayer expresses indifference but also betrays a lazy interest. Mayer bends over the body, driven by a curiosity he can't explain. In any case, he finds the expression on the German's face embarrassing. At first he doesn't see the slight movement in the rotting cloth, then his gaze fastens on something carefully groping its way over what was once a pleat in the coat. A colourful long thin caterpillar moves hesitantly forward, stopping at regular intervals to wave its feelers in the air as if suspicious of Mayer's presence in that rugged landscape of hills and valleys. Its striped body is covered with fine bristles, and its legs move with a gentle wave-like motion. Life seems to pulse nakedly under its thin skin like pale coloured liquid in a fragile bowl. Rav steps forward to join Mayer and watch the little creeping thing.

"Good God!" he says, "a Lackey moth. How did that get here?"

But this is a question none of them can answer.

COPENHAGEN,

FEBRUARY 2000

MALACOSOMA NEUSTRIA. LACKEY moth. A humble flying insect found in orchards. A hairy golden-brown little moth which as a caterpillar spins fine nets in old apple-trees and hawthorn hedges, ring-shaped cocoons which can cause the host plant to rot. In certain lights the mature moth can look almost as if it is powdered with gold. The thing creeping on the body in the bog was still a caterpillar, but Madsen had nonetheless jotted down its Latin name in pencil in a corner of his report. He must either have looked it up or asked someone. Tomas Rav and Gabriel Mayer had each handed in their evidence early on the morning of September 1. These notes were missing. By that time the archaeologist Nagler was already on his way back to Berlin via Hamburg-Altona; the other two had gone with him to the station the day before. For some reason they'd decided to drive him to the halt at Fårhus, a request stop where the train picked up passengers only if asked to do so by a signal set specially at red.

*

Police Constable Madsen's handwriting is clear, with round childish flourishes. He made a fair copy of what the other two told him. Thus Madsen's simple, gentle penmanship transforms the story, removing all rough edges and question marks: *The body was transported back to Grœnsebyen with some difficulty and is now in the old charnel house behind the church. Laid on straw over ice even though this is not strictly necessary. Such articles of clothing as could be detached from it have been laid out to dry in the police garage. No crime is suspected, even though*

the man was probably put to death long ago. Fallen in war. Grænsebyen
Town Council and Pastor Aronius are preparing a little ceremony for him,
but of course the body's nationality and age must be established first.

In Copenhagen I could hear church bells ringing as I read. At the same time it was like being in that little Danish border town in the '30s, with the heat of late August turning milk sour in milk-cans, covering sparsely paved streets with dust and making people sweat in their long flower-patterned coarse cotton dresses, berets and light-grey serge suits. An age of low-pressure tyres and creaking leather saddles, one year before the war.

In Denmark the torrential stream of refugees crossing the border had made people aware as early as 1938 of Hitler's antisemitic race laws. Many of these refugees carried passports in the name of "Sara" or "Israel", portmanteau names used by the Nazis for Jews. Folk that brought terror with them, their lost individual names a foretaste of oblivion.

Yet the topsoil was as rich as ever on the Danish acres, the sun blazed down, the townsfolk were listening to quizzes on the wireless, and someone was painting the fence that ran along the main street of Grænsebyen. In the church nearly a hundred years of ingrained dirt was being removed with soft soap and stiff scrubbing brushes, the pews were being painted grey, the gold paint and wood-carvings of the altar-piece were being dusted and the floor swept and scoured. Someone found an old hand-forged key which fitted no known lock, the church's ancient porch had rotted away long ago. The caretaker placed a tall ladder against the wall and was able at last to tear down a storks' nest which had been annoying him for years. The nest was right inside the tower, a rubbishy mess of twigs, down and dried birdshit which threatened to spread rot and decay down into the rafters. Maybe none of this ever happened. Or maybe this is exactly how it was. But one thing is certain: Pastor Aronius in his eightieth year decided the dead soldier had to have a name and a plot of consecrated ground. He began making enquiries, using young Gabriel Mayer as his eyes and ears.

*

Mayer's notes fill some twenty pages of a thin blue exercise book with spidery writing, small as though to save paper. I need my powerful desk lamp to decipher it. The paper is of poor quality, and here and there the nib of his fountain pen has caught in it and made blots. His investigations had taken him back to the 1860s and the unhappy war with Prussia.

That was just one of many occasions when the duchies of Schleswig and Holstein became a bone of contention between Denmark and Prussia. On the hills were the ruins of the Dannevirke, a fortification the ancient Vikings had built to protect them from their southern neighbours, a half-ruined earthwork that had become something of a Danish national monument and which the Danes had begun to repair now that they were faced yet again with the threat of war. This time it would see the Prussians using rifled-bore cannon. Denmark's aim was to bind Schleswig more firmly to itself by means of a new constitution, while Prussia under Bismarck wanted to preserve its route to the Baltic and hold land north of Kiel, where it planned to build a base for its Baltic fleet. If Schleswig became Prussian, it would serve to protect Kiel's harbour. Egged on by bad if catchy popular songs, free-flowing schnapps and highly emotional but poorly motivated nationalism, the armies of both states were drawn into war – first from 1848 to 1850 and then again in the spring of 1864, when the Prussians inflicted a bloody defeat on the Danes at Dybbøl and Als. Perhaps it was really then rather than in 1914 that northern Europe lost its innocence in the face of modern warfare. At the very least, this war between Denmark and Prussia was the overture.

Mayer had jotted down miscellaneous facts including dates and places which seemed relevant. Presumably Pastor Aronius was meticulous about that sort of thing. With Mayer's notes was a map printed in 1917 by the Leipzig Bibliographical Institute. This showed the territorial gains made by the German Empire in 1864, with the border running along the Kongeå River halfway between Hejls and Fjelstrup. This border survived till 1918, when Germany lost a great deal, but perhaps respectability more than anything. The map was worn and well-used; its folds had cracked open in places to expose a cloth backing. Its surface, which was coming loose, was covered with a network of fine cracks like old porcelain. It was coloured in pastel shades – Danish pink against German light green – as though time had been intent on dissolving borders and altering the shading-in of coasts and landmarks . . . But wait, I'm running ahead of events; first I must bring Gabriel Mayer to life.

METHOD

M Y LIBRARY'S NOT particularly comprehensive. The reason's simple: my space at Lille Novicegade is strictly limited. What I do have is a large old-fashioned wardrobe that I've fitted with shelves and a ladder with wide polished steps, and I keep everything I need in there. Naturally I have the standard works: Gyldendal's *Encyclopaedia*, Paulsen's two-volume *History of the Danish Wars*, and a good many diaries, some complete and some fragmentary, of the sort often printed by local societies and small publishers. Also writings by the kind of mad intellectuals who are only interested in one thing, such as whether Harald Bluetooth was murdered or Søren Kierkegaard broke off his engagement to Regine of his own accord. I've also got a growing collection of material thrown out by researchers at the Historical Institute: scraps of paper, excerpts from this or that, momentary inspirations – all sorted by subject and stored in wine boxes discarded by The Blue Grape.

Traditional researchers' obstinate refusal to go out into the field is a constant irritant to me. This fear of getting their shoes dirty or finding their shirts glued to their backs by sweat. For me, historical research is *reconstructing the past out of what exists today*. Fieldwork. I start with colour, soil, temperature, light and water as they are now and only later consult written sources. If you want to know exactly what an eggshell is made of, you should study the genealogy of the hen that laid the egg. Go back into the field again and again and study every aspect of the object of your research at different times of year and in all weathers. Only if you do this will you later be able to detect instantly any dissonance in the text, any false note when the *atmosphere* of the place doesn't ring true.

*

For example, take the battlefield of Dybbøl as it is now on a typical early summer's day. You'll find green hillsides covered with succulent grass, cows chewing their cud and watching you with vague eyes, tourists picnicking with bored or howling children; a blue sky and the Sound a hazy mist of evaporating coolness – in a word, an idyll as perfect as a canvas by a genre painter from Düsseldorf. The present turns you into a holidaymaker. War becomes as uncomplicated as moving bright tin figures around on a board.

But go to Dybbøl on a cold, raw day in early spring, one of those days when winter gives another twitch of life. Is it the same place? Of course it is, but the conditions for walking on the slopes are utterly different. The wind takes your breath away, your nose runs, tears fill your eyes. Beyond the turf-covered redoubts, waves are being whipped into spray by a wind that makes it impossible even to imagine Prussian landing-craft coming in over the rough grey water. Yet that's how it was. You can't evoke this sort of experience at your desk; you must live it. In short, you have to investigate the past with the same meticulous attention as you would investigate the scene of a crime. The researcher's job is to reconstruct a moment of history in its totality, complete with tables of wind speed and direction and temperatures. You must read contemporary diaries to discover exact times and quality of light and even, if possible, re-create clothing and food-intake and then wait for the magic moment when all the parameters coincide. *That will be your now*. Yet even this is only the beginning of understanding a moment of history. Experience must still be clothed in words that speak of borders, treaties, challenges, languages and nationalism. Strong feelings will have been forgotten, unless something of them has been preserved in some old tale or novel. Perhaps achieving so much is impossible, but it's what you must aim for. When everything comes together, you may perhaps be able to experience a specific

moment of history, like studying through a microscope a flimsy fragment of cloth cut from a body. And all this uncertainty, this sense of
the random and the haphazard and these gaps in knowledge, often
gives rise to another thought, perhaps the most exciting of all: Given
these same conditions, could things have happened differently? Is it
possible, at least in theory, for us to change history? That's what I
want to find out.

DYBBØL FORTIFICATIONS,
EARLY SPRING 1864

SPRING IS COMING, late and hesitant. A sickly red-gold sun hangs over hillsides pitted with holes. Sometimes clouds cover the sky, ragged clouds that shut out the light, make the air raw and icy and set tiny drops of water on the Danes' green wool coats, like glass beads on the costume of a ballerina at the Royal Theatre. It's like being enclosed under a heavy lampshade. Everything happens slowly or not at all. Time ticks stubbornly on like the rapid heartbeats of a pocket-watch that brings back memories of a time of warm, well-lit rooms, but the landscape of Flensburg Fjord doesn't change. The water is grey and rough with small sharp waves. A little way out, fat Prussian provision barges lie with water nearly up to their tarred gunwales, distended with food and superior power like crocodiles in a sluggish river. The roads of Jutland have turned into deep ditches full of mud, rutted by the army's wheels and the weight of its baggage train. The country folk have long since started to shift last year's harvest of half-rotten beets and potatoes by other routes. It's said they prefer to sell to the Prussians, who pay better and have Imperial gold obtained from their Austrian allies.

*

The soldiers have been lying buried among the sand dunes for more than two months now since the beginning of February, and have been enclosed within a tight ring of fire for several weeks. Little by little they've used up their supplies. Fat grey lice and brown rats from the swollen corpses outside the fortifications crawl backwards and forwards over them, bringing typhus and fever to those still vulnerable to infection. The rats are so well fed and lethargic that they are hardly capable of getting out of the way when the disgusted men throw stones or empty cartridge cases at them. Occasionally someone scores a direct hit, whereupon the other rats immediately begin to gnaw and snap at their comrade's body, exchanging excited squeaks till someone starts singing to drown out their hellish noise or maybe just to put in a word for humanity. This automatically causes the enemy's batteries to begin thundering again, as if proper order and decorum must be reimposed. Shells strike the ramparts and chisel away at the redoubt walls, turning bricks and mortar back into sand. This sequence of events is repeated so often that it assumes a kind of normality, an aura of everyday life.

*

They enlisted together, Moritz and Kristian and Gad Friis too, though strictly speaking he's under age. All three come from the suburbs of Copenhagen, from the working-class Nørrebro district. Within the course of a few hours they had to walk to several barracks, though no matter whether the buildings were sooty red brick or ochre-coloured plaster, the smell of latrines and unwashed bodies was the same. But in the army the pork ration was more reliable, at least that's what people said. At the Østerport garrison they were fitted out with jackets and trousers, but there were no shirts or boots, because these had already gone on special issue to volunteers from the Copenhagen civil guard. The jackets were dark blue with brass buttons, the trousers sky-blue. The coarse wooden shoes they got were a poor match for their uniforms, but they were told this didn't matter since they'd be transported by sea at the first opportunity, as soon as the wind came up and conditions became favourable enough for it to be worthwhile taking them out in rowing boats to the ships in the Sound. No, it was only the volunteer civil guard that would march through the city and up Amaliegade Street past the royal palace, men who knew their right from their left and how to handle a brightly polished rifle the way they do in the army. Afterwards most members of this civil guard would go home, put away their uniforms, boots and weapons and eat peaceful suppers by the light of well-trimmed candles.

*

Suddenly at the beginning of December 1863 a longish spell of mild weather made it possible for the troops to be set in motion. Boats were loaded with old men and seasick boys in gaudy uniforms, troops who looked fine so long as you viewed them from a distance through a grubby lens. They set off into the Kattegat in three of King Christian's warships, rigging creaking with frost high above steaming-hot boilers. Friis had already left the others and lay vomiting below till he got a bucketful of icy sea water thrown over him and a sharp kick in the backside. This scared him so much that he felt better and went back up on deck. The ships steamed on through a world of ice.

Off the Sjælland sandbank the sea began freezing again, moving with long sluggish dragging waves. Thin brittle ice rustled as the iron hulls cut through it. The bluish gleam of the frozen sea blended into the winter sky, and the men on the ships could see no horizon or boundary when they looked out over open sea to the north. If they screwed up their reddened eyes they could make out shadow-like elevations of land, narrow strokes of Indian ink on a white background, while after dark here and there lighthouses made spiky tracks across the ice like falling stars. To the men on Friis's boat the outlines of the other two ships were faint silhouettes in an otherwise empty world where tiny sailors in billowing clothes moved slowly and with extreme care over decks and rigging, pausing before each movement like mechanical toys that no-one had remembered to wind up. Then one night, when their ship was slowly passing the lights of Kalundborg on Sjælland with thick black smoke pouring from its funnel, even the spirit that was supposed to activate the compass grew so sluggish that the needle obstinately refused to point in any direction but south – something even the oldest sailors on board had never experienced before.

*

On January 13 they dropped anchor in the fjord off the island of Als, and 500 shivering men stepped ashore at Mommark after nearly five weeks at sea. The frozen sand beneath them seemed to sway; it was worse than being on board ship.

COPENHAGEN,

FEBRUARY 2000

I CLOSED THE exercise book. My imagination can play tricks on me, but I did have some facts to go on. The Danish–Prussian war had been one of Kai's interests; I had gone with him to the Dybbøl redoubts. Green slopes and a fine hazy blue view over Sønderborg Bay with Germany across the water. Here and there, stones in memory of the fallen can be found in the rich grass, cows with their leisurely rocking gait prowling round them. Is this disrespect, or are the cows offering the dead the indispensable warmth of life? That depends on how you see history: as something finite like a granite monument, or as a never-ending process. Mayer's notes were brief, but history always finds some way of making sure it's remembered. Old holes for you to fall into, or an unknown soldier who suddenly returns and must be given a name in the churchyard of a small town.

This soldier was buried near the Bockmeister vault on September 15 with pomp and ceremony, including a gun salute by members of the civil defence (several of them veterans of the Great War of 1914–18, when they had fought on the German side). Pastor Aronius got the parish clerk to lay out the unknown soldier's uniform on a table in the church during the service, and an elderly member of the congregation, a gentleman interested in military history, tentatively identified it as that of a Danish private, 1860 model. He couldn't name the regiment; the uniform was too badly decayed for that. In any case, the dry air in the church had twisted and shrivelled the jacket till it wouldn't even have fitted a doll-soldier from Daells department store in Copenhagen. Another member of the congregation thought a strange and slightly nauseating smell was coming from the ancient cloth, and when someone mentioned the word *blood*, the jacket was moved to a chest in the sacristy. Eventually the church caretaker carried out the rags and burned them with other junk on a heap of leaves behind the church.

By this time it was October, and the German authorities had already sent out a public notice announcing the disappearance of Dr F.A. Nagler, a document that reached Police Constable Madsen one Tuesday morning early in the month. It was an announcement that made Madsen uneasy and uncertain what action to take. Dr Nagler hadn't been seen in Berlin since leaving the German capital on August 29. His luggage was not at the Gränshållet Station Hotel in Grænsebyen, though no-one could remember seeing him leave. All he had left at the hotel was a bottle of cologne, forgotten on the washstand, and a few German coins found by the chambermaid under the bed – perhaps Nagler himself or a thief had dropped a purse. Rav had paid the hotel bill – at Nagler's request according to Rav's statement. The doctor had been travelling with nothing but his rucksack and an overnight bag, which anyone could have carried off without Fru Karin Müller, the receptionist, noticing. Both Tomas Rav and Gabriel Mayer had seen the doctor board the 6.30 train that was to carry him over the border to Germany. The platform of the country halt at Fårhus had been deserted. Rav believed the doctor had had both his rucksack and his brown leather travelling bag. Nagler had disappeared somewhere between Grænsebyen and Berlin. Somehow it seemed the dead man in the bog had given rise to yet another mystery.

I read the official German notice of disappearance, which was attached with a rusty paperclip to the back of Madsen's report. The rucksack had been found in a compartment as the train crossed the border. Its contents had been carefully recorded in the report, which had been copied into the police diary on October 11, 1938. This was followed by a short account of the facts of the case; they didn't waste words in Berlin. Nagler had been a bachelor, and it was first assumed that he had stayed several extra days in Denmark or in Hamburg, where he would have changed trains at the Hauptbahnhof. This was why the announcement of his disappearance had taken so long to arrive. He looked exactly as I'd imagined him. Short (about 1.69 metres) and stocky, with a high colour. Quite stout. Fair, with a bald patch. No known tattoos or special marks. Full name Franz Aloysius Nagler, born Munich 1904. Resident of Berlin, in ——— (the name had been obliterated). Employed in the archaeological department of the Berlin Antiquities Museum. There was no other information about him and no note of his ever having been found. F.A. Nagler was still missing. The notice of his disappearance was the last document in my bundle.

*

I turned off the light and stretched. The room lay in half-light, and music from The Blue Grape was coming through my walls. An old Sting number: "When the Angels Fall". I remembered some of the lyrics: *Take your father's cross / gently from the wall*. It was past five. This was the "happy hour" when the unhappy and lonely could console themselves with lukewarm beer and mummified beer-sausage burnt black. Maybe this comforted them. I myself had never been in the place, except during the daytime to complain when the ventilator squeaked more than usual. The music faded. *Yet all the ragged souls / of all the ragged men / looking for their lost homes / shuffle to the ruins / from the levelled plain / to search among the tombstones.* I padded out into the hall to fetch the phone book. Peter Mogensen was listed as a watchman, which I expected. More surprising was his address – a street that contained some of the city's most ambitious restoration projects. Mogensen lived at 7 Krokodillegade Street, in the vicinity of the Kastellet citadel and the old ramparts, in a building which had once formed part of a barracks complex. It was an area I remembered as characterised by austere windows decorated with globular oil lamps and Finnish glass designs. I tried to imagine Mogensen's puffy red mug in this context but couldn't. Well, I'd have to phone him later to see how the land lay. But for now I took up my atlas to have a look at Dybbøl.

*

When I'm not working I often go for walks in the city. It's easier to think some thoughts out of doors, as if cold and oxygen make memories dry and light, less personal. I'm so used to sleeping by day that darkness keeps me awake. It was now nearly nine in the evening, and the moon was hanging outside the window like a polished coin, clear and cold. Frøken Jessen's glass drop was lifeless at this time of day, nothing but a fragment of darkness on a string. As usual, I dressed warmly and sensibly in thick corduroy trousers, muffler, two wool sweaters and shoes with warm linings. The night air was cold and fresh, marred only by deep-fried fumes from the Chinese takeaway in Fjolstræde Lane. I pulled my muffler up over my face and went on my way.

*

Normally I walk along the quays at night. Not by the harbour but along the enclosed basins that are part of the city's nineteenth-century history and contain what were marshes in ancient times: Jorgens Sø, Peblinge Sø, Sortedams Sø. I leave the old town by Jernbanegade Street and Vesterport, following the straight military edges of the quays along Vestergade Street or Svineryggen on the other side of the water. The houses stand stiff as tin soldiers on either side of the quays, their windows shining into the night through glass as still as the surface of the water. I hardly ever see a human being after half-past two. It feels good to be out when you've been sitting for hours, and sometimes I hear the voices, dark or light, of people I've been reading about, and see them step forward, anxious and hesitant, from the dim streets and lose their way among the garish lights and shrill sounds of the modern city. The stooping figure of Søren Kierkegaard disappears round a corner in check coat and slouch hat. Sometimes, young and pink-cheeked, he's on the way to see his sweetheart Regine, but just as often he's old, misanthropic and sunk in on himself, yellow with bile, jealousy and too much inactivity. The young Jenny Lind, her figure like an hourglass, steps into a droshky and goes off down streets that no longer exist, the flames in the droshky's polished lanterns fluttering and sputtering in the wind. Most often I cross the water by the bridge known as Dronning Louises Bro and go through the hospital grounds and into the Botanical Gardens. At night it's as dark as a jungle among the dense rhododendron bushes with their dark leaves smoothed back against the cold. I get in by a narrow gap in the fence nobody else knows about.

But on this particular evening I took another route I knew well even though I hadn't used it for a long time. I began with a turn round the Rosenborg Gardens to breathe some evening air. I didn't go in, since you can so easily be seen there along the dead-straight paths, with their well-pruned beds of old roses which at this time of year are white with hoar frost, the fragrance of summer asleep inside black rosehips like time-bombs. I've no idea whether any fully conscious thought guided my steps, but eventually I found myself in a very individual street in front of an altogether special building. The streets round here are narrow and black as compositor's type. It's a district of greasy car-dealing businesses, bikers, billiard halls, small hotels and a multitude of pale-faced ladies who hire out rooms by the hour. Kai's garage was here too. Its pea-green wooden door had one sound window and one broken one repaired with a piece of fibreboard like a patch over a pirate's eye.

I managed to shift one side of the door after a bit of jiggling with the lock. The draught that hit me was cold and damp, saturated with dust and oil. Pliers, cables and spanners hung tidily on their hooks as if no time had passed. Holding my breath I took a step forward, trying to accustom my eyes to the gloom and protect my heart from a great mass of memories. I hadn't been in the garage for nearly three years, hadn't been able to bring myself to go there. I'd just continued to pay the rent despite the fact I could barely afford it.

The car was lurking under its covers in the middle of the oily cement floor like a wily old bat wrapped in its wings. Inherited property. I hesitated a moment longer (I've also inherited my father's timidity). In the end I groped my way inside, turned on the ceiling light and pulled the cover off the car's radiator. The dust made me sneeze. Kai

Olsen's Chevrolet Impala was just as I remembered it. Cream-coloured and softly rounded. Still shining with wax polish despite its long vigil. That car had been the apple of Dad's eye. It was probably worth a fortune, dead or alive. I pulled off more sheets, carefully opened the car door and slipped onto the leather seat, which creaked a little. The slender white bakelite wheel nearly came up to my chin. When I reached for the pedal, my foot kicked empty air. Everything was exactly as I remembered it.

*

The first time we drove down to South Jutland was in the summer of 1968, a month or two after Mum and Bobby Kennedy died. Kennedy died on the pavement outside the Los Angeles Hilton, Mum in a nursing home in Copenhagen. I read everything I could about Bobby's death and made a collection of newspaper clippings while Kai went on studying the battles of the American Civil War and drew detailed maps of places like Bull Run and Antietam. Since we had no money for a trip to America, he extended his studies to include the war between Denmark and Prussia that had taken place during the same period. He studied weapons and tactics, for example what effect the change from muzzle-loading to breech-loading had on the outcome of both wars (breech-loading rifles made it possible for soldiers to reload lying on the ground out of the enemy's line of fire. The Prussians had the new M/1841 and M/1862 rifles and thus were able to dominate the final phase of the war on Als Island).

I was six years old and had just taught myself to read. I don't remember much from before that; I can hardly remember what my mother looked like, only that she used to sleep in the afternoon, endless hours in a stuffy town flat with brown shutters that made the sounds from the street seem further away and somehow dangerous. She would lie completely still in her dark bedroom, thin eyelids fluttering like insect wings as she slept, caught up in events none of the rest of us could see. It was as if she'd become stuck in dream time. I expect death made little difference to her. I never touched her when she was asleep, because I knew that if you touch an insect's wings it can never fly again. Beside the bed stood dusty glass jars I wasn't allowed to touch and that Dad later cleared away. I've inherited my ability to sleep in the daytime from Mum, and my slender build, but I've escaped her nerves. My hair and eyes are of an indefinable colour and unlike anyone else's – uniquely my own.

*

In the summer of 1968, a month or two after the shooting in Los Angeles, my father and I took a long trip in the Chevy. Kai was thinking of buying a weekend cottage in South Jutland, and he and I planned to get there by the ancient military road – the route Danish troops had marched along ever since the days of the dithering ninth-century king Harald Klak. The modern road lies over square greystone chippings set into the hillsides to provide a foothold for small shaggy Viking horses. We expected to see at least some of this between Kolding and Åbenrå, but the old military road extends right down to the German border, so from Haderslev southwards we'd also have seen sections of original stone paving. But I don't remember much about the military road. As for the weekend cottage, it was something Kai'd seen advertised in the newspaper. He thought he was onto a good thing, but it turned out to be yet another of his many unsuccessful projects. I was only six and took my teddy bear with me and my album of cuttings about Bobby K. It didn't occur to Kai to pack anything else.

*

It was a hot, endless summer. Perhaps the longest of my life. Time moved slowly across the blue sky in the form of white clouds creeping backwards and forwards through the air like goose-down. We lived on white bread, red sausage and apricot marmalade that Kai bought on the way. He drank lager from green bottles, and I drank lemonade till my tummy seethed and bubbled. The car radio told us about a student rising in Paris and the temperature of the water and that blacks in America were making trouble because a king had been shot on a balcony somewhere. I imagined the french windows of our own flat, but in a hot damp dusk with cicadas screeching below in the jungle. Somewhere out there a sniper with a gleaming black rifle was waiting. Suddenly the summer had become dangerous, at least as long as you thought about it. But if you switched off the radio the world vanished into a Blaupunkt.

At Åbenrå we turned off along the coast and the air became close and tinted with gold by hot sun-haze and a steaming sea. The fjord was a blue stripe. By now my dress was dirty and wet with pee so we threw it in a dustbin and Kai bought me some light-blue shorts, red sunglasses and several striped tops instead. The engine purred under the bonnet like a big black cat. I wished the journey could go on for ever. The hot patched asphalt of the highway stretched ahead, endlessly winding through a sunburnt landscape. It was like making our way over a dragon's back. Time no longer existed. In the evenings we would rent a "Room for Travellers" with a sticky brown linoleum floor, or a small bathing hut with pockets of fine white sand from the beach in its corners like molehills left behind by other summer visitors. Then we continued on to the green hills of Dybbøl and the old battlefields, where Kai took photographs and drew meticulous sketches with various kinds of coloured pens. Green and red, with prussian blue for the bay. He'd brought books about the Schleswig wars with him and read aloud from them while I slept. About the retreat over to Als Island under the devastating fire of Prussian cannon and how, when the Prussians were approaching in everything that could float, the armed Danish coastal defence ship *Rolf Krake*, obeying a mistaken order, unhappily steamed off out of the bay with the national flag, the *Dannebrog*, like a limp cone in the sooty wind above her stern. The Prussians waded ashore with their weapons held high above their flat sea-caps while the smoke from the *Krake* disappeared over the horizon. It must have been a remarkable sight.

We were in no hurry, and it took us more than a week to reach the cottage. Kai had got hold of a key which strangely enough had the number 4 on it; as I remember it, the cottage stood in a field of knife-sharp sedge, not only totally isolated but beginning to subside since sand was slowly running away from beneath it into some underground furrow, filtering in fine grains as time filters through the hourglass on an old cabin mirror. I remember the tide being so far out that pools where crabs lurked were in danger of drying up and the sour smell of damp seabed had even penetrated the cottage's two rooms, permeating everything: mattresses, pillows, wallpaper. Thinking back, it may seem strange that we never mentioned Mum. But memory's always in a state of flux, especially when you've been left alone with it. When you've become its *trustee*. Maybe that's just how it was.

*

I got slowly out of the car and slammed the door behind me so that the coachwork made small noises and the window rattled. Kai wouldn't have liked that, but I didn't care. I suddenly began wondering whether Mogensen had a driving licence and the right temperament to drive a 1958 Impala. I'd ask him.

*

It was late when I got home and pushed the key into my lock. I could feel my neighbour of the larch-tree watching me through the frosted glass panel in her door. She'd never been able to discover what my work was, and this seemed to be a bittersweet torment for her. A taxonomical vacuum. I felt a bit like that myself. I jiggled a bit more than necessary with the key to give her a little more to think about, then went into my flat. The music from The Blue Grape had stopped and given way to the dry busy sound of the ventilator. No small life had been snuffed out by the fan that evening. I left the lights off and sat down in the darkness to think.

Kai and I must have visited the peat bog known as Frøslevs Mose on that trip though I had no memory of it. Wetlands, a landscape of fens. Places like that all seemed alike, caught in a kind of timelessness that suggested sacrificial sites, horses, prehistoric folk and marshlands that swallowed everything up and preserved what they swallowed: swords, pieces of bone, fermenting animal stomachs. I remembered reading some story about the area, switched on my reading-lamp and began poking about in my bookshelves. An hour later, covered in dust and sweat, I sank back into my chair. There it was, a dry, crumbling volume from 1957 shaped like a block of grey-stone in a church wall. *Four Illusions*. I caught my breath when I read the author's name: Gabriel Mayer, MA, Århus University. I let the book fall open at random.

He believes there are stories of an ancient village or settlement that existed on the peat bog long ago when there was still a lake. Before they tried to drain the land by making ditches in the 1870s, when surveyors came, surveyed, made notes and flew over the area in a balloon – they even went as far as that. German officials flying high over their new-won territory, wind howling in the balloon's ropes and the bog a swampy haze far below them. The earth suddenly transformed into a map, a projection, softly mottled like an earth-coloured woollen blanket. But there was too much ancient moisture in the bog for it ever to become good agricultural land. In the end, unable to stop water rising to the surface, even the painstaking Germans gave up.

No-one knows now exactly where the old village lay, but its story may still live somewhere in the memories of Schleswig people: memories of Romans making their way north through Germania and past the Dannevirke, alien faces speaking an alien language. Splashing through mud and listening out nervously in the darkness through long cold nights for every smallest sound. Perhaps one of them – possibly a short stocky mountain dweller from Etruria – glances to one side with eyes narrowed against the afternoon sun and all at once, some way off, sees mounds in the brown water, earthworks covered with wattle and daub, and becomes aware of a smell of hides and thin white smoke. But he can't see any people; are they all hiding? The soldiers move on past this strangely sleeping village, heavy iron-clad figures along the shore, unreal as phantoms, the stuff of dreams.

Did the Romans ever come so far north? He tries to remember. In the midst of the howling storm his peaceful memory hits on a book, Tacitus in a well-worn dark-green school edition. His eye moves calmly over the page but doesn't find the place he's looking for – the story of how people out on an artifical wooden island watched the Romans march by – blood-red wool and leather, clanking iron armour and short swords swinging rhythmically against their hips. Cloaked cohorts spread over a rugged frostbitten landscape on their way north, perhaps en route to Britain. That was their plan, to go north. Tramping heavily on soft heather-clad moorlands, the high sky enclosing them like an all-encompassing blue-grey cupola. Troops on the march, watched through narrow slits in timber walls, both then and much later. He wonders whether these sights and sounds may still exist somewhere, like pictures collected in an album. Preserved in living memory, in a time warp. He continues skimming through his imagination, moistens a finger, smooths down the page and wonders whether those balloonists up in the sky perhaps exist in the same space as the Roman army on the ground, separated only by our human notion of time, a thin layer of shared human understanding. Time. One part of it separated from another by an infinity of mechanical clocks as they tick their way onward. In some great fantasy. He leans back against the cold wall of earth, and his head begins to swim. His stomach turns. His head aches and his forehead feels hot and feverish, yes, he is undoubtedly sickening for something. The man's remains are still lying there out in the bog, they haven't managed to cover them properly. And the rain continues falling, slowly re-creating the ancient lake before their eyes as if even Nature had access to a map.

I stopped reading at this point. The story had taken me out onto the bog again. Mayer's fat little book had no subtitle to help me understand whether it was a work of scholarship, an essay or a novel – a circumstance that would have driven the Institute's librarian to impotent fury. I myself couldn't remember buying it, yet in some strange way it had found its way into my consciousness. Sometimes I buy a whole boxful of books in a second-hand bookshop simply because I've noticed a single worthwhile title among them. I never let the dealer suspect this but buy the whole boxful as if at random. It's cheaper that way. Perhaps Mayer's book had come to me as part of a job lot of this kind. The text had been set in a small crabbed font on tough greyish paper of the sort that makes the ends of your fingers itch. Many of the pages had never been cut but were still in the form of large folded sheets bound together. Here and there loose pieces of extremely thin paper filled with notes written in a small sprawling hand had been slipped between the pages. The book's title was no less cryptic: *Four Illusions*. The story from the bog seemed to be the second illusion of the four, a tale consisting of about twenty close-written pages that so far no-one had managed to get through. I deliberated for a moment as to whether to fetch a knife but felt overcome by exhaustion and decided to leave it for the moment.

*

The next day I again slept till well into the afternoon and woke with a headache lurking behind my eyes like an angry little animal with sharp teeth. Fragments of disturbing dreams lingered in my memory but as usual escaped when I looked straight at them, like slippery sea creatures avoiding an eel lantern. I stole into the kitchen, made some coffee and cut myself a slice of dry bread. As usual there was a well-filled jamjar in the cupboard (though I never buy more than the absolute minimum I need). A gulp of scalding hot coffee and a few bites of bread and I felt better. Mayer's book was still lying where I'd left it, and this time I looked through it from the beginning. Oddly enough it had been printed in Hamburg, by some small publishing firm I'd never heard of: Cerberus Buchdrucker. Something in its appearance, perhaps the artlessness of the soft white cover, made me wonder whether it had ever been published at all. Was this a printer's proof or a single bound copy made for the author? The publisher's logo was a dog with three ferocious slobbering heads, the Cerberus of myth. The stories seemed to have been arranged according to some sort of eccentric chronology which cut rhapsodically backwards and forwards in time. For example, at a casual glance most of the stories seemed to tell of strange episodes from the 1860s, while other items were short polished reflections on war and human existence. One essay dealt with the Romantic writer Hugo von Hoffroder (1809–1865) and analysed one of his stories. Gabriel Mayer seemed to have taken himself very seriously indeed. It looked as if he must have been well respected in the academic world of Århus University some forty years ago. Perhaps he was still there. Academic life is usually kind to the heart and muscles, and those who go in for it often live long lives.

I was eager to read Mayer's book, but first I had a whole lot of practical matters to attend to. *Nihil sine labore* – nothing without work, as Horace wrote, conveniently ignoring the fact that as the years went by he himself developed a preference for doing nothing but strolling up and down the paths of his vineyard. I grabbed the phone book and dialled Mogensen's number. He answered at the second ring, his voice weak. I tried to sound as severe as possible.

"Peter Mogensen? This is Dorthe Wilhelmsen, Professor Rosen's secretary."

I paused and could hear him moving, presumably to sit down: there was a sound like the groaning of bedsprings.

"Professor Rosen would like to ask you some questions about yesterday," I went on in imitation of Dorthe's clipped syllables (her nickname at the Institute was The English Bullet – a jacketed high-speed projectile). Mogensen's inarticulate reply sounded like water gurgling in a plughole. I almost felt sorry for him.

"It has to do with some documents that are missing from the Professor's room, material from the National Archive in Berlin, Herr

Mogensen. Documents the Professor is extremely anxious to find. You were on duty last night, I understand?"

Another guttural gurgle. This was no young chick he was dealing with.

"Professor Rosen wishes to talk to you about these documents."

Mogensen said nothing, but I could almost hear his mind ticking like an old-fashioned pocket-watch.

"Tomorrow at ten, Herr Mogensen. The Professor's expecting you."

I didn't wait for a final grunt but put down the phone.

*

Krokodillegade – Crocodile Street – is an ochre-coloured terrace of unsophisticated houses that have risen in the world like a poor peasant who suddenly finds himself cheek by jowl with perfumed gentlemen in polished high boots and lace frills. The buildings in the Nyboder district – a little beyond the city walls and the ancient Østerport, which had been pulled down in the seventeenth century – had once served as damp, poky housing for the crews of men-of-war. Further than a cannonball could roll, and most often to leeward of the bitter winds from the Sound, powerful gusts which sometimes blew thick smoke from ships' funnels down into the iron cooking pans of marine mechanics, tall-ships' crewmen and sailors' widows. The street names exhaled tropical heat. Crews had seen crocodiles, lions and dolphins from the sun-baked decks of frigates, sloops and long-boats in latitudes below the equator ever since the seventeenth century. The flats in this district are still small, but they are no longer as plain as they were.

It was a freezing cold afternoon with air that cut you like glass when you breathed. I could hear each breath ping into my lungs. My head was on fire inside my woollen cap. But warmer air was on the way; a damp mist was sweeping in from the Sound, creeping up perhaps somewhere near the old Steamship Quay, where the water seemed compressed between the two sides of the city. Soon, further out, foghorns would begin to sound. The door of 7 Krokodillegade was thickly covered in dark-red oil paint, and in the window next to it sat an ugly glazed ceramic dog in Chinese style, the sort of thing sailors used to bring home in their sea-chests. Round the dog's thick neck hung what looked like a beer tankard but was presumably a mug for rice-spirit. The name P. MOGENSEN had been handwritten on a piece of paper and carelessly taped to the letter-box; I picked at it and the G and a dot came off in my hand. Then a postman appeared further down the road so I left it alone. The electric bell didn't work, so I banged the brass doorknocker in the old-fashioned way; it resounded down the street like a gunshot. After a while Mogensen opened the door.

"Esmé Olsen," he croaked hoarsely. He clearly wasn't at his best but stepped politely to one side to let me in. I wondered what the matter was. I caught sight of an unusual red tinge in his small eyes, then he dropped his gaze and lumbered past me into the little hall like a great brown-bearded bear in thick wrinkled wool socks. I felt like Goldilocks as I followed him. We came into a little square room with a low ceiling like a ship's cabin, its black beams bowed under the weight of 350 years. Those oaks had once sent forth thick roots and branches and grown to the height of seven men in the royal forests of King Christian IV, in shady glades where all kinds of flying insects and other creatures of the dark flourished, a darkness somehow preserved in the wood. There was a smell of saturation, the sort that comes from ancient wood and ancient leaking drains, a mixture not altogether unpleasant. It was like breathing a fine mix of history into your lungs, and it made the past very tangible. Somewhere a clock struck five brittle chimes. Mogensen sank down onto a sofa whose wooden frame protested anxiously. The small room made a giant of him.

"Hell, Esmé, I've had a few drinks, yeh." Mogensen looked at me with bloodshot eyes, and I felt a vague compassion for him. With a shaking hand he emptied a bottle of mineral water into a beer glass and swallowed the contents in a single mouthful. A little ran out of one side of his mouth and made his russet beard droop. He looked like the Devil incarnate. I assumed his clothes were what he relaxed in: comfortable slacks sagging at the seat and a red-and-white lumber-jack-style check flannel shirt which made him look even broader than he was by several ill-fitting centimetres. There was a stain at the front which I hoped was water. He belched unhappily.

"Where's your kitchen?" I asked. He turned his eyes unhappily in the direction of the hall again, careful not to move his head. I went to look for a coffee-pot.

On the wall of his minimal but surprisingly neat kitchen hung an old engraving, a picture of the battle for the redoubts of Dybbøl that showed a clearly drawn palisade that made one think of Africa, of the illustrations in books about the travels of Stanley, Burton, Speke and other nineteenth-century madcaps who could never find peace, either at home or anywhere else in the world. Thick gunpowder smoke was billowing out over the Danish lines on the hill. The Prussians were swarming up the slope like ants on an ant-hill, and it was abun-dantly clear to everyone involved that Dybbøl was lost. A few sharply pointed stakes weren't going to hold the Prussians back. A remark-able century, the nineteenth, when humankind came to have so many new playthings.

I found the coffee and prepared a mixture as powerful as gunpowder. Everything in the little kitchen was stowed in its place, and this tidi-ness disconcerted me. Peter Mogensen must be an unexpectedly well-organised person. A pedantic troll. I put the coffee-pot and two mugs on a metal tray and took them into the front room. Mogensen was still sitting where I'd left him, holding his shaggy head in his hands like a goalkeeper gripping a football. He took his coffee in little spin-sterish sips while I walked about impatiently with the broad dark planks of the ceiling a bare ten centimetres above my head; it was a room that exactly fitted my own dimensions. Yet it seemed to change shape when Mogensen moved in it, as if like a living skin it was also capable of adapting itself to his size. Everything was tidy. Pictures of ships and sea battles on the walls, some historical literature including books about polar expeditions; an engraving of Sir John Franklin's two ships *Erebus* and *Terror*. A really good mix. I glimpsed Mogensen's bedroom through a half-open door; the bed had been neatly made with precise military corners. In truth the man was a mystery. I noticed he'd pushed his mug aside and was looking at me questioningly. It was time for business.

"So," I said, drawing the word out a little. Mogensen waited politely. "D'you live here alone?"

Mogensen gave this question some thought. Clearly it wasn't a matter of a simple yes or no.

Eventually he said, "I look after the flat for someone." This seemed to be all he had to offer on the subject. A seafarer and Nobody is his name, I thought to myself. He was extraordinarily discreet. I decided to proceed. Who he associated with was of course entirely his own business. He drew his hand through his curly red-brown hair, which was as thick as the wool on a sheep's back. Something was worrying him.

"Hell, Esmé, I've got a problem. Did you see anyone else yesterday evening, I mean was anyone up in Rosen's room at the same time as us?"

I shrugged my shoulders uncertainly. Mogensen looked as though he was in the lowest circle of Hell without a guide. I also noted that he never for a moment suspected me, the cleaning woman. He probably thought I was illiterate. This gave me the confidence to twist his arm a bit. Maybe it was I who was "Nobody" and "infinitely cunning".

"What's wrong?" I asked. "Have you lost something?" I took care not to specify whether it was a case of beer or a gob of used snuff. Even so, Mogensen was clearly rattled. He was sweating with anxiety, and his hair was beginning to look damp.

"Oh, you mean the cardboard box," I said. "I thought you opened that while I was downstairs emptying the refuse sack. Yes, there were a few old papers in it, some wine splashed on them . . ." I paused. Mogensen sweated. I rubbed my nose. "What of it? You want to know if I've thrown them away? No, just joking. They must be on Rosen's shelves. Why should that bother you?"

Mogensen forced a laugh. There are a number of profoundly disagreeable aspects to Professor Rosen, not least a crabby brother-in-law obsessed with red tape who works in the employment office of the City Council. Rosen's brother-in-law has the power to turn almost anyone in Copenhagen's administration into a non-person. A Flying Dutchman of the duty lists. Some have been reduced to the rank of temporary substitute staff for years on end for criticising the wrong people, but only death can remove anyone's name permanently from the annals of the city administration.

"Esmé," Mogensen rattled on, tiresomely insistent. "Could you do something for me?" He got up with some difficulty and splashed the last drop of coffee into my mug. Negotiations were under way.

"Could you ring Dorthe Wilhelmsen and sort this out? Tell her where those documents are and . . ." He looked at me with little red eyes. It was enough to soften a heart of stone.

"For a price," I said.

"What d'you want?" Mogensen's round eyes had suddenly grown more cunning. He picked at the skin on his nose.

"A good chauffeur," I said. "Can I interest you in a Chevy Impala?"

DYBBØL ENTRENCHMENTS,
LATE WINTER 1863-4

THEY HAVE TO wade the last bit of the way through water half a metre deep, and their legs quickly go numb. The bottom is hard and uneven, with sandy ridges and deep hollows, an invisible underwater landscape. The ships rocking on the swell out on the fjord already have steam up; their frozen three-tongued ensigns stick stiffly out in the wind, and their cables twang like the wires of a badly tuned piano. The sea's freezing cold, the swell slow and sluggish. A few metres below the surface, old water is moving to a different beat, old storms sinking slowly to the bottom. On the surface the wind sweeps down the coast, passing with a shrill whine over the dunes, carving hard-frozen sand and snow into sharp-edged waves. Friies wades ashore in his tight uniform jacket beside two greybeards, veterans of the earlier war who fought the Schleswig people at Isted as long ago as 1850 and go on and on about what they went through there, grim experiences nothing can equal. No, nothing could be worse than that, they say, often both speaking at once. But now they go quiet. On shore the men helpfully form themselves up in columns with their backs to the wind. Ice crackles on their uniforms, making all their movements stiff and somehow formal, as if what they are doing is the result of profound thought.

They spend the next two days stowing ammunition and supplies, dried meat and dried split cod from Iceland, in a bivouac made of planks and hewn timber which has already been dug in up on the heights. Outside they have the ten redoubts to protect them. From the fjord you see an uneven chain of bluntly rounded hillocks marked by criss-cross black tracks, and patches of melting snow round cooking-holes. Inside, the redoubts are dark round underground caves, each about twelve long strides across, with damp mud floors and an icy chill seemingly built into their walls.

So the men become creatures of darkness. By day grey light filters in through the gunslits where each must take his turn at gazing out over white sand and water for hours on end. Gradually the cold creeps in through their clothes, eating its way through coarse wool and thread-bare cotton, clinging to the skin like salt or fine sand. Their eyes become bloodshot and blind in the dark, and they have to grope their way back to their pallets. Everything smells of cold rancid animal grease, rape oil and waiting; so far there's no sign of the Germans. And on star-filled nights sharp moonlight pierces the slits, depriving the world of colour.

Gad Friis shares his watch with yet another old man of at least fifty, Paul Natal. They sit side by side on wooden casks, chewing tobacco and listening for time to pass. The watch is measured by the muffled chimes of a little bronze clock up on the defences. Paul is Danish though born in India, in Madras, in the former Danish colony of Tranquebar, or Tarangambadi as they call it in Tamil. His wrinkled face is dark as a hazelnut and somehow timeless. His low voice tells in a soft foreign accent of the brown meandering river Cauvery and the animals you can see there. Wild beasts with eyes that shine in the night, crocodiles and fat pale river-fish broad as a man's thigh. He tells how with a bit of cunning you can catch these light-blind creatures in your arms at night and cut up their tender quivering flesh so quickly that you can feel the fish's heart still beating in your hand. He lays his old pocket-watch in Gad's hand so the boy can feel it ticking.

As they sit in the cold and darkness by Als Sound, Gad becomes aware of the scent of spices, musk and fragrant fires. He sees mist rising from the river at daybreak and hears noises from the jungle that surrounds the town. The very names bring warmth: Coromandel, Tanjore, Tranquebar.

*

In the middle of a fierce snowstorm at the beginning of February the rest of the Danish army arrives, more than 8,000 man beating a hasty retreat from the Dannevirke and bringing the Prussians with them. The men get an extra ration of rum. At first the new Danish troops seem like warmth, life and hope. Eight thousand of them. Their boots thunder on the wooden steps, and the holes in the ground are filled with tobacco smoke, hoarse voices and endless stories of war and of women too long without men. They've seen everything, experienced everything, tasted everything. The cold sea air buzzes with voices, but however much they push and however tightly they cram themselves in, there isn't room for everyone in the bastions, and the old men and boys have to make way for the regular troops. They build compact palisades from timber that has floated up from the south with the retreating Danish army. To this they add axe-hewn oak, as they would in a forest. The palisades smell strongly of resin which despite the severe cold forces its way out of the gashed wood in yellow lumps. When they are finished, these defences under their thin covering of salt and white hoar frost look like the carvings some of the men have seen in fortified native villages in India and Africa. Newly arrived Lieutenant Kobb is reading the engineer Jules Verne's fantasy novel *Five Weeks in a Balloon* and is directing work on the defences, inspired by the French writer's detailed descriptions.

Gad Friis, Paul Natal and hundreds of others are forced to dig themselves new bivouacs in the frozen sand. They work with picks, crowbars and sharp spades, hewing and sawing their way in like travellers in Greenland working on the polar ice, though the sand isn't smooth but rough and relentless as a rasp on their skin. Now and then the sound of Prussian voices, the clink of harness and the dull rumble of gun-carriages reach them across the frozen sand. Words jerk loose and fly over the ice like wind-wrenched leaves, and the whole situation gradually instils unease in the Danish troops – a fear caused by *imponderables*, as the Prussian Bismarck puts it, fleeting things that cannot be weighed or measured. Sounds travel fast over ice and frozen fields, and seem much nearer than they really are. What the Danes are hearing is the shadow or magnified echo of the Prussian army, not the actual sound of real troops. Spirit rather than flesh and blood. Perhaps it also contains the echoes of other armies long since vanished from the fields of Europe – Napoleon's *Grande Armée* in their gaudy shakos or, even further back in memory, the iron-clad Roman legions of Varus, dispersed and terrified in the foggy forests of the German Teutoburger Wald to the south. It's all still there, even the muffled growl of bronze lurs, ancient horns heard from a great distance.

*

Large flocks of crows have begun to gather and crowd out the domesticated white gulls. Carrion birds circling over the troops, perhaps attracted by their warmth or the heaps of waste matter produced by such a large number of men and horses, which has to be shovelled into holes in the ground and covered. Piles of shit fermenting and steaming out on the snow, producing clouds of white vapour that interfere with the vision of the men looking down from the hillside. Birds land on the shit and feast together in brotherly silence. For some reason they never fight among themselves over their booty.

There are women in the baggage train too, broad sturdy matrons in stained skirts enthroned on the rearmost wagons like Nebuchadnezzar's whores on their way into some Babylonian gloom. Females with moon-faces, raucous voices and powerful arms. They run the canteen, stirring and ladling out watery soup from great steaming iron cauldrons. On the soup's surface float occasional greasy pieces of lard like lost ice-floes wandering over a turbid sea. The smell of this concoction is indescribable, rancid and nauseating, but the men accept it humbly. The women scream and shake their fists and spit at the hovering birds, cursing them as the Devil's eyes, believing such huge flocks of crows to be an evil omen. Some of them know charms in German or Latin, strange formulas they mumble repeatedly as they ladle out soup from the cauldrons, mantras to bring good fortune though no-one fully understands what they mean. They also fold small pieces of coloured cloth into triangles which they pin to their bodices and later secretly give to the soldiers they most want to protect. They make marks and draw crudely formed letters on these bits of cloth to protect the wearers from iron and steel and ward off or perhaps mislead death. Paul Natal calls them *tilsamân*, magic signs, and says folk on the great trade-routes through Persia and India do the same, though they use hide rather than cloth. But the women choose all their favourites from among the men who came from the Dannevirke, ignoring the boys and frozen veterans the ships dumped on the shore.

Suddenly in the first days of March a slushy thaw begins. Soon the ice will start to creak and crack. A thick damp mist lies heavy on land and sea, and visibility is down to a few metres. All at once there's an uncanny silence. The fog muffles sound, and all the men can hear is the regular tolling of the bell-buoy to the east on Kegnæs Point. Blinded by fog, the guards up on the redoubts become anxious during their long watches. They seem to hear cries of distress, or laughter, or seductive female voices that come to them from out on the water, but it's only bewitching high-pitched sounds made by the ice as it breaks up. They also think they see drowning human heads twisting about among the waves, but it's only small seals that have followed the cold southwards and been lured into the fjord by hunger or curiosity. They've been seen when shot at to shake their tail-fins and lash about. Lieutenant Kobb has a thick natural-history book and looks them up. He thinks they must be *phoca vitulina* and *phoca hispida*: common seal and ringed seal. When off duty, the men smoke and chatter to distract themselves from these dismal sights and sounds.

When eventually the fog lifts, they see that the ice has broken up and the Sound is lying open, bright blue like the dragoons' jackets. It's clear at once that the Prussians have come much nearer – now through binoculars you can clearly make out their uniforms, faces and weapons. A few hours later they start their first assault, a hellish bombardment that goes on for four interminable hours.

COPENHAGEN,

MARCH 2000

THE WEATHER GOT noticeably milder. Two days after my visit to Krokodillegade, there was a false spring in the air. The shrill screams of gulls came from down in the harbour, and flies which had been lying on their backs between the panes of my double-glazed windows came back to life and began to look for a way out. The warm weather lasted several days. Perhaps the wind had brought coal-smoke from Poland or the old Ruhr. Air imbued with history.

I hadn't gone back to work, didn't want to take the risk. So far as they knew I was off sick, and Dorthe Wilhelmsen was hardly likely to call on me with a bowl of broth. In any case I had a good deal of holiday outstanding, nearly three weeks. I used some of the time for packing. And thinking.

*

Kai had signed a running rental agreement for the seaside cottage. It had been a necessary compromise since he couldn't raise a loan. I suppose he wanted to get away from Copenhagen and the flat; I had to go along simply because there was nowhere else for me to go. Always the problem with children. (I'm not even sure he noticed me, but in any case it suited us both very well.) So we moved to the Amager Island district of the city and rented a smaller two-room apartment at Tårnby with walls as thin as airmail paper and neighbours with shrill voices on all sides, and began to pass our summers in the south of Jutland. We moved earlier to the cottage every spring, and Kai would drive there non-stop. He would pack the Chevy with tinned food and books as though we were heading for a siege. Having read about J.D. Salinger's interest in Indian mysticism, he would take along tomes about Indian magicians, men who could enter a room merely by thinking about it. When we reached our destination he would shut himself up for hours, treading a narrow path round the floor while he sucked at narrow dog-ends wet with saliva – cigarettes held between thumb and index finger with the glowing end imprisoned inside his hand like a firefly. I imagined Salinger doing the same in Cornish, New Hampshire. I liked to think that he too had a view out over the sea, on a coast facing east where tarry whale-hunters once took shelter to leeward, laboriously reefing in sails heavy with salt. I now know that Cornish lies in a wooded landscape, with no view of the sea at all.

*

I looked after myself, though Kai made me a list of things to avoid. DON'T GO OUT BEYOND THE FURTHEST STONES ON THE SHORE. BE CAREFUL TO AVOID THE PROBABLY BOTTOMLESS HOLES AND NARROW INLETS IN THE LINE OF BOULDERS EAST OF THE COTTAGE. NOT TO MENTION STRANGERS. This was an arrangement we both respected. We were always prepared in advance to forestall things that ought not to happen, well informed of the possibilities. Shit can always hit you, but we had no intention of letting ourselves be taken by surprise if we could avoid it. Kai's stock of tins made it possible for us to keep to ourselves for the most part. But even so, life wasn't risk-free. Kai had read accounts of botulism, the madness caused by poisoning which afflicted Sir John Franklin and his crews on the *Erebus* and *Terror* as they lay trapped in the polar ice during the interminable winter of 1846. Firmly frozen in, with little to do but chip away at the ice, read some of the 3,000 books in the ships' libraries and feast on the delicacies they'd brought with them from home. So the polar night rang with the sounds of banquet after banquet, while the lead from soldered cans slowly crept into the men's nervous systems and veins, instilling them with new and disturbing thoughts. Some believe the two ships are still there up in the north, with rigging, crews and everything else on board preserved inside an iceberg as transparent as glass. This was why Dad was most particular that our cans mustn't be even the least bit scratched or dented, despite the fact that nobody had used lead and solder as preservatives for ages. "Dented", the word suggested sharp little teeth snapping at sheet metal, and that's how I always imagined the sailors' madness. Or perhaps it was just that, wrapped up and lulled in their grey hammocks in the polar night, they slept an uncommonly deep sleep.

*

As with the garage, I'd continued paying for the cottage, a symbolic rent of 100 kroner since Dad was a close friend of the landlady, Lara P., a red-haired woman with a dark voice and acrid body odour. She used to come and see us on any pretext, problems with lighting a fire, or something she either wouldn't or couldn't carry up to her attic or down to her cellar despite the fact that she was unusually tall and powerfully built, taller than Kai. Sometimes he would spend the night at the big house, a damp villa shaded by evergreen thuya trees at the end of a dark gravel path. In former times the house had been an annexe or hunting-lodge to a larger property, and a great number of hunting lunches, arrack-punch parties and late-night continuations of other celebrations had been held there. When I asked Lara why our solitary cottage had been numbered 4, she just laughed and drew her warm damp hand through my hair so it got tangled. Her husband had died several years before, and Kai said he had thought of making money by developing some sites by the shore, but that the project had come to nothing by reason of lack of *liquidity*. I always wondered whether this word had something to do with being liquidated, since the husband had died at the same time. But the number 4 must have symbolised bold planning even if the three other cottages had only ever existed in imagination. Musky Lara P. must be a good bit over sixty now if she was a day. For the last ten years my payments had gone into an anonymous giro account. Surprisingly enough the rent had never been raised.

Viberød is an ancient estate which has sometimes been part of Denmark and sometimes part of Germany but has always been owned by the noble Schleswig family of Bockmeister. At least, for as long as anyone can remember. Its being referred to as a "farm" recalls the time when its fierce chatelaine might have rattled a heavy bunch of iron keys as her lord went off to war. Viberød has also been called a "castle" since the seventeenth century and has long been known for its orchards. The large red Christmas apple known as "Julius Bockmeister" was named after a lord of the manor in the 1780s. There are the Viberød butter-pears, too. Viberød was the name I found in the 1938 police report – the impressionable peat-cutter had been employed at Viberød farm. That's why I wanted Mogensen to drive me there.

I packed warm clothes, boots, a knife, a pocket torch, maps, dry matches and a can of paraffin in case we couldn't get the cottage's electrics to work. We'd pick up provisions on the way. Last of all I pushed Rosen's documents and Mayer's *Four Illusions* into my backpack together with a magnifying glass. I'd had another look at the book and found some illustrations in it, engravings so remarkably detailed that I wanted to examine them more closely as soon as I could. They were all signed J.H.K., initials that seemed vaguely familiar to me. I pulled the bag's drawstrings tight so that it looked like a plump Christmas pig and turned off the lamp on my writing-desk. I was ready to set out. Now it was up to Peter Mogensen to try and get Dad's car to start. I was confident he'd manage that somehow.

DYBBØL FORTIFICATIONS,
EARLY SPRING 1864

THE PRUSSIANS HAVE dug themselves in at Avnbjerg. From the heights they can see down onto the Danish positions and watch the Danes running backwards and forwards like ants on an anthill. No plan or co-operation can be discerned. On the far side of the bay lie the Vemmingbund and Gratelund batteries. The cannon have been dragged up by horses and placid Jutland oxen. The local country folk are ready to lend a hand in exchange for modest remuneration. Their dialect resembles Plattdeutsch, so the Prussians have no difficulty understanding them. This manoeuvre has severely damaged the roads, but they can be repaired. Now the ground's no longer frozen, the surface can be dug up and relaid. Occasionally they come upon bits of ancient highway a little below the surface, the stone setts of Roman roads which cause interest and discussion among the officers. They admire the techniques and adventurous spirit of a past age and draw sketches and maps of what they've discovered. A lieutenant, a young man who studied archaeology at Jena before the war, gives a talk one afternoon on the goddess Nerthus, who is believed to have been worshipped in these parts – a legendary Germanic fertility goddess who pulled people down into the bog and held them captive there. A seductive earth-maiden like the Greek Persephone. For the last thousand years such victims of the bog have been found in this area, remarkably well preserved.

*

The din of cannon, mortars and rifles lasts all day. The artillerymen are black with soot and dirt. They wash the pungent gunpowder smoke from their throats with weak beer. The new breech-loading pieces are proving very effective, and the new M-rifles have a good range. It's like hitting the target on a practice range. Easy as pie. The men bet each other French cognac, goose-liver *pâté* and cigars as to who will be the best shot. A score to add up with a pencil-stump. Not many points for hitting the windmill up on the ridge, rather more for hitting the redoubts, a bullseye for a Dane, though one tries to avoid hitting the officers. The Prussians are so near now that they can pick their targets. The Prussian officers call the Danes sitting ducks during afternoon conversations in their tents. They're in high spirits, about to win back part of the German fatherland which lies rich and welcoming in the spring sun.

*

Around April 17 they begin making serious preparations behind the lines to celebrate their victory. Already a covered wagon drawn by four horses has been en route from Lübeck for a week carrying everything the merchants of that city can offer in the way of delicacies. Oysters in gelatin and frozen quails, preserves, joints of meat and raisin puddings plus cognac, champagne and vintage wines, all carefully packed in wood shavings and felt. Also candles and candelabra, cold-mangled linen cloths and starched napkins decorated with the Prussian national coat of arms. And several Hamburg girls of easy virtue to provide company and make up the numbers at the senior officers' table.

The wagon has to travel very slowly over the bad roads if the expensive entertainment it's carrying is not to be wasted. What the girls get to eat during the journey is basic: bread and cheese with a dab of butter. As they get further north, the sanded roads turn into winding paths used by livestock with deep muddy ditches on either side; the driver has to cling firmly to his seat. The road heaves itself over hills and dips deep into hollows. Inside the wagon the women try to socialise among baskets and hampers and the overpowering fragrance of well-hung game and spicy stuffing. The wagon rocks onward over tussocks and muddy ditches like an overloaded ship on the open sea. But three-quarters of the way there, out on Jardelunder Moor, it gets hopelessly stuck. Round about midday, lunchtime. Still revolving, the wheels sink right down to their axle hubs before the driver finally gives up and assembles his passengers outside the wagon. The girls are not at all easy-going now but sulky and frightened at the thought of the approaching night. They're not used to spending much time in the open air. The exotic food-smells have made them all ravenously hungry, but the driver makes it clear that if they touch the delicacies they could be court-martialled. He sinks to the sodden ground exhausted, his face still a greenish yellow from the rocking motion of the journey. The coats of the four army horses harnessed to the wagon are grey with lather and dirt; they twitch their ears and snort, worn out by the heavy mucky going, and one of them breaks wind noisily. Five people marooned in the middle of Jardelunder Moor. Around them the bog, deserted but for a few thin cows huddled under a solitary tree a few kilometres away. They can't see the cows clearly, but they can smell them. The driver gets up and wanders off to look for help; perhaps some farmworker might be able to pull them out of the mire.

Time passes. The road's deserted too. How can this be? The cows move off, and the road remains empty. By six in the evening of April 17, 1864, the four women have had enough. It's time for dinner.

*

Jutland country folk still tell the story years later. Four stunningly beautiful women eating at a table spread with a white linen cloth out in the middle of Jardelund and Frøslevs Mose. An unusually still, mild evening. The rumble of cannon reduced by distance to a dull popping that mingles with the sound of champagne corks flying up into the night and with all the unfamiliar night-noises from the bog. Candles flicker in a light breeze. Bodies are warmed by wine, and skin gleams. Expensive cigar-smoke rises to the sky while not far away the Prussians are preparing to storm the Dybbøl redoubts. Four thousand eight hundred Danes are going to die tomorrow. And I don't know how many Prussians. A thousand? It's difficult to imagine so many bodies. The imagination isn't equal to the job of comprehending reality.

There's more than one version of the end of the story. Some say the driver returned towards dawn with a farmhand and an ox and that eventually the wagon (lightened of its heavy cargo) was pulled free. And that the women were taken home to Hamburg, though no court martial ever took place because the Prussian authorities, drunk with victory, were magnanimous even to four thieving whores. And that the women went back to their normal occupation, perhaps punishment enough in itself. But other people tell a different tale, something so fantastic as to be almost beyond belief . . .

In this second version, a light mist lies over the bog just before dawn, damp but not unpleasant. The women have completely emptied the hampers and bottles, so that there's plenty of room now inside the wagon for them to wrap themselves up in the felt packaging from the wine and doze off. One of them is snoring loudly. Outside the horses are tethered to the wagon-wheels that caused all the trouble in the first place. The driver hasn't come back and never will, because in the darkness he stumbled straight into the Prussian positions and a nervous sentry accidentally shot off his head.

Just as the sun begins to rise, the horses become restless, pull at their harness and rock the wagon, abruptly waking the four women. The man who reported this saw it all from a considerable distance; he was a simple peasant with the typical childlike imagination of the uneducated. They say he was on his way to get the cows in when to his surprise he came upon the covered wagon and neighing horses out on the road and hid in the heather to see what would happen. The wagon door opened, and four women slowly got out as if half asleep: "My sister walks in her sleep," said the man, "so I know what that looks like. They were city girls in thin dresses with expensive lace – something we don't often see in these parts." Despite their fine clothes the four women confidently untied the horses and mounted them as if it was something they'd been doing all their lives. Then, riding bareback like men, they set off into the mist in a straight line as if along a road or track. As if following someone. The man ran forward but didn't get far over the wet ground while the mist thickened and turned white and milky. No-one ever saw the four women again. Local folk say they must have been riders of Nerthus.

*

I suppose this isn't true. Decide for yourself.

ON THE ROAD

W E FIDDLED WITH the Chevy for more than an hour. To be more precise, Mogensen did the fiddling with the upper part of his body hidden under the bonnet and his bum in the air while I sat on a stool in Kai's garage reading. I'd got a good way into my book. The story of the food wagon was included as a detailed note to the third of the four illusions. The print was painfully small and seemed to be getting smaller, though of course this can't have been possible. My eye must have been deceived by the demanding style. I couldn't be sure the story wasn't just one of Mayer's inventions, and this irritated me.

Finally Mogensen straightened up, leaned heavily against the workbench and stuck a battered cigarette between his thick red lips. A shiny adjustable spanner protruded from his check breast-pocket, and his great paws were black with lubricating oil, a sight not only colourful but confidence-inspiring. Between breathless puffs of smoke, he explained the situation.

"Her battery needed charging – but we'll still be able to get her going." He gave the cream-painted metal a friendly pat. It sounded like a tin can, and his hand left a sticky mark. "The steering wheel was loose, and there was a noise in the gearbox, the leads are decayed and might go at any moment – or last the whole way, no guarantees."

That was only to be expected; I have lifelong experience of being without guarantee. So I just nodded and said nothing, trying to look as if I was considering the situation. I have no views on car engines.

"But will we be able to drive down there?" I asked finally.

"Of course," said Mogensen. "Just can't say how far we'll get. Could end up in a ditch or field, yeh." He inhaled; the smoke leaked out of him slowly and drifted in grey eddies round his curly head. He seemed to be radiating heat. Then he dropped the cigarette on the floor and put his foot on it. He looked very much at home in Kai's garage, and as we stood there I felt a remarkable sense of fellowship with him. It's always seemed important to me to talk to people I scarcely know or hardly have any interest in. Mogensen presumably felt the same.

"I can fix this one," he said with satisfaction, grinding his fag-end to a pulp. "When do we leave?"

"An hour," I said. "We leave in an hour."

*

In fact it took us more than an hour to fill the Chevy with oil and decant petrol into her bottomless tank, to prise the heavy vehicle out into the road and get her engine running (the word *deadweight* suddenly came to have real meaning for me). I sat at the wheel, half-lying in order to reach the gas, while Mogensen huffed and puffed behind with his paws on her backside. Some of the street's more scantily clad girls came out and goggled at us with interest, a hairy giant and a pale dwarf struggling with an antiquated cream-coloured car that didn't want to start. The Chevy was just about the only thing in the district not in motion so far as I could see. I could sense disappointed souls brooding behind unwashed windows, mortified to learn that an American vintage car had been hidden in the garage without their knowledge. A 1958 Chevrolet Impala isn't the least valuable thing in the world.

The engine started just before we reached the end of the street, and I jammed on the brakes for all I was worth. The controls seemed set in stone, locked in a dead man's grip. The Chevy rattled as it ticked over while Mogensen climbed in and took the wheel. He was horribly red in the face and smelt of beer or sweat (perhaps there wasn't much difference between the two). He was wearing a crumpled wool sweater and had thrown his only luggage on the back seat, a black plastic bag decorated with the words *SPECIAL OFFER* in fiery red letters. As far as I could see, this bag contained another crumpled sweater, a check shirt and something I assumed to be underpants – I avoided looking too closely. He had the wreck of yet another cigarette in the corner of his mouth, and I guessed that the fag was at least as important to him as the car's gear lever. For a moment he seemed to have lost his nerve. Then he wrenched her into second and we were on our way.

If you've ever had to drive out of a big city, you'll know that you have to be wise to all the tricks: short cuts, lane changes and the day's programme for digging holes in the road. (Urban hole-diggers wage permanent war on motorists, with the hole-diggers usually a step ahead. A single leak can be enough to generate five or six evil-smelling holes, preferably drilled through earth frozen as hard as granite and in accordance with the dictum *He who seeks shall find*. It's impossible to get past these holes even on foot, and they never stay in the same place for two days in succession. The men who dig them assert their claim to newly conquered territory with heaps of earth, blinking red lights and straggling wooden fences.)

Mogensen proved a model chauffeur. He neatly extracted us from Copenhagen in next to no time, and I was soon able to return calmly to my reading. The Chevy's engine thundered under the bonnet, and the tyres hissed and howled on the wet asphalt. The suburbs passed as quickly as patches of farmland seen from a broomstick-ride in a fairy tale. Redbrick villas in upmarket districts and straight lines of terraced housing: all seemed deserted, as if some pestilence had come and swept everyone away in their prime. Though I expect they were just sitting indoors waiting for spring. Those who had no homes or had been thrown out of them had conveniently died, decimated each winter by the cold weather. As I see it, poverty, drink and drugs are just another form of plague, a pale lean death that transforms its victims enough for us not to have to face mirror images of ourselves sitting on park benches. So everything's taken care of.

The curvature of the car seat was familiar and filled me with a mix of feelings I preferred not to try to analyse. After a while I was no longer sure what age I was living in. In his narrative, Gabriel Mayer had tried to structure time and existence in his own way by returning to the past. Just as I was turning a page, a thin handwritten piece of paper fell out of the book and started to fly away, but I managed to catch it at the last moment.

FRØSLEVS MOSE,
THURSDAY, AUGUST 31, 1938

MAYER AND RAV dig a shallow ditch round the body. Their spades cut easily into the earth, but suction makes it difficult to pull them out, and they have to be twisted this way and that before they can be extracted. The crows have moved nearer and sit jabbering discordantly among themselves, snapping their sharp beaks right beside the hole. With their shiny button eyes and rapid movements they seem remarkably free from fear. The German, still miscalculating the body's age, waits above on firm ground. He picks up a lump of earth and throws it among the crows. They take flight, and for a time all that can be heard is the dry flapping of a hundred wings as they rasp the air. F.A. Nagler has exhausted his vocabulary by now, both Danish and German. With jerky movements he gets out his flat cigarette-case again and smokes with short little puffs.

Mayer and Rav work in silence. After a while they remove their jackets and continue in shirtsleeves. Flies and mosquitoes buzz obstinately round them, attracted by the sweaty warmth of their bodies. Apart from the sound of insects and spades it's remarkably quiet. The sun has gone in, leaving a stifling calm like that at the bottom of a well. From the bog's higher ground comes a sharp aromatic scent from dense thickets of bog-myrtle and broom, making the men drowsy. They dig slowly and carefully. Swamp water runs quickly into the hole, creating a narrow moat round the dead man, something not to be stepped over. Rav stops, lays down his spade and dries his strong hands carefully on a large white cotton handkerchief with a red border. When he's finished, he folds the handkerchief into a neat triangle and tucks it back into his trouser pocket, which it shares with the tin containing the Lackey moth larva, which is still alive. Franz Nagler watches him in irritation. Young Mayer rests on the handle of his spade, glad of the break. Rav decides to take a few more pictures and picks up an egg-shaped light-meter which he holds at arm's length till he gets the right reading. His powerful nose is shining with sweat so that he looks as if he's been inhaling light. He's pushed his felt hat back on his head till the brim nearly touches his yellowing shirt collar. There are wet marks from his hand on the felt. Before he presses the shutter, he lays thin white measuring sticks marked with simple hand-written scales for length and breadth round the body so as to record the dead man's dimensions. Having been so strongly compressed, almost like a herb in a plant-press, the body is now quite small. Rav checks the points of the compass and finds the head's pointing south and the legs, what's left of them, north. The unseasoned wood of the measuring sticks stands out against the dark ripeness of the bog. When he's finished, the police chief bundles the sticks together again and ties a piece of string round them. The dead man accepts all this activity in silence, stiff as a piece of wood as if waiting patiently.

Gabriel Mayer enters all the measurements on an official form as required by the state in cases of sudden death – particularly unexpected deaths, but then perhaps every death is unexpected. He begins wondering whether a tongue and teeth still exist behind the stiff brown lips, and what the dead man's voice was like. Danish or German? Dark or light? Loud or soft? This is an ancient border area. The dead man could now be a foreigner in his own land, since the border has moved so often. Mayer imagines the tongue probably rotted away before the salts and other substances in the bog had a chance to preserve the body. A nauseating thought that he immediately pushes aside. Perhaps the district medical officer will come; Aronius and Rav will probably send for him. Yes, there's bound to be an investigation if they manage to move the body in one piece, though this is a matter for the Danish police, just as it was with the dead woman believed to have committed suicide early that spring. He was in on that too, as witness and recorder with Madsen and Rav. The ground had just thawed, and the fields were soft and spongy when he crossed them in the icy wind. Mud stuck to his boots in thick green lumps – ancient seabed which had worked its way to the surface. The body was found in an outhouse a good distance from the nearest farm, a draughty shed where a farm-worker kept old tools. They took the same stretcher with them that time, and it was heavy going across the fields on the way back.

Water's still bubbling up round the dead man. Mayer can feel the damp forcing its way through his thin leather shoes; he moves back a little to a flat raised area where the ground is dryer. He's read some-where that humans are 60 per cent water. So we must be more likely to return to water and air than to dust, no matter what the priests say.

Rav has unrolled the canvas stretcher, which is still stained with dried clay. This is the first time it's been used since the spring; here in Grænsebyen most folk live hardworking, God-fearing lives and die in their beds. He motions to Mayer to put down his notes and come nearer to help with the lifting. They need to get their spades under the body and either shift or cut through a network of old roots and tightly packed turf in a single movement. Not an easy manoeuvre, in fact a balancing act, and the German must help too or the platform of earth may break up and the body with it. None of them is prepared to touch this horrifying object with his hands, so the work goes slowly. At the third attempt they manage to get it onto the stretcher, and Rav covers it with pieces of fine cotton, including two white lengths crossed over the breast like a pair of soiled wings. Mayer is suddenly reminded of tacked-together angel costumes lying on a bench behind the choir at Christmas celebrations in the church. They lift the stretcher and are surprised to find the body is almost weightless.

TO SOUTH JUTLAND

S OME WAY BEYOND Slagelse, the engine coughed and died. Its last gasp carried us onto a slushy hard shoulder, and that was that. The rest of the traffic thundered by like a noisy herd of wild animals, some drivers blinking their lights to make sure we realised we'd come to a halt. Mogensen swore and climbed out of the car with a grunt. I smiled through the window to encourage him. The icy wind emphasised the ripe colour of his face; he looked as if he was about to have a stroke. I leaned forward and grabbed the control I was most familiar with, the lever that opened the bonnet, which rose into the wind. I felt I was lifting the lid on a boxful of trouble; Mogensen was going to be kept busy for a good long time.

Among Rosen's documents was a paper from Pastor Aronius, to be more exact a letter from the autumn of 1939 that I wanted to study more closely now I'd read Mayer's story. Something about the examination of a body. Age had made Aronius rather confused, and in his letter he was obviously mixing up two separate events, one being the discovery of the body of the unknown woman.

*

Writing to Munch, the district medical officer, he starts with general comments about recent illnesses and deaths, about how many fruit trees in the vicarage garden suffered frost damage the previous winter and how the cold caused him severe pain in his joints and bones. Then he comes to his real reason for writing: how in February 1938 a macabre discovery had been made not far from Grænsebyen. On the

18th of that month a farmworker called Bue Hatt had found the body of a young woman in a farm shed. And "since it was a bitterly cold winter of the sort that makes birds fall dead from the trees and blights ancient willows with frost, the body was frozen solid so that it was impossible to tell how long it had been there." What had most troubled God-fearing old Aronius was that the woman had been almost naked, dressed in nothing but a thin embroidered vest. She had had a white complexion and looked well nourished, almost plump. There'd been no outward sign of injury, but her bare feet had been stained with earth and marked by sores and signs of frostbite as if she'd walked a long way. There had also been superficial cuts on her soles, believed to have been caused by the sharp crust on the snow that lay over the fields. Across each instep had been a deeper gash, but there seemed no obvious explanation for this. These wounds had not been new (at this point the pastor loses his thread and witters on about old Danish myths collected in the area; he was a member of the South Jutland Antiquarian Association, a learned society founded as long ago as 1865 by the father of prehistoric archaeology, Jacob Asmussen Worsaae).

The woman had had fine fiery red hair and regular features. She hadn't been tied up or locked in, since it was impossible to lock the shed from either inside or outside, and its wooden walls were in such bad shape that it would have been easy to break through them (and the shed was full of tools). The only explanation anyone in Grænsebyen could come up with was that the woman must have gone into the shed with the express purpose of freezing to death. But *de mortuis nil nisi bene* (speak no ill of the dead), as the anxious pastor puts it. After a superficial examination, her body had been placed on a block of ice in the church mortuary or charnel house to await Dr Munch's post-mortem (Aronius himself kept the key to this building). Apparently the body had to be left there longer than intended since Munch had been busy with a severe flu epidemic at Tønder.

Then there had been the year's second unknown body, the soldier from Frøslev. On this subject Aronius has difficulty keeping his facts straight. It appears from what he says that Munch had examined the soldier but not the woman; the pastor doesn't explain why. The red-haired woman had been placed in a locked inner chamber on her own, since the church caretaker kept his tools in the outer room of the charnel house (where it was the custom to park the deceased in their screwed-down coffins but never for more than a few days so as not to show them disrespect). Too much coming and going in the small inner chamber had been discouraged for fear it might cause the body to thaw out. But when one day in early March the door to the inner room had finally been unlocked, the body was found to have vanished without trace. There'd been nothing left but sodden straw and a piece of ice that hadn't melted. Aronius' response had been to hold an extra prayer meeting that evening, while Police Constable Madsen had fine-combed the churchyard for footprints but found nothing unusual. The matter had been set to rest a week later when Munch, with Rav and Aronius as witnesses, had written out a death certificate in the absence of the woman's body.

The examination of the soldier had been performed quickly because his body had begun decomposing with disturbing speed – like when last year's apples roll under the bench in the pantry and rot on the stone floor. Munch had removed the heart, some half-decomposed lung tissue and the stomach and preserved them in formalin (in glass jars reluctantly lent by Aronius' housekeeper from among the ones she used for conserving fruit). He'd also cut off two locks of the dead man's red hair and sealed them in an envelope together with his nails. An attempt had also been made to take his fingerprints, but this had come to nothing since substances in the bog had obviously contracted and dissolved the delicate whorls on his fingertips; when pressed on paper the only mark they made was a smudge like a dried water-stain. The woman's fingerprints had already been sent to national police HQ in Copenhagen (Rav had so far received no response). Thus the only physical evidence that she had ever been in Grænsebyen at all was the ten prints taken from her frozen fingers. For what it's worth, comments Aronius, her hands had been small and well-formed. He ends by thanking the doctor for sending a wreath to the soldier's interment *Pro Patria* in Grænsebyen churchyard.

*

The rest of the letter dealt with the problem of parasites in the meagre apple harvest and was of no interest to me. I folded it away. Mogensen was still busy under the bonnet so I decided to stretch my legs. The car squeaked when I got out, but he didn't look up and I set off along the edge of the road. The sky hung over us like a metal lid, but I could see a turn-off to a layby some way ahead. Cars hooted at me as they passed, followed by five juggernauts from Wrocław proceeding bumper to bumper like a dirty grey moving wall, infuriating drivers who couldn't pass them. I struggled on half in the ditch, inhaling air saturated with diesel fumes. The Polish lorries reminded me of Rosen's box and of documents in general and the realities they represent. Wrocław used to be called Breslau and was part of the German Empire and old Prussia. It was Prussia's second largest city after Berlin. In 1945 it became one of Hitler's fortresses in his final battles against the Russians. This was followed by nearly forty years behind the Iron Curtain, the result of lines drawn on a map to indicate borders and lines of words written into a peace treaty that altered people's lives, languages and memories (naturally there were some things they wanted to forget). Fictive things can become more real than grass, warm sun, fields, muddy rivers and cool forest glades, which can all be made invisible. Agreements which stick can even change the past or our image of it through a suggestive choice of words, self-interest, guilt and silences. By means of something we are in the habit of identifying as human that is in fact as impersonal as chess moves. Reality can be changed, phased out and eased in as if following a French curve. The strange thing is that this usually works.

The layby had been constructed to conform with the commonly accepted view that all we need for a sense of comfort and well-being is an overful dustbin, a couple of toilets with metal doors that have been kicked in so that they won't close properly and a piece of grey fibreglass furniture screwed to the ground just in case we might feel tempted to enjoy a picnic after our trip to the toilet. This scene overlooked a large windswept field where grey ice persisted in the furrows left by last autumn's ploughing as though the earth had forgotten to take winter out of its pocket. Everything breathed cold mist, mud and desolation. Right on the edge of the field stood a mighty oak with gnarled branches, and under this oak sat a dog.

*

It was the ugliest mongrel I'd ever seen. It had a large square head with narrow, slightly slanting eyes and a powerful snout marked by a white scar from some forgotten battle. The front part of its body was as muscular as a boxer's but led to a spindly rear end with a thin ratlike tail. Its paws were astonishingly small and dainty, and its coat, apparently black, looked to be buried under several layers of ingrained mud. The dog had a wide leather collar round its neck but apparently no owner; in fact, there was no human being in sight. The only person I could see was Mogensen in the distance still bent over the car's engine, holding up an adjustable spanner like a tuning-fork and deaf to all else. The mongrel contemplated me with calm indulgence, making me feel I was being judged. It flared its nostrils rhythmically as it inhaled my odour. I stood still, my heart beating a strict-tempo drum solo under my woollen sweater. Then it got to its feet in a leisurely manner and, to my astonishment, wagged its tail lazily and came trotting straight towards me on bandy legs.

I have nothing against dogs – on the contrary, they seem more decent than most human beings I've known – but I prefer to watch them from a distance. From the other side of a street or park. Now this cur had chosen me, there could be no doubt about that. Close up it looked even more fiendish, with congealing strings of snot round its muzzle and purulent yellow eyes. Perhaps it had a cold; I have no experience of animal ailments. Otherwise it seemed in prime condition. When I held out my hand in formal greeting it licked my woollen glove voluptuously. It was enough to bring tears to the eyes. A small metal plate riveted to its collar told me its name was Terror.

*

Terror lay down on the back seat of the car. The Chevy's upholstered in light sheepskin, which must have felt comfortable after the field. To my satisfaction, he paid no attention whatever to Mogensen but followed me with moist eyes. In no time at all the car began to smell of wet dog. I rooted about in my backpack and pulled a packet of biscuits from my little survival kit (biscuits, raisins, nuts, dark choco-late and a pocket-flask of brandy). Terror swallowed the biscuits in a couple of gulps and belched with contentment. He was like a ship that had come into harbour.

DYBBØL,
APRIL 20, 1864

THE VAN ROCKS on through a grey foggy landscape. Its axles creak and screech as they turn, their monotonous song interrupted only when the man on the box is forced to rein in his horse before some exceptionally large hole. Skirting such hazards can be a slow business, and he often has to jump down from the box and lead the horse round in the sucking mud, while the van tilts and threatens to overturn. The glass bottles in its dark interior clink and slop at each dip and stone. Every now and then the man stops to make sure they are still properly corked. The road has been churned up into little more than a muddy ditch twisting and turning its way between the hills. God only knows whether one can call it a road at all, Käsemann tells himself. Fog lies like a wet cloth on the slopes. The horse is disturbed by the strange scents drifting through the haze, the acrid smell of gunpowder and burning and something else too, something putrid and sweetish. These odours prevent both driver and horse from feeling hungry. From time to time the photographer takes a swig from his pocket-flask of French cognac to deaden his sense of smell.

The van's only cover is an oilcloth painted black and stretched like a tent over a wooden frame. The whole outfit vibrates just as ladies' hats used to do on the promenade at Ostend, where Käsemann used to go to paint in the North Sea light. The van is in fact a mobile darkroom, a curiosity hired from a friend (Käsemann handed over his gold watch as security for it). The name of his friend's studio – IMAGO – has been carefully painted in silver on both sides of the oilcloth cover together with the studio's address, F——strasse No. 10. The thin grey mare struggling to pull the van is an army reject. Heinrich Käsemann is a landscape painter from Berlin who also dabbles in the new art of photography. The goal of his uncomfortable journey is the battlefield at Dybbøl, where he plans to photograph the glory of victory.

Käsemann is a well-built man, a good one metre seventy tall, clean-shaven apart from the thin military moustache under his powerful nose. His fair, almost white, hair is clipped *en brosse*. His blue eyes sit close together under strong brows, giving him a thoughtful, concentrated look, though he's usually neither thoughtful nor concentrated. He wears a snuff-coloured knee-length cotton coat, half-length elasticated boots, check trousers and a red neckerchief arranged in a careless knot. For the moment he's taken off his hat and put it beside him on the box, carefully clamping the brim down with his strong thigh to stop it falling into the mud. He has taken a lot of trouble over his appearance, because he knows Prince Friedrich Karl of Prussia is at Dybbøl. He intends to take a portrait photograph of the prince if he gets the chance.

*

As the van nears the battlefield, the stench gets ever stronger. The mare lays back her ears, quivers and hesitates even when Käsemann strikes her bony back with his whip. He's sweating despite the clammy mist and takes off his coat. The alcohol causes him to exaggerate his movements, making him unsteady so that he has to hold fast to the iron rail of his narrow seat. The screeching and creaking of the van are giving him a headache. His friend Loser in Berlin is seriously ill with typhus, and he wonders – if the worst comes to the worst – whether Loser's wife, Clara, might not be willing to sell her husband's cameras and other equipment for a fair price. He cracks his whip over the horse's rump and thinks for a moment. The van sinks into yet another hole. Clara can keep the darkroom.

Soon figures begin to materialise in front of the van, their voices muffled and monotonous in the damp. The road's no longer empty, and Käsemann is forced to move to one side repeatedly to let open carts through carrying the wounded and the dead. The wounded groan, cry out and swear when the cartwheels jolt into holes in the road. But other carts are silent and covered with grey tarpaulins, their solitary drivers stiffly hunched like death sentries, each with a neckerchief round his face. Only the tobacco smoke from their pipes, intended to mask the smell, detracts from the atmosphere of ceremonial solemnity. The carts move slowly for fear the bodies will roll over and fall off – dealing with this if it does happen is not pleasant. After the carts come columns of soldiers on their way home, grey-faced and silent. It is hard to see any difference between victors and vanquished in this sad, exhausted crowd. The mist makes everything theatrical, unreal.

Heinrich Käsemann isn't unfamiliar with death, far from it. He has taken death portraits for Berlin's best families, in dark silent apartments with drawn curtains and funeral meats laid out on dishes adorned with lace. He has spent long hours alone with the dead in the presence of wax candles and sticks of incense, especially in summer when relatives prefer not to stay too long in the stuffy rooms. And he has often photographed suicides in the cellar at the morgue, pale wretches dragged from the dark waters of the river Spree, taking shots of their faces partly to help the police with possible identification but most of all for character studies. A number of active researchers at Berlin University are compiling systematic collections of noses, eyes and mouths. An Archive of the People. They are interested in correspondences between features, and in whether unrest in the structure and harmony of the face may also lead to unrest in the soul. All in an attempt to establish whether perhaps the suicidal and the depressive make up a race of their own. The city's imbeciles are being catalogued in the same way, but Käsemann has never been to the lunatic asylum. Only to the morgue in ——strasse; assignments of this kind are of course confidential and must be carried out with discretion and tact. In the morgue the dead are laid out on marble benches, still wearing their sodden rags. Sometimes appalling gases emanate from their bodies. Sometimes nothing is left but sodden cloth, as if a whole personality has vanished but for a bright red skirt, a pair of shoes with broken heels or a velvet waistcoat that survive like items forgotten on the left-luggage shelf at a railway station. But usually such people are very poorly dressed.

When a photographer has the opportunity to use light and time exactly as he wants to, his pictures come out good and sharp. The drowned never complain of cold or exhaustion. But on one occasion Käsemann's work was disrupted when a dead body suddenly came to life again, a young girl so thin that every rib stood out with horrifying clarity. He can still remember her deep sigh when he laid her on her side, her pale face blue from the cold river. Rushing for help, he nearly knocked his camera off its tripod. When she finally realised where she was, the girl became hysterical. She was a visitor from the land of the dead, and his photograph came out blurred, the shutter open at the very moment life revived in her. A few hours later, for all he knew, she was back on the streets of Berlin. Resurrected only to fall back into the depths.

On the floor above the morgue, two duty attendants sit in their office, stocky red-faced men as like one another as twins or sun-dried berries, Heinz and Fritz, smoking and playing cards, usually rummy for low stakes, and he can hear their excited voices, harsh as rusty saws on splitting wood, as the game reaches its climax. When, having put on his coat and hat, he turns quickly in the doorway to say goodbye, Käsemann sees Heinz or Fritz placing copper coins on the eyes of the dead to stop them staring, worn pfennigs to serve as travel-tokens till the bodies have been placed in wooden boxes and nailed down. Heinz and Fritz are veterans of the first Schleswig war; they are used to death but can't stand the stare of the dead. The boxes are constructed from packing cases supplied by local businesses, marked with freight-stamps and product names in large black letters that can be seen here and there among the knots on the wood; "Mayer & Co.", perhaps, or "Weislinger Sekt – Prima Qualität", as if the dead have been granted the aliases or newly stamped travel passes they will need before they can go any further (Käsemann thinks of them as a sort of refugee). The hollow sound of hammer blows in short bursts like drum rolls follows him up the broad stone staircase. The pfennigs are kept in a tin on the caretaker's desk. The belongings of the drowned, when they have any, are sold to the Jews of Alexanderplatz, so the dead pay their own way with their rings, necklaces and hair. This will buy them a pauper's burial in an unmarked grave, two or three coffins in the same hole when someone has found time to dig one.

*

The mare stops abruptly and refuses to go a step further. Neither the crack of the whip, friendly words nor oaths can get the stubborn wretch to change her mind. An idea has taken root and grown in the simple horse's head, and in the end all the photographer can do is to jump down to the ground. Mud splashes his shoes and too late he remembers his hat, which glides down on its broad brim like a dying chicken and lands beside his foot. An expensive hat made of real American buffalo hide, bought in one of Berlin's finest stores. He swears silently to himself, quickly snatches it up and puts it safely on his head.

Käsemann knows why the mare is uneasy. He can hear a jingling and rattling, and some way off a light captures metallic reflections in the damp air. Spurs and gold, eagles and snaffle bridles. A detachment of the prince's hussars is riding along the muddy road. Men in the saddle as tense as steel springs jolting along out of time with one another on the deplorable surface. The horses snort and break wind anxiously when their hoofs fail to find a foothold on the slope. Their eyes are bloodshot after a hard ride. This movement of troops presumably means that the prince is already on his way home. If this is so, it means Käsemann is too late. He gropes stupidly for his pocket-watch until he remembers that he left it in Berlin, on his friend Loser's bedside table.

The first contingent of hussars passes with a light smell of gunpowder, sweating horses and leather. Then comes a battered vehicle, a covered travelling-carriage with blinds carefully pulled down behind its polished windows. It alternately rolls and slithers along the churned-up track, its four wheels clogged with clinging bluish mud so thick that their spokes can barely be distinguished. The carriage has been badly splashed too. Its doors carry no coat of arms or name. On the coachman's box a sallow man in a grey-green cloak shakes the reins over two tired geldings with lathered flanks. Both carriage and horses look as if they've emerged from the bottom of the sea, like Neptune's coach with two seahorses in the traces. This is definitely not the prince's coach but something else, maybe something secret. Does it contain the prince's mistress? Or Bismarck himself? Or money? No, they would never entrust anything so valuable to a miserable post-chaise that threatens to overturn at any moment. Käsemann stares with curiosity as this equipage passes. The hussars coming after it are expressionless as it rocks unsteadily on a special temporary pair of wheels. Click, clack, click, clack, a sound like knocking at the Sea King's gate. The cavalry horses, normally so fearless, lay back their ears at the sound. Not until long after the troop has passed can Käsemann manage to coax his obstinate mare to move. And when she does, she pulls as if what has passed and is now behind her is the Devil himself.

TO SOUTH JUTLAND

B Y THE TIME Mogensen had finished working on the car, the mongrel was deep in an untroubled slumber that – his scar notwithstanding – indicated a clear conscience. Together the three of us created a close, strong-smelling atmosphere. Despite the cold the nightwatchman was greasy, sweaty and red, and it was only after he'd sworn a long string of fruity oaths that he managed to squeeze us out onto the road again, in the smoking wake of a German long-distance lorry. Its load was described as fertiliser, which I could well believe. The Chevy coughed a couple of times but kept going. The muck seemed to have left the carburettor and established itself somewhere else. I had no confidence that we would ever get to the cottage.

The bridge over the broad waterway of the Great Belt is like an endless runway for planes to land on without the relief of any facility for them to take off again. Our tyres hammered monotonously on its asphalt and concrete, and I looked out over a rail streaky with gull-shit. The fertiliser lorry had vanished. The sky was a constant grey.

*

When I was a child, we sometimes used to spend the night in Christiansfeld, a town once associated with the Moravians. We always booked in at Brødremenighedens Hotel at 25 Lindegade Street. The old border between Denmark and Prussia used to run through here. I have a vivid memory of the place. Birds would crowd chattering on its ramshackle weather-vane. The building has been damaged by damp and is extremely old; it leans in towards its own centre as if crossing its arms to hide a rotten heart. Its roof is curved like a dragoon's saddle long weighed down by convex containers. The entrance hall is a mixture of various rich smells, somehow timeless as if someone had opened the lid of a forgotten chemist's chest. At the foot of the stairs stands an old long-case clock, which runs slow and has a tick that sounds like it is marking off the years in quicksilver. In a room on the first floor, just to the right of the stairs, a truce between Denmark and Prussia was signed in 1864, during the night of July 17–18. Colonels Kauffman and von Stiehle and their adjutants toast the armistice in vintage red wine, in sultry heat in which the candles in the two brass candlesticks burn right down without flickering. Insects of the night come in through the window, singe their wings in the flames, flare up and vanish, spreading an unpleasant smell. The two men stand in front of the window silhouetted against a light sky. The Prussian, Gustav von Stiehle, has trimmed his full beard carefully to sharpen his profile and wears an Iron Cross round his neck on a short ribbon. Heinrich August Theodor Kauffman wears his hair in the style of the German-British Prince Albert, with a soft side parting over a high fore-head, a twisted moustache and long, carefully combed whiskers. In the doorway stands a maid holding a dusty bottle wrapped in a linen cloth; this is mine host's 15-year-old daughter Tanne, ready to pour more wine into the two men's glasses. The wine's an 1845 burgundy she has fetched up from the cellar, and she hopes not to have to go down again, since people have several times seen ghosts and other spooky things there. She's red in the face because the room's so hot and oppressive, and there seems to be thunder in the air. But the gentlemen only drink one glass together and thereafter hurriedly with-draw each to his own side of the long corridor. The clock on the wall, which at this date still works, strikes two.

*

There are a table and four chairs in the room and, by the wall, a four-sided white porcelain stove decorated with a plaster flower-medallion. Within this medallion sits a lady wearing nothing but a thin white shift and an indifferent smile. The medallion must have come from somewhere else, for in the fashion of the early nineteenth century the woman's charms are easily visible through the cloth of her shift. Her small, well-formed feet hang outside the roundel in dainty shoes, as if she were about to climb out and run off. I like to think she's only there when we're looking at her. On the adjacent wall hangs a clock with motionless pendulum, its long hands doing the splits over time. On summer evenings the town is deserted as though it too is fashioned in plaster with a dusty golden light falling over cracked façades and bright windowpanes. There's hardly anyone to be seen; in the churchyard brothers and sisters rest like strict, taciturn custodians of the living, while the church spire threatens every sinful thought like a chastising cane. At nightfall the churchyard pathways are full of the stupefying aroma of thuya, growing in neat hedges clipped into tight blocks. There are also gravestones in memory of the fallen, soldier boys who fought for Denmark or Germany for reasons no-one can remember.

The hotel seems to be waiting for Kai and me, silent and patient, with polished stone steps leading down into the street. But the bottom step is invisible now; it disappeared long ago under layers of setts and asphalt, and the gate has been reset. To get in we have to cross the yard at the back, an open space where stage-coaches and carriages once used to stop, their exhausted horses stooping in a row at the water-trough. We go to bed early, and under the beds in our room we always find dead insects, mummified little creepy-crawlies rolled into balls with their legs drawn in tightly to their bodies. Kai spends a long time reading, the book leaning against his scraggy knees. He chain-smokes, making the air in the room heavy and pungent. I sleep badly in my bed by the wall, disturbed by unfamiliar noises and footsteps in the night, and on one occasion I even imagine I can hear the tinkle of glass.

*

Next morning, July 18, 1864, confident in victory, von Stiehle returns to Berlin. The crowing cocks still sound heavy with sleep as he climbs into his carriage with his portfolio of documents and goes on his way behind a glossy, well-groomed four-in-hand. The period after the armistice is characterised by confusion, with military units marching in all directions along the sandy country roads in response to muddled orders. At night people notice a reddish corona round the moon, and many take this as a sign of new unrest ahead. Officers of a more scientific bent believe it has been caused by all the fighting, gunpowder smoke and agitation which have disturbed the surface of the earth and set particles dancing in the moonlight like dander caught in the beam of a stable lantern. The farmworkers of Jutland are in the fields taking in the harvest while the troops parade backwards and forwards, ever fewer in number since many of them, deciding that getting in the harvest is more important than continuing to serve in the Danish army, have unbuttoned their tunics, rolled up their sleeves and gone home to their villages and farms. In August the dust kicked up by horses' hoofs still lies tight as mist over the hot summer landscape, whitewashing the greenery in the ditches like a cattleshed. The sky is as light a blue as the jacket of a Danish dragoon, the dog days are beginning, and all seems just as it always was. But gradually the laws, language and justice of the new masters gain a foothold, and South Jutland, at least superficially, becomes Prussian for the next fifty years and more.

*

This time we didn't stop at Christiansfeld. The motorway rolled out the landscape, transforming the past into advertisement hoardings and slip roads easy to miss. We were still a long way from the Viberød estate and even further from the road to the beach cottage. I don't know what Mogensen had done to the Chevy, but its motor was now going as steadily as clockwork. Its windows slowly misted over again, and the mongrel continued snoozing on the back seat. He had a lot of sleep to catch up on, that dog, there could be no two opinions about that. Now and then he emitted little sounds as if hunting in his dreams. I closed my eyes and nodded off too.

*

It was late evening and dark when we swung off onto the last narrow exit road. A sharp crescent moon hung in front of the car, evidence that the weather had finally cleared. The road was exactly as I remembered it, full of sharp bends and shadows where it pushed its way forward through low shrubbery dotted with occasional pines bent by the wind. The sea was just beyond, an icy surging immensity that always both scared and attracted me. It seemed to be roaring weakly, as if it was holding itself in check but wanted to let me know what it was capable of. I didn't need reminding. Mogensen was singing quietly to himself, something about beer and birds, maybe something he'd made up himself. Terror had woken and was sitting upright on the back seat looking expectant. He had wet rings round his eyes and whimpered now and then. But he was glad we'd arrived.

The cottage stood by itself, a bungalow knocked together from brown boards with a rickety veranda built on the wrong side and an unstylish pair of windows in either gable, looking rather as if made from a '60s do-it-yourself building kit. The hardboard shutters Kai had fixed over the windows made it look as if it were anxiously screwing up its eyes in the glare of our headlights. The hardboard had swollen in the sea air so that the shutters bulged downwards like bags under the eyes. A slender tin chimney stuck up like a periscope from the central ridge of the black tarred-felt roof. The whole structure reminded me of Kai himself, shabby but perfect in the right places. Alert too. Between the bungalow and the sea a sparse fragment of pine forest served as an inadequate windbreak. On windy days every gust extracted a shrill flute-like sound from the chimney as if using its own signalling system to communicate with the sea. A narrow path that probably dated from before the bungalow was built went down through the trees to the water and had been trodden deep into the ground like a tiny ravine. Across the fjord you could see the northern tip of the island of Als.

We parked on the open space by the bungalow, which had been nearly repossessed by rough grass, making the ground bumpy and uncomfortable to walk on. It was as if small angry fists had scraped together the sandy soil and were holding it in their grip, mean and suspicious. When trodden on, it gave out a dry crunching sound. Terror had immediately got out of the car and lifted his leg with unhurried enjoyment against the wall of the bungalow. He appeared thoughtful, which I could well understand. Mogensen had stopped singing when he saw the building.

"Real primitive, yeh," he said, finally dragging himself out of the Chevy. He stroked his fleshy nose, searching for the right word. "Sort of basic, yeh."

He looked around in confusion as though he'd expected a full-scale pub or at least some unpretentious shop where you could get a beer. I wondered whether he'd had the foresight to cram a few bottles of Pils into his bag. Presumably not. He was a child of the city and used to easy access to life's small comforts. I marched purposefully onto the little veranda and felt under the eaves for the key. It was still there, a bit sticky with sea-damp. The floorboards were green with decay and bent under even my slight weight. But Mogensen wouldn't fall far if they gave way under him; the bungalow had been constructed directly onto the hillside, which made it a second home to sandflies and beach ants. Presumably these were asleep somewhere in the house, unaware that they'd just got company.

We'd stocked up with some provisions along the way: candles, jam, pasta, tinned food and mineral water since there was nothing but brackish water in the nearest well. Mogensen began unloading cardboard boxes from the boot while I stuck the key in the lock and turned it.

*

The cottage had been built to a simple plan: a large living-room, two smaller bedrooms and a minimal kitchen containing a wood-burning brick stove. It was pitch-dark inside, but I still remembered exactly how it looked. A sofabed with a table beside it, a dining-table and two chairs in front of the window facing the sea, and a shelf holding my collection of stones and some decaying books. Above the sofa hung a map of the coast from Åbenrå to Flensburg. I knew that somewhere there must be a needle with a length of red thread attached to it, since it was Kai's habit to measure distances before we went anywhere. The thread was exactly twenty centimetres long, at least in dry weather.

In one room there was a camp-bed and a chest of drawers. A permanently wobbling stool stood by the bed, and there was a clay pot with a withered bunch of flowers in the window: my room. Icy trapped air hit me. It was colder inside than out, and the mongrel, who had followed me in, turned back and sat down expressionless in the doorway. I tried the light-switch, but nothing happened. Probably some cable had blown down. Mogensen came lumbering in with a rusty paraffin lamp he'd found in Kai's store at the back of the house. He managed to light the damp wick at the fourth attempt. Even the flame smelt damp, if that's possible. He thumped the lamp down on the table. The light summoned up high shadows which stood motionless along the walls as if they'd been waiting for us. Mogensen disappeared outside with a hammer to take down Kai's shutters. A well-organised man in his way.

*

The hunting lodge is about three kilometres from the shore if you take the narrow path that leads over grass meadows and along cultivated fields and through clumps of trees. Sometimes it's nothing more than a track that can hardly be made out as it crosses damp glades and old patches of cultivated ground overgrown with moss and ferns. Here and there, half concealed by greenery, you can see the foundations of old buildings. As I force my way through thickets of fern, the small hard sori on the back of the fronds strike my hot face. I have to run to keep up because Kai's in a hurry. Now and then I catch a glimpse of his white nylon shirt ahead of me in the gloom and the flash of his pocket torch among the trees. The slender trunks are like a fence made of poles. I know his shirt has a dark sweat-stain on the back. He's rolled up his sleeves in his usual way, a bloke's way he calls it. I try and do the same with my blouse. It's the middle of the night, and I can hardly see where to put my feet, but I'm not afraid, I'm certain of that. I run so fast it hurts when I breathe. Kai has stopped to light a cigarette: I can see it glowing.

It's further from the shore to the hunting lodge if you go by the main road, as you have to use a tangle of small paths which on the map seem to lead nowhere.

*

I found two more paraffin lamps in the kitchen cupboard and managed to light them. Bright white moonlight was shining in over the window-ledges, and I carefully drew the dusty cotton curtains to shut out the glare. Terror crept close behind me, sniffing and taking stock of the situation. The bungalow put him in a bad mood, that was obvious, and his eyes were slanting more than usual. A true china dog. In the end I opened a tin of ham and emptied it onto a plate to give him something else to think about. He ate it and fell asleep on the sofa, stomach rumbling. I hoped he was house-trained. Then Mogensen and I lit a fire together. The nightwatchman's round face was wrinkled with worry; the city, and The Blue Grape, were far away. The wind had got up and was blowing smoke back down the chimney in irritating small puffs. Over on the sofa the mongrel was himself puffing and blowing. It was still cold enough for your bum to freeze if you sat down in the wrong place. Things could indeed have been better.

"Now, Esmé . . ." said Mogensen finally, peering at me through the greyness. We were both in tears after long struggles with matches, damp newspaper and kindling. *Tempus fugit*, whatever you do. Mogensen's voice was thick and muffled. ". . . Is there something you haven't told me?"

The question made me smile so that when I incautiously opened my mouth I swallowed a mouthful of acrid smoke. It was a while before I could get a word out. Mogensen lumbered off to fetch a bottle of mineral water, and we sat down at the table to dry our tears and have a talk, "man to man" as Kai would have said. With some difficulty I opened the damp-swollen window, fastened the hasp and watched smoke ooze out through the chink. As soon as it was outside, a powerful blast immediately swept it round the gable while the chimney pipe whined in the westerly wind. I could hear the sea too, rustling in over the stones on the beach. Lift, collapse, run back, over and over again, as the waves reckoned up their harvest. Over stones shining like dark green glass. The sound was like holding your ear against a large shell with the sea inside its innermost whorl. I drew breath, more cautiously this time.

"Quite a lot . . ." I said with a certain understatement. I blew my nose with care on a paper handkerchief Mogensen helpfully offered me. "Mogensen, have you ever lost a memory? Something you really ought to be able to remember, but which has somehow ended up in the wrong place, sort of as if you put it tidily away in a box and then forgot it. I mean, you do remember it of course, but not as it was."

Mogensen was troubled and wrinkled his broad brow. He spread his hairy hands on the table and studied them closely. His nails had black oily edges, but he seemed relieved to find he still had five fingers on each hand. He picked his nose carefully with his little finger. He was embarrassed. What I'd said sounded damned stupid, I could hear that myself. I tried again.

"I mean, I wanted to come here to see if I could remember. And that business with the old documents has something to do with it, I just don't know exactly how."

He looked up and met my gaze. The paraffin lamp hissed between us, flickering when the flame reached old uneven bits in the fabric of the wick as it burned down.

"I've nothing against being here, yeh," said Mogensen, withdrawing his hands and clasping them neatly over his stomach. Suddenly he looked at peace. As though he belonged in the bungalow; remarkably enough, it no longer felt so chilly. I shut the window since most of the smoke had gone. Mogensen leaned towards me, his eyes red from the smoke.

"Hell, Esmé, I'm no psychologist, but I can tell something's bugging you, like . . . We're doing this trip together, yeh. Would you be able to sell me the car afterwards for a special price between friends? Say no more if that's not on." He fell silent. "Then we can sort it all out with Dorthe and the papers later, yeh," he added, looking satisfied.

I nodded. It was all quite simple, really.

*

Kai's room's a little bigger than mine. It's simply furnished: a bed thrown out by some hospital, a work-table, bookcase, chest of drawers and wardrobe, that's all it has in it. On the floor a rag rug so ingrained with dirt that it's lost all its colour. Above the writing-table a calendar from the early '90s, and nailed up beside it a black-and-white photo that shows J.D. Salinger taking a walk in New York in February 1964. The camera has caught him on the pavement at the corner of 72nd Street and Central Park West; the collar of his dark ulster's turned up, and he's caught sight of the photographer at the very moment the camera clicks. His gaze is so naked it's almost embarrassing to look at the picture. He'd just ended his marriage. Rumours of domestic violence were circulating in the press, and he was feeling persecuted. In the background stand the Dakota Apartments like a spiky silhouette, a rugged massif in the middle of the city. Once they stood alone at the corner of the park, and people thought of them then as being as far from the centre of the city as the northern Indian territory it was named after. Between 1861 and 1864 the Dakota and Cheyenne Indians in the northern territory had had a few years' respite from the white immigrants, who were busy killing each other in the bloodiest war the world had so far seen, the American Civil War, which left more than 600,000 dead in places with names like Bull Run, Gettysburg and Appomattox. On muddy fields or in clumps of gunfire-shattered trees. It was a time when many new weapons were invented and old ones refined and then immediately exported to Europe and the conflicts there. Repeater rifles and a new kind of cartridge which fired with great accuracy. As usual, war was a profitable business for some.

Now it's 1964. The war in Vietnam, and a flood of memoranda and maps in the White House operations room; the great troop offensive on the ground hasn't started yet. Jerome David Salinger, author, former professional soldier and unloved son, has noticed the camera a split second too late and has only had time to lift his arm halfway. His pale, rather pasty face, round as an August moon, betrays the fact that he hardly goes out any more, and that when he does he ventures no further than the fence round his muddy backyard in Cornish. From where he can see mountains but no sea. On this occasion his publishers, Grosset & Dunlap, have made him come to New York. He refuses to speak to reporters, but his shyness and desire to keep himself to himself have turned him into someone reporters want to hunt down.

*

Kai's bookcase was nearly empty; there were several odd volumes from an antiquated reference work, a book of maps, nothing of interest. The bed was made up with an austere grey blanket neatly tucked in with military corners. I sat down and rumpled it and got a rapid memory-glimpse of Kai barefoot in nothing but his underpants one hot summer afternoon. He's telling me he's thinking of going down to the shore and that while he's away I must stay in. The room is stuffy, the window locked shut despite the blazing afternoon sun. He sweats all the time because it really is an unusually hot day, somewhere around the end of July, I think. If I close my eyes I can see the calendar above the writing-table, but I can't read the date. His light-coloured trousers and shirt are crumpled together in a heap on the bed. I detect a strange smell, but I can't put a name to it in my memory. He's looking for something and has pulled out the brown suitcase he always keeps under his bed . . . I bent down and looked into the dusty gloom. Nothing there now. The picture faded, and I could hear Mogensen busy in the tiny kitchen. He'd rigged up the spirit cooker on the bench. The tin-opener screeched on thin tin. The mongrel whimpered from the sofa. Soon it would be dinnertime.

GRÆNSEBYEN,
MONDAY, DECEMBER 12, 1938

MADSEN WAS FREEZING. The tin of throat pastilles was irritatingly empty, and his obstinate cold showed no sign of releasing its grip. It was late afternoon, and they'd started lighting the lamps. Outside, the raw, damp Danish late autumn had settled over meadows and cultivated fields, and an icy wind penetrated the police station through tiny chinks and cracks invisible to the eye. It whistled and howled in every corner. Over the road the signboard creaked and banged in the wind above the confectioner's door, and his shop window glowed with warm inviting light. Madsen imagined that from where he was sitting he could smell vanilla and cream flavoured with berries. At home his wife would be waiting with piping-hot oxtail soup full of pieces of meat heavy with fat, to be followed by hot tea laced with a generous shot of brandy and several spoonfuls of sugar, just as he liked it. In imagination he could see the sky-blue cup in front of him and sighed; the seat of his desk chair was always icy now when he arrived in the morning, even though outside it wasn't freezing yet. His hernia was bound to be worse before the winter was over. The police station was badly heated by a single stove in the inner room, where Police Chief Rav sat behind a closed door. Madsen had to cope with the cold as best he could. Rav had recently been absorbed in butterfly hand-books and the entomology of butterflies and moths. He had brought one of his books to the office and was glancing through it. "*Lepidoptera*", the police chief called these insects, putting on a serious expression as he pronounced the word. He'd lectured Madsen on the various stages of their lives, how they were characterised by *total transformation*. Perhaps this new interest would keep Rav in Grænsebyen; then his subordinate would not have to undertake such long spells of duty. Earlier Rav had often gone to Copenhagen to ferret out one thing or another. People said he went round churchyards. God knows what he did there. A fresh blast of wind made the window rattle in its frame. It needed new putty and a general check-up like everything else. Police Constable Madsen blew his nose loudly in his handkerchief and hoped Rav would hear.

*

The Berlin police authorities had written again. A buff envelope had come containing two typewritten pages with a new name Jens Madsen couldn't decipher scratched at the bottom. Rausch . . . something like that. It was all *Über* something or other. There was still no sign of Dr F.A. Nagler, but a stream of contradictory evidence had diverted the Berlin police's attention in another direction. Nagler had been seen in all sorts of places on both sides of the border. Each time this happened, a new report had to be drawn up. Madsen got the impression that they were more interested in sending out papers than travelling to a little place like Grænsebyen to investigate the matter thoroughly. You could say the investigation was living its own life in what looked like a neat series of diary entries. Things were getting done, there could be no doubt about that, and here was written evidence of the fact. This time the runaway Dr Nagler had been sighted in Hamburg by a woman of his acquaintance who had given her professional name as Lola, which surprised no-one (except perhaps Fru Müller of the Station Hotel, who had classified Dr Nagler as a "fine gentleman"). This was the twelfth report in the series, and it was beginning to seem as if the whole business could well be written off. All the documents had been rubber-stamped with nasty grimacing eagles and looked very official. Madsen blew his nose again. That Nagler must be a disagreeable devil since no-one really seemed to miss him. Madsen pushed the report aside and looked out at the street. Young Gabriel Mayer was struggling past into the wind, unsuitably dressed as always in a jacket too small for him and trousers that were too thin (where had he left his coat?). Madsen shivered. Mayer spent hours working in the parish office and was presumably now on his way home to his sick mother. She hadn't much time left, so Madsen understood.

*

The Mayers, mother and son, lived in a lane off the town's main thoroughfare. Madsen watched the hatless young man disappear round the corner, jacket flapping. They were of course Jewish and kept themselves very much to themselves. But contrary to what one expected of Jews, the late father had been a failure as a businessman. His wine and spirits business had gone bust in May 1932. People said his bankruptcy coincided with the death of a Swedish businessman called Kreuger in Paris. One of the Swede's subsidiaries had imported large quantities of German wines on credit using Kreuger shares as security – shares which turned out to be worthless. So the Mayers lost all their money and now had to rent one of their own former storehouses to live in (Grethe Mayer was a Dane from Grænsebyen and still had friends in the town; the rent was not exorbitant). Thinking of this, Madsen pursed his lips. Pride before a fall, always the same story. Then Josef Mayer had accidentally shot himself on the Bockmeister estate near the coast . . . while hunting hares, it was said. Out in an isolated field, no witnesses. Josef Mayer had been a slender effeminate man, very much a city person, and no-one had ever before heard of him hunting. Even so, the investigation was suspended; Rav decided there wasn't enough to go on. Bockmeister was another of Mayer's customers, and it was said that he too owed rather a lot of money to his wine-merchant. Gabriel was all right, except that he always had his nose in a book. Still, that was what Police Chief Rav liked, a studious young man willing to learn and ready to help with drawing up reports.

Madsen got up to heat himself a little tea on the spirit stove.

Besides, the boy was good at knowing when to keep his mouth shut and mind his own business. Madsen moved carefully so as not to suffer yet another spasm of pain, but it hit him all the same. He groaned loudly but cut his groan short; he would end up under the knife before spring if the cold weather continued.

Rav and Mayer had together certified the facts in the case of the German Nagler, and there was nothing more to be said about it. Madsen took the caddy down from the shelf and spooned tea leaves into the pot. He hoped strong tea might drive out his head cold. They still had Nagler's belongings at the police station since Madsen had received no instructions about where to send them. He poured hot water into the teapot and put it under a tea-towel to draw for at least five minutes. As luck would have it there were still some oatcakes in the tin, and Madsen put four on a plate. He licked crumbs off his fat fingers with a preoccupied air. Then he went quickly to the large grey steel safe, unlocked it and took out Nagler's rucksack. He stopped a moment to listen, but Rav seemed deeply buried in his butterflies. Not so much as the creak of a board or the scrape of a steel nib could be heard from the inner room. The police chief was unlikely to emerge before closing-time at six, and there was still an hour to go before then.

The rucksack had been sealed, but the seal could be fixed again. Madsen had been through its contents once before, together with Rav, but now he'd had an idea, an unusual exercise of thought for this slow-moving policeman. He slowly took the objects out of the ruck-sack and set them carefully in a row on the writing-table. There wasn't much: a soiled handkerchief, a penknife, a cigarette case, the bottle of cologne from the hotel room, a notebook with a black leather cover, a thin grey woollen sweater creased with damp, and the object which Madsen had been brooding on, a crumpled railway ticket. He stopped and poured himself a cup of tea, strong and steaming. The cup rattled lightly on its saucer as he put it down on the table. The date on the ticket was clear. His memory hadn't deceived him. Nagler was meant to have travelled back to Berlin on September 3. But he'd actually gone on August 31, and his ticket hadn't been punched by the guard. That was what Madsen called a strange story.

*

Gabriel Mayer saw that lights were still on in the police station. The outline of Madsen's spherical head was visible through the window like a carelessly exposed photograph. The round pink face was turned towards him. He took care not to look too long for fear Madsen might beckon him over. He turned off into the lane and trotted the last bit of the way to the gate. The simple house with its now neglected lawn bordered on the massive church, which made the house and yard look like a pretty miniature in decay. A doll's house someone had finished playing with and pushed aside. Nearly opposite, between the church and the house, on what had now become an untidy bit of open ground, stood the church's mortuary or charnel house, a compact mass of grey stone in the dim light, its form dictated more by the nature of the material from which it had been constructed than by any architectural theories. This outhouse was older than the church and had been allowed to survive leaning at an angle, presumably because at some stage they'd had second thoughts about pulling it down. Close to the charnel house was an ancient well that was no longer used, its mouth closed by a padlocked wooden lid. The remains of an old churchyard wall also survived in the form of a row of stones along one wall of the charnel house, with two surviving steps from a demolished stair once used when moving bodies. This was where Jup, who looked after the churchyard, kept his wheelbarrow in autumn so as not to have to wheel it constantly back into the charnel house during the period when the great lime-trees were shedding their leaves and transforming the churchyard into a thick springy carpet of decay.

Gabriel opened the front door of his home and stood for a moment in the chilly entrance hall to listen. All was calm and quiet; his mother must be asleep already. In front of the door to the little living-room a rolled-up mat had been placed to keep out the draught. He moved it aside as he always did, opened the door and stepped inside. As always, too, he was surprised at how cramped and stuffy the room was, with heavy dark furniture from his parents' old home taking up every square centimetre of its surface. Tall German cupboards, tables and lathe-turned chests of drawers, once acquired for their spacious Berlin town apartment in ——strasse, now stood head to toe like boots in a cramped wardrobe. This arrangement did make the place look more like a store than a home.

Everything was permeated by the sour smell of medicaments with its stale, musty undertone. In a moment he would stop noticing it, but at first it was strong. As always he felt an impulse to leave immediately, as if his present life were a mistake that could easily be rectified. But instead he pressed on and entered his mother's bedroom, hardly more than a cubbyhole overlooking the churchyard and completely filled by a Biedermeyer double bed like a raft cast up after a shipwreck. A little bedside table contained a washbasin holding water full of dregs and a folded towel. The wallpaper behind the table had been discoloured by splashed liquid. Above the bed hung a picture that always made him uncomfortable. In former times it had been over the sideboard in the dining-room. It showed a narrow empty country road winding its way through a plain, with dreary desolation stretching into the distance on either side. The colours were dull as though covered by a misty membrane. He was unsure whether the artist had intended this or whether they had dulled with time. Scattered daubs of paint in the background sometimes seemed like figures seen from a great distance, at other times like flat bits of woodland or banks of mist. Sometimes he imagined he could also see the roof of a building sticking up in the middle of the forest or beyond it, though in the clear light of day he thought the same shadows looked like nothing more than old soot from the age of smelly smoky oil lamps. (This was what his mother had often told him when he was a child unable to sleep for thinking about the gloomy picture. Sometimes he liked to think that Hans Christian Andersen's soldier, the one with the tinder-box, would come marching down the road with his kitbag on his back and his sabre rattling at his side. Thinking of the soldier made the road less frightening, because of course Gabriel was familiar with the rest of the story.) This unremarkable picture had long ago been set in a heavy and pretentious gold frame like a great work of art. It came from his mother's parents' home and had been painted some-time in the 1860s. He'd forgotten the artist's name.

Grethe Constance Mayer was asleep in the middle of the bed. Her hair, still auburn, was spread over the pillow and made her skin look paler; her thin arms were stretched out as if clinging to the thread-bare bedspread. Her breath came in little puffs like an animal greedily snatching for air from just beneath a hole in the ice. Sitting down on the edge of the bed, her son laid his hand on her brow. He could feel the cold sticky sweat he'd learnt to expect, but under this there was still a reassuring warmth. Her face was a greyish-white plaster mask against the sheet. Only her cheeks had any colour, two sharply defined red patches that reminded him of spots painted on a cheap ragdoll. Disease was gnawing away at her bodily functions – heartbeat, breathing, violent attacks of sweating – destroying her with a frenzy that seemed a simulacrum of health. Soon all life would suddenly burn out. He pulled back his hand before she could interpret his gesture as a caress. He felt a need to maintain a certain distance from her, as if his mother and the evil of her illness were separate things. As if she would still be there when the alien smells of sickness were finally gone. He got up and left her. She hadn't even moved in her sleep: she was now being given very large doses of morphine.

*

Gabriel's room, in contrast, faced the main street, and by day he could hear the noise of traffic. But at this hour all was quiet and still. The autumn chill had driven people indoors to huddle over stoves and fires. The street lights hinted at warmth and comfort like small hot flames in the illuminated landscape of a table set for Christmas. Ignoring the raw cold in the room, Gabriel curled up on his bed. The sheets felt damp, a layered chill that crept slowly through his clothes just as it might have done if he'd been lying out on the ground. As in those autumns when during some long break from school they'd slept out of doors in a tent after a long train journey through the sooty suburbs of Berlin, wheels clattering "Ba-bels-berg" and canting over at the curves on rain-wet rails. Wearing shorts even though autumn was well advanced. He remembered his skin rough and blue with cold.

Strengthening and character-building, in the words of Herr Schiller, the school's crew-cut youth leader. A world that survived intact so long as he didn't look directly at it. He imagined his friends still living in the same street and doing the same things with the stifling comfort and wonderful predictability of everyday life, drinking tea or coffee from large cups in the morning before going off through the wakening city with brown satchels strapped to their shoulders, the sun a golden haze hovering in the sooty Berlin air. Orange clouds. And the smell of dark-roast coffee, beer and cat-piss. He knew every curve and angle in the dark chessboard-patterned entrance hall and remembered the smell of sour cabbage soup outside the caretaker's door on the ground floor, muffled hammer blows from the shoemaker's workshop in the yard and the plonking of the piano as his little sister practised. The piano in need of tuning, and his sister crossly attacking the keys. *Fünf leichte Übungen für das Klavier* . . .

Some light forced its way in from the street, but otherwise it was dark in Gabriel's room. He could make out his clothes-cupboard, chair and table, the single shelf over his bed and, on his writing-table, the brass and green-glass reading lamp that had once belonged to his father. On his shelf stood one single book and another work in two volumes, Andersen's *Fairy Tales and Stories* in the Danish first edition of 1864. Gabriel remembered "The Tinder-Box" and "The Galoshes of Fortune", tales read over and over again in his mother's parents' home. Beside them a novel by Jules Verne that was his own. Nothing else in the room stirred memories. This was why Gabriel always kept the door closed and locked it when he went out. His mother had a carer, a woman from Grænsebyen who sat with her every day till four. She was an old school friend, he'd learnt. He hated her fresh round cheeks and meddlesome manner, her stocky body laced into a tight woollen dress like spiced sausage on a Danish Christmas table. This woman saw his mother's illness as the natural result of the way she had chosen to live; it was only to be expected that marrying a German Jew (even an assimilated one) and settling in Berlin would lead to cancer, that was the natural order of things. Justice was always done sooner or later just as bonds and annuities always matured eventually. Grethe Constance Mayer had been born with a shiny gold spoon in her mouth which sooner or later would be taken from her and laid in the memory cabinet of the little town for everyone to see. Gabriel was freckled and ruddy in appearance and looked like his mother, and for this reason he was welcome to stay. At least for the time being.

*

He sat up abruptly. If he kept perfectly still and concentrated on nothing or on the monotonous ribbing of the rag rug, perhaps these thoughts would go away. He could hear sounds from the street; the confectioner and his wife were locking up their shop and making their way home. The confectioner limped from a bullet wound in the Great War, and his clogs scraped roughly over the stone setts. His wife stole silently after him on rubber soles. Then all that could be heard was the wind, hungrily pulling and tearing at the gilded wooden figure-of-eight biscuit over that bakery door just up the street.

The suitcase that belonged to the German was hidden right at the back of Gabriel's wardrobe, an expensive case in dark brown leather with Nagler's initials stamped on the lid, F.A.N. in gold lettering. One corner had split open and gaped like a sore. He had shoved that end furthest in against the bottom of the cupboard. Following Police Chief Rav's instructions, he'd made no attempt to open the case. In any case it was locked, and he hadn't been given a key for it. Rav had come by late on the night of August 31, his screeching Ford dusty and splashed with mud even though they'd separated only a few hours earlier on a dry country road. It had been a sultry evening, and the windows overlooking the neglected lawn were still open. It had been one of his mother's good days, and she had sat up late, her emaciated body almost drowning in her ample bolster. Despite the heat she was always cold. Gabriel had just helped her into bed and was about to close the windows. Crane flies and other long-legged insects of the sort that flourish in the heat of overripe late summer swarmed round him, attracted by the whitewashed wall and the lamp burning in his mother's room. If you killed an insect of this kind, its remains spread a sour stench on your skin, a smell it was very hard to get rid of.

Rav had driven into the lane and come to meet him hat in hand with his coat thrown over one shoulder. In his other hand he'd been carrying a smart, elegant suitcase of a type Gabriel remembered from his childhood home. The police chief's face had been shining with sweat, and his lank hair, grey with dirt, had been falling into his eyes. This gave him a more informal look, as if for a moment he'd abandoned his official role and been revealed as a human being, the boy with a fringe Police Chief Rav had once been. When he came closer he hastily put his hat back on his head out of ingrained habit and instantly recaptured something of his authority. Gabriel could see the wretched Ford parked a little way off, next to the gable of the ancient charnel house. (The car had been positioned so that it interrupted his view of the churchyard and the charnel-house door, something he would remember later. So he couldn't see whether the door was open or not.)

Rav had deliberately left the car's headlights on and walked round the house with weary steps. A mass of flying insects immediately gathered in the light, dancing in the blinding rays as if this were the very moment they'd been waiting for, but Rav seemed not to notice them. Gabriel came out on the front steps to meet him. He didn't want the police officer to see the living-room and its massive contents, but Rav quickly drew him into its still, stuffy gloom. For a moment it was as if both men were underwater, shut inside a deep-sea diving-bell with the dark furniture as a labyrinthine but invisible reef. Gabriel could smell the other man's odour, rank and heavy as if saturated with fear.

"I want you to do something for me, son." Rav's voice was hoarse and he seemed out of breath. His words came in a rapid continuous stream. "Don't ask any questions, just look after this for me. For a while."

He gestured vaguely towards the suitcase, which he'd put down on the floor some distance from himself, a presence Gabriel could not so much see as sense in the darkness. A rectangle of deeper darkness.

Gabriel took the case without voicing the query that hovered in the air between them. It was by grace and favour that the Mayers lived in prosperous Grænsebyen at all; it wasn't his business to question anything and certainly not the police chief's words. It was only when he laid the case on the bed in his own room that he saw the initials on it and understood whose it was.

Rav didn't leave immediately. He went out for a minute and switched off the car's lights; Gabriel thought he heard a door close. By the time he came back, Rav had regained his composure. With the suitcase out of the way, he seemed to relax and become unusually talkative and Gabriel felt able to invite him to share a couple of bottles of wine, one of them an easy-drinking, sensuous 1921 Mosel with a spicy nose that came from his father's plundered cellar. And with three candles burning in the brass candlestick on the table, the room was transformed yet again and now became a warm, sheltering cave, a place for mutual trust where secrets could be shared. A place on the frontier between reality and imagination. The wine soon put colour into Rav's grey cheeks, and eventually he told a story about something that had happened the previous spring. It was a memory he often returned to.

*

It had happened in April, about two months after they had found the unknown dead woman in a shed in the fields. Rav and Madsen patrolled the railway station at Grænsebyen nearly every afternoon, and they liked to drive through the woods along a gravel road that followed the railway track for a kilometre and a half. Madsen would have his lunchbox with him and would usually lay his ample packet of sandwiches on the dashboard while he drove, a greasy concoction wrapped in sandwich-paper which his wife would have prepared and brought over to the police station at lunchtime. This habit of eating in the car irritated Rav, but he always refrained from making any comments because Madsen was capable of sulking for hours, which was even worse than having the closed car full of the stink of onion-sausage and pickled gherkins. This particular afternoon was like every other apart from a thick milk-white fog which had enveloped the land-scape in an all but impenetrable shroud. It was like making your way through whipped cream, and Madsen drove extremely slowly while he ate. The windscreen wipers laboriously traced a narrow path on each side of the windscreen, like the viewing slit in a tank. It had been raining for days, and the many holes in the road were full of water into which the heavy and clumsy Ford repeatedly sank with a bump. The only way they knew they were still on the road at all was the crunch of tyres on gravel. It came as a shock when they suddenly hit something neither of them could see.

"Shit," said Madsen. "Got to be a hare." He pulled on the hand-brake and climbed out with a good deal of fuss. The coachwork rocked like a ship in a storm; Rav, battling with car sickness, stayed put.

It wasn't a hare but some thin wretch who'd been hobbling on the verge. He'd been struggling along hampered by a full rucksack, but the car had been too quick for him. Nonetheless, he seemed unhurt. Rav straightened his hat and followed Madsen out of the car. Recently Jewish refugees had been crossing the border from Germany in a steady stream, but most had managed to arrange things better for themselves than this poor individual. In the early '30s they'd rolled in in Hubmobiles, Studebakers and other luxury cars wearing furs and trailing heavy clouds of perfume.

"Papers," snapped Madsen, adding in a rather milder voice, "*Ihre Ausweis, bitte.*"

Rav was aware of movement in the corner of his eye and next moment saw it was a young woman running away a bit further down the road. When the fog parted for a moment he clearly saw pale bare legs and well-worn pumps. The sound of her running, muffled by the fog, seemed to come from a great distance. Her broken-down shoes made a strange slapping sound which Rav likened to someone running ankle-deep in water along a shore. She went up onto the railway track; he heard the rails ring and the ballast under them crunch at every step, and she kept turning round, uncertain whether to go on by herself, he could tell. He raised his hand to beckon her, but Madsen was already running along the road, his round face red with heat and excitement. So Rav thrust his hands deep into his coat pockets and studied the man before him instead. About thirty years old, he judged, more likely a little under than a little over. Of slender build, stooping slightly. Accountant type. A good-quality suit now so threadbare and baggy that he probably wouldn't be admitted to even the humblest café. He'd abandoned his rucksack on the road, and several spotted and crushed apples had fallen out of it. Looking at the apples, Rav was reminded of the desiccated heads prized by headhunters that he'd seen in the Ethnographical Museum in Copenhagen. This was exactly what they looked like, small, shrunken and earth-coloured with the same spotted and hollowed appearance. He began to feel sick again and tried not to think about it. The apples were of the sort local farming folk threw away at harvest time when they drove around in Bue Hatt's lorry filling their coats with fruit from the stores. That was probably where the two refugees had spent the night, in one of those humble sheds which here and there offered some sort of shelter. The man's thin face had a pale, washed-out appearance, and his straggling black hair fell over one eye. His mouth was so red and badly chapped that it looked like a sore. Much later Rav was to remember those swollen, split lips. Someone had struck him across the jaw too. Hard. The sight made Rav look away.

Madsen came back with the woman. He didn't touch her but even so seemed to be protecting her as if from a blow. Her unwashed fair hair was pulled up into a knot from which some coils had come loose and fallen over her face. She was dressed in a ragged cardigan buttoned over a dirty grey blouse. It irritated Rav that she had put one of her buttons into the wrong buttonhole, and it was all he could do not to reach out a hand to put it right. He didn't know why this feeling came over him. As if he wanted to reprimand a child and at the same time protect it. Her skirt was thin and made of fine silk-like material. Impractical. They must have set out in whatever they happened to be wearing at the time. (This may have been the moment Rav's big idea first came to him, but later he couldn't be quite sure about this.)

The man and the woman stood close together. He took her hand in what must have been a brave attempt to show himself protective. He held his identification papers in his other hand. His fist shook and seemed to flutter like a bird's wing as he held them out to Rav, at the same time contemplating his own hand as if it were an alien object, beyond the control of his own body and will. He has slender wrists like a girl, thought Rav.

"*Bitte*," said the man. "Please." Even his voice seemed thin, too small for someone full-grown. Rav took the crumpled documents, put his glasses on his nose and read, taking his time. "August 1934." They had expired long ago. The man was twenty-eight; Rav had been right about his age. He said nothing but folded the papers and handed them back. The man's violent shaking had stopped.

"*Gott*," said Rav. "Good." He pronounced the word very deliberately and trusted the other to understand him. He motioned the two into the car, trying to smile though he could tell this merely bewildered them. He heard Madsen draw a sharp breath at the sight of Rav's gesture. Refugees often brought lice and every imaginable illness with them, and Madsen was clearly not looking forward to washing the back seat with carbolic. The couple hesitated and whispered something inaudible to each other before climbing obediently into the car. She first and he after her. Rav noticed that the man had a limp. But he couldn't possibly take him to a doctor, not yet. He adjusted his hat and got into the car. Madsen followed, muttering, but offered what was left of his sandwiches to the couple in the back seat. Rav looked all round; he could see the forest on the far side of the railway now. No-one was visible, but the fog was beginning to lift or at least thin out and change into small light wisps, which passed on over the muddy fields and into the woods. A gentle wind brought a smell of earth and of the tender vegetation which the wet weather was causing to germinate and grow on the slopes.

"Spring's on the way," announced Madsen, turning the key in the ignition.

*

Rav fell silent and leaned forward on the sofa with his chin in his hands. Gabriel waited for him to continue.

"We didn't drive them back to Grænsebyen, but to a small weekend cottage I'd inherited a few kilometres from town. It's isolated; no near neighbours, but not too far from the main road. People knew I went there sometimes, so if they saw lights they wouldn't think anything of it. Madsen did not comment. He'd already made arrangements to go on holiday with his wife for some days in Easter week, and I granted him extra leave on condition that what had happened stayed between the two of us. A week later the young couple had gone." Rav fell silent again. It was as if he was trying to decide how much to tell.

"I wonder where they went," said Gabriel.

"Oh, they went on their way . . ." Rav clearly felt he ought to add something further in clarification. He leaned a little nearer, and Gabriel could smell his breath, a bit sour and surprisingly hot.

"Tell me, son. Have you ever read the German writer Hugo von Hoffroder?"

THE HUNTING LODGE

T HE FIRST NIGHT in the bungalow I couldn't sleep. Mogensen and the dog each snoozed in his own room, and their snores would have been enough to lift the house and send it on its way over the sea like a message in a bottle or a dried split-cod. So I kept my door shut and did some reading by the light of my pocket torch, with a cup of hot tea beside me to sharpen my concentration. Now and then I heard Terror wandering about and scratching cautiously at my door. I had Mayer's bulky *Four Illusions* propped against my knees. I started at page 42 because the heading on that page, "The Hunting Lodge", immediately caught my eye. Mayer started with a few lines about the troops who had fought at Dybbøl:

(From Knudsen, H., Copenhagen 1950): "During the war of 1864, pipes and tobacco pouches formed part of the regular troops' equipment. Both pouches and pipes – when not in use – were fastened by a cord to the buttons of their uniforms. These uniforms were green and blue. In addition the soldiers wore their own civilian scarves against the cold." I think it must have been a remarkable sight, home-knitted woollen scarves of all colours set against their strict formal uniforms. In more recent wars such an open expression of individuality has been impossible. But if we look back at earlier times, to the hastily assembled military forces of the seventeeth and eighteenth centuries, we find mercenary militias in ragged clothes fighting in territories of uncertain nationality for whoever paid them the most. Men who killed for pay, marching over muddy European fields that had become a sort of common land for war and battles. War was conducted outside normal life, so to speak. It had its own choreography of marches, uniforms, parades and formations, things that contradict normal behaviour. Moving directly towards death by right-angled paths. Allowing oneself to be shot to pieces or ripped open by bayonets. Crossing fields covered with dead men and trampling them as if they were wood or soil. Things we can't imagine doing so long as we remain in our everyday lives. Is that the way it was?

In earlier times villages, watering holes, castles, lords of the manor and dialects made up a microcosmic social world, something the ordinary man or woman was capable of understanding, with cultivated land they could cross on foot or on horseback by means of winding roads, until in the nineteenth century railways and balloon flights enabled us to get a rapid overview of nature in an abridged form and from a considerable distance. Now perspective seems to have been compressed as though seen through an astronomer's telescope. But perhaps the truth is that we are really still living on a local scale, we only think things have changed. As if we were to believe modern people have better sight simply because stronger lenses allow us to make out barren mountains and quiet valleys on the moon or Mars. But our human eyes are just as weak as they always were. And often they are wolf's eyes, even though we think of ourselves as civilised. We flourish in herds but don't hesitate to hit out if this is required – and sometimes we hit out for no reason at all. We don't like those who drop out of the herd. Perhaps it's our nature. I don't know . . . Or perhaps war has made possible a new way of thinking that has reduced the individual to insignificance in favour of groups, armies and nations. Technology has left us without individual responsibility. There were to be no more gaudy scarves in the next war. Or visible tobacco pouches. All that would remain was this extraordinary delight in killing. That was enough.

At this point Mayer changed course and began telling a story with mythical-romantic overtones. The two principal characters in this story are well known: the writers Hans Christian Andersen and Hugo von Hoffroder.

One spring evening in May 1864 the writer Hans Christian Andersen steps into a closed coach and leaves his home in Nyhavn, Copenhagen. Ships chafe against the quays like a line of fat matrons on their way to market, their furled sails like starched petticoats or Sunday-best mothproofed in bags in a wardrobe. The coach rolls along the quayside behind two nimble, beautifully groomed roans.

Andersen is 59 years old and deeply depressed. His luggage, in the form of two capacious trunks made of thick ox-leather, is tightly lashed to the roof of the coach to withstand the dreadful surfaces of the main country roads. These trunks have been with him on all his travels round Europe; Sweden, Germany, England, Italy, O! the campagna . . . his heart's joy. Inside the coach, the hatbox containing the high hat he wears in cities jolts along on the seat next to the smaller case in which he keeps his notebooks, a piece of rope, a dangerously sharp pair of scissors, charcoal for drawing and a sketchblock. He doesn't trouble his mind with the German question even though his destination is South Jutland.

The writer has received a letter now in his portmanteau. A woman he knew as a young girl in Copenhagen has written fervently begging him to favour her with a last visit. A secret sweetheart. One of many . . . Andersen barely hesitated a moment before ordering a coach. His packing went quickly, like a dance, and for a while he forgot his melancholy. His rooms in Nyhavn seemed permeated by a wonderful fragrance of roses, a memory of youth that hovered round his bedroom and drawing room like a fresh sweet breath, reminding him of walks along the crunching gravel paths of a rose-garden. It must have been twelve years ago, at least. But, now he's in the coach, darkness and sadness have returned even though blackbirds are singing and there are wonderful magnolias in bloom in the Botanical Gardens, and he bleeds with the Danish people for the loss of Schleswig, Holstein and Lauenburg. And he's beginning to grow old, and his muse has deserted him.

The journey takes four days. Stages and inns come one after the other. His nose is constantly alert for fire. The same anxiety and mortal fear always torment him. He is oversensitive. He has brought with him a number of letters which he reads and rereads again and again. Compliments from all the royal houses of Europe and moving little expressions of friendship from women and children. These letters keep him warm in the evenings, when he doesn't dare have a fire lit in his hotel room. He reads them often because the spring nights are chilly.

The sea passages across the Belts are a trial, with cramped cabins, and noisy fellow-travellers on the spree to be avoided. Regression threatens, but Andersen gets a grip, then with great care and concentration combs his curly hair in his travel-mirror and straightens his already irreproachable cravat. Mr Bulwer-Lytton would call him a "self-made man". He sees himself as a *sommerfugl*, a butterfly.

For the last few kilometres the roads are intolerable, with the coach slipping in and out of old wheel-tracks. He scans the ditches in vain for spring flowers; everything has been devastated, trampled down, laid waste. His heart bleeds for the army horses and oxen that have fallen by the wayside and been left there to die. When he sees a wounded horse some way off in a field, he orders the coachman to stop, but the poor beast moves away with a terrible limp when Andersen crosses fields and ditches to bring help and comfort. A headlong march at the double over muddy ditches that reminds him of his youth.

Once the gelding has been caught, the coachman has to shoot it with his pistol since nothing more can be done for it. Andersen weeps.

Gradually they approach their destination, the Bockmeister family estate of Viberød in what used to be Denmark. Henriette Honorine Bockmeister has gone on living there alone since her elder brother Claus fell at the Dybbøl redoubts. She has never married. The coach is stopped at regular intervals by roadblocks manned by military pickets, both Danish and German, and an exhaustive examination of papers follows until the writer steps out and lifts his hat. Then it's schnapps with the officers (which Andersen usually declines), well-thumbed copies of the *Fairy Tales* to be signed and three cheers on departure. They've all read his insignificant little stories! They know his light entertainments and major works for the stage too. The simple language of a writer is universal, that's a paradox he's taught himself to live with. After this the journey gets a bit bumpy since the coachman is not a man to decline offers of refreshment. But Andersen says nothing, as the many encounters warm his tired senses like a spring fire.

On the final night of the journey, May 7, a note reaches him at his lodging-place, its sealing-wax embossed with the Bockmeister seal, which features a flowering spray of bell heather (*Erica tetralix*) in a medallion. Henriette Honorine is at the hunting lodge by the coast, where she hopes the sea air will check the headlong course of her illness (he never discovers what exactly is wrong with her). He arrives on the morning of May 8.

The hunting lodge is in the middle of a dense fir plantation. The road meanders on between the trees; nothing has been done to prune back nature for a very long time (thirty, forty years? he's forgotten), and long heavy branches sweep against the coach and knock hard on its eggshell-thin sides with bark-clad knuckles. It's like driving into a darkness where thousands of voices whisper and wail when the wind pierces the forest screen. Andersen lowers the window and inhales the aromatic scent of fir. Here and there paths run among the trees; he glimpses them as the coach passes, tracks that seem to materialise from nowhere, since the manor no longer employs forester or farmhand to clear a way through the undergrowth. Andersen imagines that the Lady of the Forest and the young maidens who help her have staked out these paths among the firs, a network of lanes designed by her own sap-intoxicated nature for reasons no mortal may know. But then the coach rounds a bend, the coachwheels ring out on cobblestones, and suddenly the forest is past and the hunting lodge lies before them.

It's strange to see one's own memory re-created before one's eyes in the grey pointed mountain-style panels and mansard roofs and the fairy-tale griffin weathercock at the end of the roof-ridge! The griffin's beak points east. For comfort. The castle – as they also call it – has been neglected too, he can see that at once. And the shutters on many of the windows are closed, which surprises him. But thin smoke is rising from one of the chimneys, so someone's at home. The "castle" isn't the least bit imposing despite its name.

It was the master-builder Justus Theodor Bockmeister, Henriette's great-grandfather, who had the ground staked out and started the plantation in 1814, just after Napoleon was shipped off to Elba and order seemed to have been restored in Europe (the Bockmeisters never took sides in the wars, not even in 1807 when the English anchored their ships in the Sound off Copenhagen and began to bombard the city). At that time all that stood here was a simple summer cottage. A day's journey from Viberød. Henriette's father and grandfather were gripped by their nation's romantic past and constantly enlarged and added to the building, creating a hybrid, a dodo in Andersen's view, a Nordic mountain cottage worthy of a German knight. (In fact, the family had roots on both sides of the border: they owned a house and land in Copenhagen and another house in Berlin. To begin with they'd made their money from colonial trade. Ivory or guano, Andersen can't remember which; just that it was profitable.) Now the male line is on the point of dying out.

Andersen, feeling a little giddy, steps out of the coach onto the drive in front of the house. He goes up to the door while the coachman begins the complicated task of taking down the luggage. He'd stopped in a small market town along the way to buy a few delicacies and five bottles of surprisingly good red wine. He's also brought sweets and confectionery and other good things from shops in Copenhagen. All this is in a large closed hamper which the coachman must now struggle to take down. (The man's face is pale and moist; he spent the previous evening at the bar in the inn. His breath smells sour, and it's clear that a throng of extremely energetic copper-beaters are hammering away in his head. Andersen hopes the man isn't about to be ill.) In his breast pocket, over his heart, Andersen carries enclosed in a pretty little oval ivory frame the cut-out profile he once made of Henriette Honorine. Snip, snip, all his own work. He knows her fine features like the lines on the palm of his hand. Just as he lifts his hand to knock at the double door, one side of it opens.

She's very much changed. Almost unrecognisable. Her beautiful features have given way to an unhealthy flabbiness. Her bosom is half bare in a manner very much out of fashion and covered with little greyish marks, scars left by some unknown illness. Her breasts are framed by a piece of thin material titivated with fluffy thread. Andersen takes out a handkerchief, presses it to his mouth and pretends to blow his nose. The woman has small suspicious eyes but they light up when she looks at him. It suddenly occurs to him that she looks cunning. Nature has given her a mean mouth, but she has sweetened its shape artificially for the occasion. Nor is she alone. At her side, half hidden by her wide skirts, is a small urchin with a sandy forelock and a stupid expression. The braces on his lederhosen are loose, and a soiled shirt much too big for him has been left hanging outside his trousers. His bare feet are reasonably clean, but for a moment it seems to Andersen that they are covered with rough fur, though this vision disappears when he blinks. The boy is clearly a child of the forest and smells as rank as a fox. A window above the front door is flung open with a crash, and a shaggy head looks down on Andersen, who instantly recognises the red swollen drinker's face, hopelessly tangled grey hair and big round glistening grey eyes – like melted tin in a scoop – of the writer Hugo von Hoffroder. The man directs a yelp in his direction, an inarticulate cry Andersen believes may signify "good morning". He politely lifts his hat to the figure in the window. The woman at the door makes a cooing sound.

"Henriette?" says Andersen, hoping against hope for a negative answer. The woman's smile widens, exposing a row of neglected teeth. Now he can see a sore on her thin lip. With a touch of her old grace, she offers her hand. He stifles an impulse to pull out his medallion for comparison. Time has his way with us all. Andersen is cautious enough to keep on his glove when he accepts the offered hand.

He stays four whole days. An eternity. The coachman has been allowed to stay too and sleeps in a corner of the attic. Andersen prefers the ground floor, as close to the earth as possible. Every night he wedges a chair under his doorhandle, but even with this security his sleep is spasmodic and troubled. What he most fears is entirely irrational – that the boy will sneak into his room. Henriette Honorine's indisposition usually begins with a jug of wine at breakfast and is fortified as the day goes on by progressively stronger forms of refreshment. Sometimes Hoffroder keeps her company. In the evening the lady of the castle usually slumbers heavily in her chair in front of the open fire with the wild child at her feet, while the German holds his wine – he drinks only wine – appreciably better and stays awake. This is the time, during the long spring evenings, when von Hoffroder and Andersen talk. The German is by no means uninteresting. Until the previous month he was sleeping out in the field with the Prussian army. He was wounded at Fredericia, not by a Danish bullet but in a drunken brawl at a wayside tavern when he got the point of a sabre shoved up his back-side. Since then he has been unable to sit but leans on the chimney-piece while he talks (the wound has not healed prop-erly and has gone septic). He is unwilling to talk about the war, but Andersen still manages to coax a few scraps of infor-mation out of him.

On April 20 Hoffroder was on reconnaissance among the Dybbøl redoubts with several fellow-officers. The sun was shining; it was a pleasant spring day though the seven men had to soak their neckerchiefs in vinegar and tie them over their mouths and noses so as not to choke on the gases from the shallow graves. People were afraid of epidemics, and there was talk of spreading quicklime over the worst areas. Here and there fat glossy rats scampered about, entirely unafraid of humans – but then why should they fear the creatures who served every day as their favourite dish and had done so for several months? Hoffroder takes a deep draught from his wine glass and crosses the floor. He stands by one of the large windows and looks out at the light spring evening. The sky is whitish, shining like the flesh of a mussel. A little beyond the courtyard the fir plantation stands like a wall. They can both see the boy at the edge of the wood. He seems to have caught something and to be playing with it, a baby hare perhaps, or a kitten. Lets it go and catches it again . . . a simple game. Hoffroder puts down his glass so heavily in the splayed window-space that its foot rings out; it's a wonder it doesn't break.

Well, the seven officers made their observations, drew up a common report that evening and then got drunk. The Prussian losses hadn't been excessive, perhaps 200 or 250 killed. The names of the dead hadn't yet been registered, so it could be claimed that on paper they were still alive. To all intents and purposes, the regimental clerk was their executioner. It was worse for the Danes. The Prussian army camp was a couple of kilometres from the battlefield, but even so Hoffroder had the sickening sweet smell in his nose all evening. He couldn't bring himself to eat anything. Just after midnight he left the tent and went out on the hillside to relieve himself. Here and there fires were burning where men had crept together, more as a protection from darkness than cold, since it was a warm evening. Someone was playing a simple melody on an accordion. The notes flew round at random in the damp night air, but he couldn't recognise the tune. Ti-da-dam. He tried to sing along, but his tongue refused. He wasn't a sentimental man, but the music made him want to weep.

A little way off was his own refuge, the tent where tonight he would sleep alone since the two fellow-officers he shared it with had gone to Hamburg on leave. There was no wind, but the tent was flapping like a loose sail, making a considerable noise though no-one but himself seemed to be aware of it. He buttoned his flies and staggered off to find out what the cause of this strange phenomenon might be, and what he saw still made the hairs on his neck stand on end. In his tent, on the pallet, sat a young soldier, a Danish private so far as

Hoffroder could make out. The extraordinary thing was that though he could clearly see the boy sitting there on the bed, he was able at the same time to look right through the slim body as clearly as if it had been a window. Through it he could see his own trunk and open kitbag and a lamp with a smoking wick that he'd carelessly left burning. The young soldier said nothing. Seemingly unaware of the German's presence, he got to his feet, straight as a poker, as if he had suddenly had second thoughts about something, and walked straight out through the side of the tent without causing the slightest damage to the cloth. The lad had seemed simultaneously real and unreal, and Hoffroder thought he could hear his breath as he passed, short and hissing slightly just like the breath of a living person. Had he been a mere spectrum caused by Hoffroder's intoxicated condition? An optical illusion consisting in equal parts of alcohol, mist, humidity and light? Hoffroder feels he'd recognise the boy if he ever saw him again. At the same time he can't quite re-create the boy's features in his memory. (Just as it's often impossible to re-create the face of the woman you love in her absence. What's nearest you is often what's most difficult to reach.) When he saw the young Dane, what seemed familiar was simply a strong emotion. Recognition? Sympathy? Guilt? He can't decide.

"And the lad's uniform. Did you see that clearly?"

"Very clearly, it was green, and the jacket was partly unbuttoned. No bag or baldric." Hoffroder rubs his eyes.

"And he was fair-haired, I think. Hair brushed back from his face . . . very young. It looked to me as if he was crying."

Whatever the truth of the matter, that night Hoffroder went back to his friends and said not a word about what he'd seen – or thought he'd seen. But, true or not, what happened had given him the idea for a story which – he holds up an ink-stained hand dramatically – he is just now in the process of writing (at this point he suddenly becomes reticent again, afraid of talking his precious material away).

"And you'd never seen him before?"

"Never."

Andersen is careful not to rush ahead. The story grips him, but life has taught him patience. He pours himself some wine – first wiping his glass clean with his handkerchief – and sips cautiously while he watches the other man. It is still not dark, and the white spring light falls obliquely across the German's face, sharply chiselling his features. At that moment, standing there, Hoffroder looks like a lion – one of those animals that saunter restlessly up and down along the iron bars of their enclosure in the Zoological Gardens, a stinking old male resembling the imprisoned beast Andersen saw in the strange menagerie at the Tower of London nearly twenty years before, sunk below ground level in a thirty-foot cage – he'd been able to see the prints made by the great paws as they paced to and fro. The old lion's paws had been lacerated and infected, his eyes filmed over by a white membrane. With time he had become blind in the semi-darkness. It was said he tried to dig himself out every night, as if he thought the wild he remembered was waiting for him on the other side of the bars. Going home. To the keeper, who had roared with laughter at the thought of the animal's stupidity, the story of him trying to dig his way home had merely been another curiosity. Andersen is only lightly touched by the memory.

Hugo von Hoffroder has combed his greying hair, which falls over his collar. Andersen knows a terrible disease exists that can slowly draw the facial muscles together and transform a human face into a monstrosity, a rigid grimacing mask, but Hoffroder's expression is so sensitive that he immediately pushes away the thought. Anyway, where do you draw the boundary between human and beast? Those men who used to frequent the poor women in the tenement block in Odense were worse than the male lion in his cage. Their cage was a projection of pleasure and fantasy constructed from the lowest instincts of humanity. The same ability to imagine enables a theatregoer to accept the stage and its limitations as reality for a couple of hours, as the world or the wild; nothing more is needed so long as the piece is skilfully written. Black or white, culture or something contrary to nature? Who can say where the boundary lies?

Andersen watches Hoffroder watching the boy out in the yard. Is he the boy's father? One can't tell. A lion begetting a fox-cub, stranger things have been known. And the boy's mother? The thought sickens him but won't leave him alone. His imagination presents him with unwelcome and disturbing scenes. Pictures he put aside long ago like some old well-thumbed childhood card game with a pattern of red squares, corners folded down by cheating until it became unusable in well-lit drawing rooms. Andersen takes a deeper draught of wine, but suddenly its taste seems to have become dense, bitter. Like iron or blood, or the bitter vinegary wine they used to serve in clay pitchers in the humbler drinking-places of his youth. You could get a mugful for a few coppers, he remembers. He looks round for a cup or pot so he can spit the revolting liquid out, and his eye falls on an extremely old mirror in a corner, almost completely corroded by black oxidising stains which have pushed their way up to the surface like holes made by seawater in thawing spring ice. He starts when he catches sight of his own bent, grizzled figure and suddenly knows the answer to his question: what separates man from beast is man's self-confidence. And with this insight he swallows a mouthful of wine.

Next day is the day of departure, and Andersen gets up early. The air is fresh, and the previous evening's melancholy has gone as if blown away. The coachman rummages in the kitchen trying to assemble enough drink, bread and butter to make up a single bag of food. Henriette Honorine is not to be seen, and Andersen feels relieved. He has avoided her throughout the visit; now he can put the miniature back in its place on his wall in Copenhagen again. All that's happened is that now there's a small thorn in his memory of her. Something he can deal with. The "fox-cub", as Andersen calls the boy to himself, constantly slinks about at the writer's heels, remarkably attached to the tall friendly man despite the fact that they haven't spoken to one another. The boy never speaks, and Andersen suspects he's dumb. Or perhaps imbecile, hard to tell. But his eyes are the most beautiful the writer has ever seen, blue as the sky in high summer. This morning the child has sticky dark stains round his mouth, and for one terrible moment Andersen thinks it must be blood from some little animal he has trapped in the wood, then he realises the stains come from the goodies he brought in the gift hamper. This last morning the boy seems to have realised the time for saying goodbye is near, and he hangs round Andersen's pocket as if he would like to creep into it and hide from the world. The writer pushes him gently away, but in no time the boy is back, more importunate than before. In the end all the writer can do is give him a sharp box on the ear of the kind his mother used to administer, with hand open and fingers rigid. Andersen feels the blow on his own cheek at the same moment as his hand strikes the boy's slender face. He has hit him hard, much harder than he intended, and the child falls to the floor. He doesn't make a single sound, and this is worse. Now Andersen has to get away from this house. At once! His palm is burning, and he sticks his hand into his coat pocket, a safe hiding place after all. The boy has vanished somewhere into the house or garden. Andersen never saw him go.

The boy is still not to be seen when the coach finally rolls out onto the road and heads north. Von Hoffroder waves from his window just as on the first morning, a wooden bird emerging from a dirty cuckoo-clock. Andersen flaps his handkerchief backwards and forwards a few times, then draws down the blinds on the coach windows and closes his eyes till they are out of the forest. In one of his trunks lies Hoffroder's half-finished manuscript, *Transformations*.

ON TOUR

I WAS WOKEN by the sound of Terror yapping. The mongrel had come into my room during the night and was now snoozing at the foot of my bed, apparently just about to sink his teeth into some dream-prey, the prospect of which was making his mouth water. He had grabbed most of the blanket for himself so I was freezing. It was six o'clock. I got up carefully and crept out of the room. My feet followed an old familiar track across the cold floor and wandered as if of their own volition over to the window. The sight of the Chevy in the morning light made me start; everything was just as it had been before, as if no time had passed at all. I went back into the bedroom and pulled on my shirt and jeans together with a jacket I found in the wardrobe. Terror had woken and was watching me with approval. To go out for a walk was just what he wanted. I tied a piece of cord through the eye on his collar, jumped into my shoes at the door and off we went.

The path down to the sea zigzags between windswept pines. The dog made the most of the corners, and all I had to do was hang on. I glanced back at the bungalow before it vanished behind the trees. It had a rumpled appearance in the early morning, as if the rising sun had surprised it doing something it shouldn't have been. The blinds in Mogensen's room were still drawn. Then the house disappeared behind a bend, and the smell of the sea reached me.

The sea has an entirely different smell at different times of year. Summer is ripeness, fermentation, a satisfied blanket of organisms that makes the waves comfortably sleek and oily. They lick the pebbles and sand of the shore like gentle cats' tongues and deposit drifts of rustling dry seaweed like cast-off black lace underskirts. The smell leaves a taste of rotting algae on your lips. A cloud of tiny seaweed-flies the wind whisks away.

In spring, on the other hand, clarity and chill bring a solemn rigour that in anticipation of summer measures out equal quantities of sweet and salt into the bailers rolling about in inshore boats as water slowly slaps their swelling wooden sides. You only become aware of spring's tentative smells when you've already moved some distance from the sea. Then there are other spring days when aggressive storm-waves carrying ice on their rugged tops anaesthetise nose, mouth and lungs.

Today was a normal day, and a weak chilly wind was roughing up the surface of the water without really paying much attention to what it was doing. "I could do this if I wanted to," it seemed to be saying, "but I can't be bothered." The waves folded over one another like table napkins tidily arranged in a basket. Terror's senses absorbed all this; maybe he'd never seen the sea before. I took off his lead and let him rush the last bit of the way to the water. He sank his teeth into several waves before realising that this new element was wet and cold. Then he trotted back and gave me a look as if to say "I knew that all along, of course." I didn't bother to contradict him, but dried his snout with a handkerchief I found in one of the pockets of the jacket while he laid his head on my knee. When I folded the handkerchief I saw from a childlike monogram that it had been my mother's. Presumably the jacket had been hers too, though I had no memory of it. It was an old-fashioned blue windcheater with a hood and kept out the wind remarkably well. I felt warm and, surprisingly enough, thoroughly rested. Gabriel Mayer's strange story was going round in my head. I wondered if perhaps it was true. I knew the place he'd written about. Viberød's present-day hunting lodge was only a few kilometres from where we were now. Less if you walked along the shore. For a moment I wondered whether to go back to the bungalow and Mogensen, but all things considered he needed his sleep. The dog gave me a yellow sidelong look then bundled his bandy legs along the shore in the right direction. All I had to do was follow.

*

It was by no means a difficult path to find, and gradually my memory returned, just like when you manage to fit several jigsaw pieces together in a row so they reveal a motif though you can't be sure what it represents. It must have been fifteen years since I'd last walked here. I passed several large sailing boats moored a little way out on the fjord. They were snatching and pulling at their chains and plunging their bows into the water as if to curtsy deeply to the waves, but I saw no sign of any human being. The wind freshened, and Terror danced ahead of me on light paws, sometimes at the water's edge but taking care now not to get wet and skilfully avoiding the waves as they rolled in. The sun was hidden; now and then a ragged fragment of strong sunlight escaped only to be covered immediately by a new bank of cloud – as if the light had been the result of an accidental oversight. Eventually we reached a point where my memory told me we should leave the shore and go upwards. Several scrappy thickets obstructing our way were evidence that this particular path was hardly used any more. In fact, it was virtually invisible, and I could only detect it because I already knew it was there. Again I thought of a jigsaw, but this time it was the whole picture I had in mind rather than the individual cut-out pieces. I could see what I expected to see. Finally we left the sea a little way behind us, and the smells changed. The forest smelled of imprisoned cold. The wind blew through the upper branches high above our heads with a sound that seemed simultaneously far away and near. Sometimes dry branches whined and moaned as they scraped against one another. The firs hadn't been thinned for years. Terror wasn't so keen on going in among the trees, so I fastened the cord to his collar again and pulled him along with me. He kept his snout to the ground as though he thought this was how you forestalled disagreeable encounters – and he may have been right. I had to be satisfied with taking a good look round.

The wood was not at all large, but its impenetrability made it difficult for one to get a general impression of it. It was a plantation, the result of a romantically inspired early nineteenth-century land project, though of course new plants had grown up since then. (The nation had been unwilling to lose more of its territory to the sea. Conifers grow quickly, though it's unusual to find whole forests of them in this part of the world, where they are not native.) But at some point the forest's innate wildness, its primitive nature, had got the upper hand, and as you tried to force a way through between the closely packed trees it was hard to grasp that there had ever been any plan behind this venture. This was the forest's own territory. Light from outside was virtually excluded, yet the thick trunks glowed with a strange light of their own. Kai used to explain this by saying that the trunks produced an exceptionally sticky yellow resin which reflected the little daylight that did manage to get through the network of branches. Insects stuck in this sticky mass and fluids from a multitude of small decomposing bodies produced a chemical light-effect. Phosphorus. Under the trees a sterile carpet of needles made the ground soft and springy. In the early days they planted every type of conifer here, including rare varieties the Bockmeisters brought back from their business trips to Russia and northern Turkey. Presumably these were still there somewhere among the forest's green federation of foreigners, together with the brick grotto built at the time of the first plantings. But all paths had long since been obliterated, and the exotic plants had been assimilated into the Danish landscape.

*

If I remembered right, it was going to be about a kilometre's walk from the shore to the hunting lodge. The forest had sent out runners in the form of feeble conifers which had overstepped the boundary of their own domain. Down by the shore their counterparts had stood like a crowd of stunted pale-green guard-posts set in an uneven line. Now as I came nearer to the house, gaps began to open out, round spaces created by some heavy-handed thinning process. This must have happened a good many years ago, because even here young trees were beginning to fill the gaps. Light filtered down from a pale sky. The hunting lodge wasn't the house Hans Christian Andersen may have visited but a smaller villa built in a traditional style following a fire sometime in the 1920s. Parts of the foundations of the old building were still there, transformed into tennis courts. At least, that's how I remembered it. This was where the Bockmeisters had entertained their German guests during the long hot interwar summers of the 1930s.

It came almost as a surprise when the house appeared suddenly from behind a dense thicket. It had been built as an octagon, an eight-sided box. Nearest to the brick terraces were thick hedges of thuya which had been allowed to grow untrimmed and thus almost totally concealed any possible traces of humanity. Now this tough greenery was climbing up the red brick and approaching the terrace doors. It smelled like a churchyard: damp gravel, wet vegetation and decay. The villa's empty windows gaped. Terror repeatedly stopped to press himself against my leg and look up into my face out of the corner of his eye – perhaps to see whether I was afraid.

There was a gravel path round the house, just as I remembered it. I could hear rather than see the gravel under my feet. We set off to find the main entrance. At an angle off to the left I could see what remained of the tennis courts, their red surfaces almost eaten away by whitish moss and grass, as though they'd been struck down by some exotic disease, some Indian fever shipped home in one of the family firm's wooden packing-cases. Here and there long yellow grass from last year and dry bushes showed where the courts had been trans-formed into wilderness again. The wind moved through the bushes with a rustling sound that made Terror back off uneasily. It was a remarkable feeling to find myself at the house again, like moving through my own memory and finding everything familiar yet at the same time unfamiliar. I thought I could detect smoke; perhaps someone was burning twigs and leaves somewhere in the grounds. There could be no doubt the place was still inhabited even if I could see no sign of life. The dog could smell the smoke too, sniffing the air as though he'd detected a string of sausages hanging just above his square head. His short coat seemed rumpled with worry.

The last time I'd been here, the very last, it had been a stiflingly hot summer evening. My memory of it lay where I usually found it. Kai was in a dazzling white shirt which made it easy for me to follow him through the forest. He couldn't see me.

*

Lara has taken out the grill and set it on the terrace at the back of the house. She's prepared meat on a chequered plastic plate. Blood has gathered in a pool in one corner. Something my father normally never eats. Her odour reaches all the way to me. Nauseating, warm and rank like an animal's. I lie hidden behind one of the walls left over from the old house. If I put my nose against the crumbling brick, I can smell smoke and something else, iron or blood. Lying completely still is uncomfortable; my knees and elbows hurt, but I have my role-models: supremely self-confident polar explorers like Sir John Franklin on deck one May morning as the *Erebus* makes her way through the muddy Thames Estuary. Franklin is uneasy because his wife had used the Union Jack as a bed-cover one evening a few days before he set out. A sign of death, but a woman wouldn't know a thing like that. A shadow crosses his face too quickly to be a passing cloud. He is reassured when a dazzling white pigeon lands on the mast-top; it hesitates a moment but eventually settles peacefully on one of the yard-arms. This is a mark of good fortune, and the crew cheer. The stone paving grazes my elbows, but that's nothing compared to the suffering that awaits Franklin. The *Erebus*' sister-ship *Terror* follows in her wake with the river-pilot still on board, but Franklin knows the river like the back of his hand, every sandbank of it, and stands beside the *Erebus*' helmsman whispering orders. Depth five fathoms by lead and line. The line's disappearing astern, which means their speed is greater than that of the tidal water. The ships' bows are reinforced with iron plates, the structure of their hulls is extra thick. The rigging will creak when the new sails fill, thirty-three squares waiting to unfurl like crumpled butterfly wings. The river babbles along the ships' sides. The wind freshens, and the heavily laden ships gain speed. You set sail when the tide's out. Franklin never admits that he later finds the dove beside the binnacle with her neck broken, her round pearl eyes open but covered by a milk-white film. On the deck she is no longer white but a dirty grey, and he drops her into the estuary when no-one is looking.

*

Lara's wearing a light summer dress. Short and square. On her large feet are elegant silver sandals with low heels that make her look coarse, mutton dressed as lamb. As for me, I'm as small and supple as a weasel, silent and invisible. My silence is strength, not shyness. My hair has been cut short like a boy's by Dad's "gentlemen's hairdresser", a heavy pair of trimming scissors he keeps in a cardboard box in a cupboard. My body is light and dry. I can run silently in my thin white rubber shoes. The way Dad's standing obstructs my view of Lara; his arm is round her, and she laughs at something he says. At everything he says. Her laughter clucks deep in her throat like the cooing of a pigeon. She has no idea what to do, and he has to look after the grill for her. The meat hisses and starts burning. Lara's not at all like Mum, she has a heavy and immobile body with feet planted firmly on the ground. I have my notebook with me so I won't forget anything. The rough stones are hurting and numbing my thin legs.

*

It was on May 19, 1845, in the eighth year of Queen Victoria's reign, that Franklin's expedition sailed down the Thames on its way to search for the North-West Passage. *Erebus* and her sister-ship *Terror* (commander Francis Crozier) had what they needed and more to keep them going for five years – longer if they were strict with their rations. They carried the latest navigation aids. Compasses with cardanic suspension made by John Bruce & Son of Liverpool, together with marine clocks and other state-of-the-art measuring apparatus. Each ship was equipped with a twenty-horsepower auxiliary engine (manu-factured by The London Railway Company, which was already boring its way with precision under London's streets); the ships were also the first polar exploration vessels to be fitted with screws. With steel blades like wings. In short, they were excellently equipped to measure themselves against darkness, ice, cold and desolation, powers of the polar regions. Which is why the Admiralty sent no relief expedition to find out what had happened to them until May 1848, though by that time there had been no news of the ships for more than two years. The last to sight *Erebus* and *Terror* were two whalers who saw them both going full steam ahead into pack ice and shortly afterwards disappearing from view. When he put in at Julianehåb in Greenland two months later, one of the whalers reported the sighting as having been at 74° 48' north (the details are uncertain). *Erebus*, perhaps named after Homer's cold and desolate region of the dead, was the first to enter the ice and vanish. The sister of the ancient Greek Erebos was Nyx, the night. An endless polar night was what awaited Franklin, Crozier and their crews in Lancaster Sound and Barrow Strait.

*

I walked round the last gable and looked up at the outer door. There was nothing there. Or rather no door, only an empty rectangle of air. From where I was standing I could see into the hall and also a bit of the living-room. Last year's dry leaves littered the corners, as if the forest had continued right into the house and left bits of its foliage behind there. There were big dark patches of damp on the wallpaper, and a grey sky gaped directly into the room through an irregular hole in the roof. Light from outside was filtered through remarkably fine-ground dust as if the whole structure were in a state of disintegration. Perhaps the nibbling grubs of small insignificant vermin were attacking the wooden framework; I know nothing of such things. Whatever the truth of the matter, the dust gave the damage a physical body, as if every speck had its place in a specific gliding time-rhythm on its way down to the floor. In its transformation from one form into another.

It wasn't free fall since a number of factors – weight, air resistance, wind, humidity – affected the particles and thus seemed to make time go round in circles or at least sideways. For a short moment the sun broke through the cloud cover and gilded the air inside the house, turning it to cloth of gold. The fabric of dreams. Terror whimpered anxiously and sat down, firmly determined to stay outside. With him on the other end of the lead I'd never be able to explore the ruin. I was struggling to call up an image that refused to come to the surface: I couldn't remember how that evening had ended.

*

When we got back to the bungalow, we found Mogensen busy in the kitchen. He'd opened the window for a much-needed bit of fresh air and put on the pot to make coffee. Some of Kai's old military journals were piled on the table together with a few yellowed daily papers. I sat down and began absent-mindedly glancing through the first page of the *Jutland Post* from August 23, 1971 – to all intents and purposes an antique. Its brittle pages crackled like old pieces of thin unleavened bread. I turned them with care: ads for sun cream, Dubonnet with ice and deckchairs. I could hear Terror gobbling noisily from a bowl in the kitchen. Mogensen set out a simple breakfast using chipped cups and an assortment of plates he'd found in a cupboard. He didn't ask where I'd been. Inside the paper were the usual "Indian summer" beach photos, plus pictures from a war – Vietnam in this case – and a news item about a woman's body washed ashore in an inlet used by bathers. I immediately knew I'd read about this before.

It was a brief paragraph some way down one side of the page, so the news must already have been old by late August. All it said was that the police hadn't yet been able to identify the dead woman, not helped by the fact that she had no face, but that "a disappearance in the district had been linked to the discovery". The body had been sent to Copenhagen for further investigation at the Institute for Forensic Medicine. I burrowed into the pile and found a paper from three weeks earlier. Kai must have kept them deliberately. Here I found some news at the top of page two; the reporter had talked to the parents of the Copenhagen youngsters on holiday who had made the macabre find. The mother, Fru Mette Rasmussen, was angry that so little trouble was taken to keep the beaches clean. Her husband took the same view. The body had been found in an inlet not far from a cluster of summer cottages known by the name of "Sunbeam". A grainy grey photo showed a shapeless sack being loaded into an ambulance with two carelessly and shabbily dressed children in the foreground who didn't look the least bit affected by all the attention. Or indifferent to it either. The press-photographer's camera narrowed the perspective, cleverly emphasising the link – in reality the children must have been standing a fair distance from the vehicle. A girl and a boy, but you needed to read the caption to understand that. Hans and Jytte Rasmussen in matching shorts and striped shirts. Either could have been me, but I didn't recognise them. They certainly didn't come from my home district in Tårnby. They were staring unblinking and unsmiling into the camera.

I remembered there was a dead fox I used to go and look at every day during one boiling-hot summer. It became a sort of ritual or compulsion. The body lay a little way inside the wood, in a small hollow to which the animal had apparently dragged itself. It lay there grimacing with half-open jaws and sharp teeth. At first I wondered whether I should bury it, but curiosity got the upper hand and instead I studied the process of putrefaction. The greedy hunger of the small carrion-eaters had a sort of disciplined order which was interesting to observe. They seemed to know exactly how to go about their job, just like the butcher in our old street in Copenhagen who always managed to get the most out of his sides of pork. A sensitive way with the knife, that was his speciality, as he cut through cartilage, tendons and bone. Knowing which bits to take particular care over. Eventually the stench from the fox's corpse got too strong for me to go near it. But I could see the tracks. Insects tramping up like armies to carry away the body in small neat morsels. Lines of bearers in ordered single file marching over roots, needles and stones, their loads tilting like sails.

Children are explorers too in their way, cold, matter-of-fact observers. It takes time and experience to soften us. Gradually we begin to understand that a day will come when we ourselves will be weak and defenceless again. When you're a child you know you're going to grow bigger and stronger, even if sheer toughness often turns out to be an illusion. Other factors enter in and affect our strength, altering the opportunities open to us, our choice of direction and our limited freedom. Perhaps being human is simply something we learn, a necessary social trick like wearing clothes or taking care not to pick our noses in public. I drank Mogensen's hot coffee. I still couldn't remember that evening.

"TELL ME, SON, have you ever read the German writer Hugo von Hoffroder?"

Rav stared at Gabriel across the dim room amid the furniture that stood, covered in sheets, silent and motionless along the walls. The younger man shook his head.

"Well." Rav leaned even further forward. "Hoffroder was your *echt* German Romantic. An educated man steeped in Goethe's early work *Götz von Berlichingen* and Schiller's *Die Räuber* and thus in search of what was fundamentally and truly German, the original basic peasant culture and, well, what people call the folk soul. He travelled round the villages of northern Germany collecting fairy tales and legends which he then used in the fantastical stories he wrote. He absorbed what he collected then did a bit of grafting to suit himself. I found one of his stories by chance in a shed in the country – the last place you'd expect to find such a thing. Its German title was *Verwandlungen*, which means 'Transformations', but this was a Danish copy dated 1871, several years after the author's death." Rav clapped his hands as though he had scored a point. "Hoffroder died in 1865, the year after the last Schleswig war."

Gabriel nodded, unsure what the other man was driving at.

"Well, it's no great work, only forty pages, but for me that made the subject all the more interesting. He writes of a bargain concerning souls. Long ago, he doesn't specify when, there was a certain village in the northern part of the Duchy of Holstein. A simple place, four or five farms and some thirty people who'd decided to settle there and make a modest living from farming and raising cattle. They also grew small hard apples of a green unripe appearance that they pressed to make extremely potent cider, which they stored in large oak barrels. Their orchards covered many acres, and it was these apples, or rather the powerful cider that came from them, that were the village's principal source of income. The village itself lay in the damp misty shelter of a ridge from which they had a wide view of their surroundings, not far from the old abandoned border defences known as the Dannevirke. From time to time their thin inbred cattle fell into empty spaces that remained under the earth where ancient structures of wood and wattle-and-daub had rotted away. Sometimes the beasts broke through the orchard fencing in autumn and ate windfalls till their stomachs swelled with colic and they went mad. In fact I know the district so the story interested me more than it might have done otherwise. No main roads or important paths passed near the village, so the inhabitants naturally became a bit isolated and introverted. If once in a while some wanderer came near, which happened very seldom, they hid and put out their fires so as not to attract the stranger's attention. Yet the village was extremely ancient, despite or perhaps because of the fact that it was cut off from the surrounding world, sheltering like a soft snail in its shell. Perhaps you could say it wasn't even real, since only one of the villagers ever had contact with the world as the rest of us know it. This link-figure was the Wagoner, who each year took the cider-barrels to market.

"One altogether special tradition was kept alive by the villagers. Since every one of them, little girls, small boys, men, women and old people alike, was incapable of reading a single word, they would tell each other about the village's customs in rich detail though also with a certain toughness and lack of sentimentality. The past became an endless chain of voices built up link by link, sometimes mumbled by the weak tongues of the elderly, sometimes offered by young voices just beginning to learn how to venture into the slippery and treacherous labyrinth of memory. The villagers considered their people to consist not only of those still alive but also of all the dead whose names could be recalled through the memories of the living. The highest honour and status in the village went to the longest and most complicated genealogy. They had a burial ground as near as possible to the crest of the ridge; each grey stone carried only the special mark of a particular family with an additional small stone splinter for each body buried there. In this way these simple village folk became masters of memory while many outsiders might have dismissed them as mostly idiots even though they were by no means stupid."

Rav cleared his throat and poured himself more wine but did not drink.

"All this changed during the last century. You see, a schoolteacher walked into the village. Hoffroder does give his name, but I've forgotten it, I'm afraid."

Rav tapped his head and smiled.

"This teacher was a tall, thin, short-sighted bloke. In fact he was heading somewhere quite different, but a strong wind and icy whiplash rain had forced him to look for a more sheltered route. So he made his way through undergrowth and brushwood and over soft marsh-land by a path he found which was less open to weather and wind and seemed more like a tunnel or perhaps the way to a burrow. Then suddenly there he was in the village. Because of the foul weather the villagers were not aware of the intruder till he was right in their midst, a presence as unexpected as the appearance of eels in a rain-water tank (one local even claimed he'd emerged from a thunderclap). Now this schoolteacher was an enlightened and educated man who had studied pedagogy with the famous Grundtvig at Borch's College in Copenhagen. He was amazed and delighted with the 'primal Danes' he imagined he'd discovered in the village. Here was the classic inde-pendent Danish smallholder – strong, honest and genuine – with his sharp scythe, toothless mouth and long home-woven smock drenched in sweat, who sowed, harvested and brought small grey babies into the world and spread human and animal dung over narrow strips of ploughed land in the eternally rotating cycle of nature. The schoolteacher was excited and attracted by this perfect simplicity, this self-sufficiency and ability to adapt. He didn't notice that the village was actually a matriarchy. His heredity and education hadn't prepared him for this possibility, and the blue-tinted glasses he habitually wore limited his sight. That spring, like an industrious shepherd who quite by chance has found himself with a new and needy flock, he taught the villagers to read. He stayed with them into the early summer, coughing and sneezing with a cold he seemed unable to shake off in their smoky, draughty cottages, and when at midsummer he packed his knapsack and books to leave, they killed him with a single well-directed cudgel blow behind Old Ole's outhouse. From gratitude, you understand, because they were now so much better equipped to defend themselves against the outside world. They didn't bury him in the village burial ground but under a long narrow mound of stones at the edge of the forest. Young-Young-Ole was far-sighted enough to carve a large A on a piece of board which he stuck in among the stones, since that was the very first character their teacher had taught them. It was the beginning of a new age in the village." Rav leaned back on the sofa and sipped his wine. "It was also the beginning of my idea," he added, "but I'm getting ahead of myself."

The police chief got to his feet and started pacing. Shadows moved across the walls by fits and starts, magnifying his movements as if there was a restless giant wandering in the low-ceilinged room.

"The villagers began writing down their genealogies," continued Rav when he had once again sat down opposite Gabriel. "They knew no other field in which to make use of their new skill. They weren't at all romantic. They looked at life from a strictly utilitarian point of view, and, as we have seen, the longer and more complex your network of relatives, the higher your status in the village. Now that they were slowly beginning to weave what they knew for certain together with other things people 'thought they'd heard', they named the whole thing THE TREE after a mighty and ancient ash which grew on the outskirts of the village. Thus, though what was written down might not always be accurate, it was thought to have greater authenticity, since the written characters themselves seemed to lend knowledge extra weight and dignity (most of the villagers had simple names which could be written with three letters, but in writing them down they would add one, two or three family names). It was not long before a girl known as Ib from Nedangården attracted attention for her exceptionally quick mind and particular skill and nimble fingers with the drawing-pencil. They gave her the job of making a fair, final and permanent copy on goatskin of what the others had scratched on pieces of wood and scraps of cloth. This gave a substance to the written words which no-one could question even if the letters, both the illuminated capitals and the plain ones, seemed in Ib's small hands to hover like a flock of swifts over the vellum. Also, they would never correct a mistake or alter an uncertain piece of information but go carefully round it and assimilate it, making it their own in exactly the same way as a peasant does when he has a difficult bit of land in the middle of his property. People noted things down on their own account too, bits of new information that didn't need to be either absorbed or rejected by the collective memory. Notes just 'arose', and since no-one ever dated or signed these additions, it became impossible to establish their veracity. Eventually the little village had a table of family connections worthy of a German noble house, so complicated had it become with all its ramifications and links. Naturally all this took an enormous amount of time. But even when they'd achieved it, the villagers weren't happy, and the reason for their unhappiness was the failure of their apple-harvest."

Rav groped in his pocket and conjured up a tin.

"D'you recognise this little fellow, Gabriel?" he said. In the tin, on a bit of white linen, lay the caterpillar from the bog, the Lackey moth, rolled up in a hard grey ring. It had lost all its colour, and the tin smelled strongly of ether.

"*Malacosoma neustria*. The villagers taught themselves to recognise it. While they had been calculating and working their way back generation by generation, recalling to memory names that existed before such concepts as Danish, German or Schleswigish even existed, the Lackey moths had been nibbling away at their trees. The bark remained and deceived the eye, but underneath, the heart of each tree was being gnawed to yellow dust. Where the fruit should have been growing and ripening was a moths' nursery full of grey cocoons. The same thing happened in orchard after orchard. Only a few hardy cuttings that had been crossed with another species survived."

Rav shook the caterpillar out onto his big palm. As Gabriel watched it seemed to move as if it were about to stretch itself, twitch and be off.

"No apples, no cider," said Rav, shaking the caterpillar back into the tin. He shut the lid noisily and put it back in his pocket. "It so happened that in that year, 1863, war threatened again. Some say Bismarck lured the Danes into a trap. I expect you know your history. The duchies of Schleswig and Holstein refused to accept the new liberal constitution adopted by Denmark, to which they belonged. Or rather, a more liberal regime didn't suit the conservative landed gentry of Holstein, who preferred to make common cause with Prussia and Bismarck if they weren't to be allowed to continue the autocratic ways the Danish king had permitted them till then. War was kindled by riffraff in the streets of Copenhagen who thought that all you needed to defeat Germany was abuse and patriotic ranting in the beer-halls and town squares of Denmark. Some enlisted out of nationalism or a longing for adventure, or were tempted by the promise of fine military clothes. So off they marched in a stinking cloud of beer, horseshit and unaired uniforms. And Bismarck parried and feinted so rapidly and cleverly in his constitutional fencing with the new Danish king, Christian IX, that this ill-prepared army assembled for the greater honour and glory of Denmark eventually found itself at the Dannevirke, only a few tens of kilometres from the village we have been talking of, to fight for a cause hardly anyone really understood. They didn't stay there long since – this is hardly surprising – the ancient defences were in a state of collapse and totally impossible to defend.

"But it was when the armies needed to send home dispatches that the villagers, so rich in family connections but otherwise poorest of the poor, saw their chance to make a little money. All they harvested that autumn was sackfuls of dead moths and shrivelled grey cocoons. They spent several days caring for lost and confused soldiers before they summoned up the nerve to come forward with their proposal. They chose the Wagoner to do the talking, as he knew how to be as smooth as sweetened cream and was used to dealing with folk from the outside world. So he put on his best suit, spat, rubbed the dust off his black top hat and walked over to the Danish lines.

"What they proposed was simple. That a whole company of infantrymen should be formed from among the villagers' own dead relatives and that the names and dates of these should be entered on detailed rolls that would actually exist only in Ib's beautiful hand-writing, and that this company should be sold to the Danish commissariat – officially to one of its junior civil servants, but Hoffroder implies that the commander-in-chief himself, General Christian Julius de Meza, knew all about the scheme. Soon Ib began to add individual characteristics and personalities to her lists of names, so that these simple men from Schleswig were transformed into colourful, fully rounded figures. In this way were created brave men who had remained longer than anyone else at the Dannevirke and been the last to march over the wooden bridge from Holstein to Schleswig, men whose true *esprit de corps* would rescue something of the badly tarnished reputation of the Danish army leadership. It was in the breasts of these fictitious soldiers that the Danish heart beat most strongly, and Copenhagen poets wrote sentimental ballads in their honour. Before and after performances at the Royal Theatre, claques made up from the city's rabble led cheers for the Schleswig Company. The young ladies of Copenhagen day-dreamed about them, and some of their names even ended up on gravestones in the garrison cemetery, where they remained until 1886, when all the bones there were collected and reburied in a single common grave. All documents concerning this company's movements, together with the names of those who died in action and details of medals awarded for bravery, were taken to HQ at top speed in a carriage specially chosen for the purpose and supplied with a mounted guard to ensure that the material should not fall into the wrong hands.

Better still, these fictitious peasant-soldiers naturally had no living relatives who might want to know how each had died or ask awkward questions about what exactly their brave and unselfish deeds had been. The battered Danish nation needed heroes, and the people needed to believe that Schleswig and Holstein still had Danish hearts. So far so good. A few months later, the villagers made the same offer to the Prussians, but the senile Prussian commander, Field-Marshal Wrangel, gave the game away, which is how Hugo von Hoffroder got the idea for his story. At least that's what he says."

Rav took a large mouthful of wine and leaned back, his face red with satisfaction.

"So that's what you do too," said Gabriel. "You give new names to Jewish refugees."

"Danish names, son, the very best old Danish names. I provide them with family trees. Not even the Germans can question *that*."

DYBBØL,

APRIL 20, 1864

OUT ON THE coast the weather clears and the sun comes out.
Käsemann parks his van on the edge of the Prussian army camp,
in a field cleared by the troops. The ground is uneven, and it's hard
work wedging the wheels with pieces of wood; soon he's running with
sweat in the intense spring heat and has flies buzzing persistently
round his head. The heavy supply wagons have cut up the turf, exposing
a rich topsoil full of worms which gives off a warm damp earthy smell
so long as the wind isn't coming from the battlefield. Large flocks of
seabirds have arrived from the Sound and are circling with shrill cries
over the slopes of Dybbøl. Their strong slender wings almost touching
as if the whole flock were one mighty body, the birds rise and fall in
ever tighter circles round the troops, who are collecting the dead on
open-sided carts. The soil round the redoubts has been churned into
a crater of mud, an open sore that looks as if it must be the result of
an explosion within the earth, with mud everywhere and shattered
wood that has been flung up into the air. Sheets of tent-canvas have
been stretched over the dead lying where they fell on the hillside to
keep off the greedy birds. Boots, baldrics and tunics are being salvaged
wherever possible. The soldiers work with pieces of cloth soaked in
vinegar knotted round their faces. The heat makes the cloth stick to
their skin. Their grey cotton masks make them look unreal, like figures
created from cloth rather than flesh and blood. They bury the dead
in hurriedly dug ditches which serve as large graves, to discourage the
spread of infection in the spring heat. Käsemann has passed several
of these mass graves on his way up to the slopes. In them the men

have been laid in ranks as if formed up in marching order for a journey down to an underground landscape, a journey the living can't make. Here and there where fires have been lit, smoke and sunshine mix to create a haze that makes it difficult to see.

In the camp, order rules with sharp shouts of command and the jingle of bridles and harness, as if discipline, leather straps and a few dabs of grease will suffice to bring back the dead. Here too fires have been lit in special bowls, and pungent herbs have been thrown onto the embers to reduce the stench of death, because Prince Friedrich Karl is in fact still staying as a guest in Field-Marshal Wrangel's tent. It's well known that he has a sensitive nose. Above the tent the Prussian royal standard with its eagle is flapping hard in the wind. The plan is that tomorrow, as soon as the area has been cleared by sappers, Friedrich Karl will visit the ruins of a mill destroyed by the artillery. Heinrich Käsemann's in luck.

*

Käsemann tours the battlefield and tries to understand the philosophy and strategy of war, but all he sees is disorder and chaos. And he is followed everywhere by that stench, so close and tangible that it almost seems to have a body of its own now that nearly all the dead have been taken away. Sometimes as he walks he is forced to press a handkerchief over his nose and mouth. He must make a long detour to avoid the swollen corpse of a horse. The ground is slippery and treacherous with holes, all that remain of ruined saps, plank-lined pathways that lead nowhere. He still tries to work methodically, making sketches for compositions and angles, pacing out and noting down distances. Now and then he has to step aside to let men pass with stretchers. From a distance he makes hasty charcoal sketches of faces, weapons, uniforms, empty spaces. All done in an instant like capturing a butterfly in a net, catching it fast in the filigree.

Käsemann isn't alone in his mission; Graf from Berlin's here already with his big American camera. Käsemann has seen him at a distance in the camp, with an assistant in tow and as self-important as ever.

But Graf is no artist; his pictures show no sensitive understanding but simply reflect reality in a dry, flat, matter-of-fact way. Käsemann ponders the question of how best to present his own work: should he shape it like a novelist with a narrative, creating an emotional retelling of war? He counts twenty steps from a shattered wall to a trench and nearly falls over a wrecked gun-carriage. What a pity they've already got round to carrying away the dead.

He has come some way now from the centre of the action. He can just see the tops of the hospital tents and, beyond them, the road to Sønderborg winding its way down the slope. Several mucky young-sters are running about on the edge of the devastated area, and Käsemann thinks why not photograph them too. Pictures of peasant children are in demand in the capital. As simple people do, these chil-dren are likely to stare straight into the camera, so perhaps he'll manage to capture a fragment of their souls with his lens. In fact they do stare at the photographer, inquisitive and impudent, before continuing to root about in the rubbish like skinny backyard rats in the seedy Moabit district of Berlin. Käsemann thinks of pictures he has seen from India, images of the very poorest people set against a background of ancient buildings, houses of porous stone and deep, uninviting pits. A play of light and dark in which one can no longer determine what was built by human hands and what was capriciously created by nature. One of the youngsters, a half-grown boy, suddenly pulls up his long shirt, bends over and shows Käsemann his dirty arsehole. Thin white legs and a firm bum. Then the boy turns and looks him straight in the eye. Käsemann gets angry despite himself and at the same time strongly excited. His sex springs to life and rises hard and importunate; it must be the heat, he waves to drive the group away before they see he's lost control of himself. They're like small and indescribably dirty animals. Even so his blood has inflated him with lust. Humanity at its most primitive. He straightens his hat and goes back up to the redoubts by a different route, sweating and licking salt from his lips. His heart calms down a bit. Stupidly, it hasn't occurred to him to bring a field water-bottle. And it really is unnaturally hot.

Up on the slopes again, the sun burns Käsemann's back as he works. His thin cotton jacket feels like the thickest worsted. He needs to stop to scrape mud off his boots, even the upper parts of them. At a little distance, perhaps twenty metres away – it's hard to judge distances in the haze – he sees a group of soldiers sitting round a fire. They are almost motionless, slowly lifting tin mugs but saying nothing. At least Käsemann can't detect any sound. Maybe seven men, sitting in a tight ring. Sunlight flashes momentarily from a buckle. The heat is affecting his eyesight; he blinks and tries to focus. Are they Danes or Germans? Suddenly their uniforms all seem alike, the drab colour of earth. He can't make out an individual face. Should he go over to them? He decides to take a short walk first, but when a moment later he returns to the same point – he can see the prints his boots made in the mud – the soldiers have vanished without trace. And where they were the ground is trampled flat: there was clearly never a fire there.

*

Käsemann continues his tour for more than an hour. He cautiously follows a narrow path behind the redoubts. Here too the ground is churned up and muddy, and from time to time he has to climb over splintered logs that have been blown up behind the lines, lightly tossed into the air as if by the hand of a playful giant. They still smell of fir resin, to him a forest smell. Here and there are bloodstained rags, twisted iron and ruined weapons. He wonders what the time might be; to judge by the sun certainly later than three in the afternoon. He suddenly feels faint, and there's a nasty taste in his mouth. He's a broad-shouldered man with plenty of flesh on him. It's long past midday; the sun is slowly beginning to lose its heat, and the shirt clinging to his back is cold. He can no longer remember what he came here for. He passes a mound of earth, carefully avoiding holes that lead down into the redoubts. It's not a big area, but even so he seems to have lost his way. A disgusting rotting smell rises from the darkness: he has come on a food store whose seal has been blown apart, and he can hear rats running about underground, their little paws rasping on wood. All at once he isn't hungry any more. Suddenly he thinks he can hear a low murmur of voices from inside the earth, and despite the stench he goes nearer. Sometimes he seems to identify German words, at other times the syllables seem meaningless. Yet the sound lures him on. A half-demolished set of wooden steps leads into the earth. Käsemann covers his mouth and nose with his handkerchief and carefully begins to climb down. The steps rock under his weight but hold firm. He can hear his own quick breaths. A frightened Orpheus with nothing in his waistcoat pocket but a box of sulphur matches. Just that.

*

At first Käsemann can see nothing in the darkness. The steps seem to be leading him down into a place where time becomes infinite. Small stones clatter past, continuing to the bottom with abrupt tapping sounds. The atmosphere is stuffy, and he realises what he's doing is absurd. No-one knows where he is. He can still hear the voices. He counts the steps down, one, two, three . . . and stops when he gets to twenty. He gropes the rough walls and feels them crumble at his touch. His skin feels dry yet at the same time greasy. A little further down the passage narrows, and he has to breathe in to get by. Then it widens again, and he feels as if he's inside some huge hourglass where time rustles by like fine sand. There's a taste of earth in his mouth. His eyes smart and fill with tears. A sharp curve in the wall shuts out the light. An odour of sulphur and putrefaction closes him in, and Käsemann has the feeling he has been buried. This is just how it must be: this smell of decay, this tight lid of darkness over one's eyes, this *nothing*. He takes a deep breath at the thought and at the same moment reaches the bottom of the hole. Hesitantly he puts his feet on the ground, still holding onto the steps with both hands. The ground is soft and crackles as if he were walking on shells. Now the silence is absolute. He quickly strikes a match and looks around: a round hole, smooth mud walls, a space as empty as if it had been swept thoroughly clean. Yet before the match goes out, he thinks he sees tracks on the floor. The air is in motion, amazingly fresh, the stench almost gone. His little flame seems to have caused unease among the inhabitants of the hole. He can hear the rats again, shrieking angrily behind the walls and falling with heavy thuds as they scramble over one another. He's sure his next match will show him small eyes glittering like buttons.

A voice comes from above, loud but distorted by the walls on its way down. "Haallooo!" Someone is shouting, drawing the word out at length, their voice nearly drowned by the sound of loose falling earth. He suddenly panics and regains the steps in one terrified stride, all but falling through them on the way up. A moment later he's back in the light and looks around, almost blind from the darkness. It's late afternoon now, and the sunlight is stretching listlessly along the slopes. Up on the heights they're beginning to erect yet another tent for the coming victory celebrations. Käsemann needs time to regain his composure. Standing before him is a dirty female child dressed in rags. She has a thin face, extraordinarily old-fashioned grey clothes and hair tied back with string. One of the youngsters from the crowd? She stares unblinking at him. Though his face grows hot at the thought, he reaches for her hand, just to feel living warmth, and she responds with her name.

"Ib," she says.

RESEARCHING THE SOURCES I

THERE WAS NO Mayer in the phone book, no Rav either. We'd stopped off at the Co-op, and in no time at all Mogensen was inside cruising the aisles in search of special offers. Terror gazed at me from the back seat of the Chevy while I glanced through the phone book – or what was left of it – that I'd borrowed from the shop's games corner. Inside by the garish red counter the usual collection of the overweight, the overage and the overlonely were hanging out, their insipid gazes fastened on screens where athletic men or maybe horses were heading for the finishing line. The sound on the games had been turned down, and the nags were running to the accompaniment of Death-Ninjas orchestrated by an attenuated and pimply youth behind the counter. The computer games ground on. Blip, blop. Apart from this there was no noise; as usual, life was happening somewhere else, and none of these boys had been invited. A man scratched his balls thoughtfully as he concentrated on filling in a lotto coupon; we all have our lucky numbers and their attendant rituals. I cut the phone book like a pack of greasy playing-cards and this time chose the upper half. There turned out to be five Madsens in Grænsebyen, but none of them called Jens. Even so I noted down their addresses and shoved the phone book back on its shelf above the counter while the Ninja kicked ten of his enemies to kingdom come. The creatures vanished with an electronic crash. The pimply youth laughed, displaying a row of sharp white teeth. I didn't laugh with him.

*

Mogensen met me outside the entrance, clutching four carrier bags full of liquid special offers. He looked happy.

"We should check the addresses in the police report," I said. "In 1938 the police station was in the main street. We can at least have a look and see whether it's still there. Just for old times' sake." Mogensen shrugged and his bottles clunked against one another. Behind us the mongrel pressed his nose against the car window, anxious to get going. I assumed I'd taken a generally agreeable decision.

Grænsebyen is hardly more than a single street that winds through the community on its way to Germany. There didn't seem to be much left of the town Jens Madsen had known. On the other hand the year 1864 must still have been visible in Madsen's Grænsebyen, with its stucco façades, wheel tracks and stone setts. I had the document folded in my pocket but I knew most of it by heart. *Reporting the discovery of a body . . .*

*

Madsen got up from his chair and stretched, putting his hands on his head as recommended in the civil defence drills. This pulled his trousers uncomfortably tight over his buttocks, and he hastily lowered his arms again. It was his long woollen underpants that made him fat, but he had to wear them or his hernia would get worse. He couldn't afford a new uniform just at the moment, now his wife was expecting. It was bad enough having to live in that old-fashioned flat two floors up with its outside toilet and icy water always freezing in the pipes in winter. Soon there'd be three of them sharing two rooms and a kitchen. That morning the hand-pump had produced nothing but a long-drawn-out gurgling sound, and he'd had to go to the nosy old woman on the ground floor to fill a bucket. Half the water had splashed out as he climbed back up the narrow stairs, and he'd been forced to change his long johns and socks.

Madsen sighed and sat down again heavily. Outside his window the street was beginning to come to life. He opened the register, dipped his pen in ink and neatly wrote the date at the top: *Tuesday, January*

14, 1939. Yesterday Jup the church caretaker had come to report that a hand-barrow had disappeared; it was the only entry for the day, and Rav had made it himself. The caretaker had flown into a rage; Madsen had met him on his way out. Ole Jup had always been a bad-tempered man, of course. Last autumn it had been the crypt he'd been raging about. Something about a padlock that had been changed, how the hell could he distinguish one rusty old lump of metal from another? "There was nothing wrong with the old lock," Jup had insisted. "The outside has nothing to do with the mechanism inside." It seemed a strange thing to do, stealing an old padlock, but even so Pastor Aronius had been worried and had agreed the crypt could be opened. It was of course Jens Madsen who'd had to do this unpleasant job; he'd heard that even ancient corpses could be carriers of disease. They had to saw through the lock with a hacksaw, since Jup insisted the key wouldn't work. Madsen wasn't surprised. As far as he could make out, there was no keyhole.

Down in the crypt nothing had been disturbed; a thick layer of dust covered the floor and the old coffins of the count and countess. There were six lead coffins in all, the oldest from the end of the eighteenth century. If someone had been in the crypt they must have flown through the air. He'd shone a light on the walls where the six white children's coffins lay in their niches, but he hadn't seen so much as a rat-dropping. The air in there had been stale, and afterwards he'd developed a bad cold. Not that he'd complained. Jup was like an old goat with his ragged dark hair, like the Devil himself. It's true he'd grown up in the district, but of course his mother's skin was even darker . . . Jup had got the idea into his head that someone had been moving things about in the toolshed and charnel house. And that dead woman had disappeared, which was remarkable. Later the caretaker had discovered that the lock on the well was missing, but neither he nor Aronius had bothered about that. Enough was enough. Jup had found a new lock for the well, fixed it on and then manoeuvred a large stone into place on top of the lid. In the autumn the confectioner's ugly black mongrel had regularly done its business round the lid, and its owner had been afraid the creature might fall in and break its neck (the well had been drained half a century earlier). The confectioner had grumbled about the matter to the church caretaker, since when the two hadn't been on speaking terms. Madsen ruled a line under the date and laid a sheet of blotting-paper over the text. Then he leaned back in his chair and waited for the morning to end.

There was always a lull in Grænsebyen after Christmas and New Year. People were slow to adapt to normal daily life again. It was no different at the Madsens'. Not only that, but the wife was in a bad mood in the mornings because Madsen's mother was about to come to town and stay with them. In any case her moods had become unpredictable. Dinner wasn't always punctually on the table when Madsen got home. At the police station life was as it always was. The case of the disappearance of Dr F.A. Nagler had been laid aside together with the case of the missing body of the unknown woman. Filed away at the bottom of the cupboard under "Miscellaneous", a category that covered everything other than feuding neighbours, complaints about animals or disputes over pastureland. Grænsebyen was too small for anything else. Quite simply, there was no *time* for the locals to raise their eyes from their own little world. In Copenhagen they'd failed to identify the missing woman and had sent the relevant documents back. She'd probably been a refugee. Strangely enough, they hadn't been able to find any fingerprints on the paper Madsen and Rav had sent, despite the fact that both men could certify that there *had* been fingerprints there to begin with.

Madsen wondered whether to go over to the confectioner's for some freshly baked rolls, but fear of slipping on the icy street put him off. The door of the shop was constantly opening and shutting, and the tinkle of its bell made his mouth water. The street shone slippery as a slide in the morning light. People crept cautiously along the house walls, ready to grab hold of the railings and awnings outside the building next door to the bakery, where Jup had put up his ladder in order to knock down icicles. He never strung a warning rope below where he was working, and all passers-by got was "Bloody hell, look out!" Madsen suspected that the church caretaker nourished a secret longing to impale one of the good citizens of Grænsebyen on a particularly sharp icicle. Jup loathed them all: "Arseholes the lot," he'd say. Madsen got up, went to the window and stood on tiptoe to see over the frosted part of the glass. Up on his ladder the caretaker was swinging his hammer like a swarthy Hercules. Bareheaded and gloveless, his black hair a restless cloud round his head. He seemed unable to feel the cold. A piece of ice crashed to the street without hitting anyone. Fragments clattered over the stone paving, a shower of glass-hard splinters. Jup still had a lot to do. It had alternately frozen and thawed several times; the weather seemed reluctant to decide which season it was, and today was really cold.

Madsen concentrated on the face of the clock above the office door; its big hand was moving with a loud dry tick and soon it would be nine. Police Chief Rav hadn't come in yet, and time was dawdling unwillingly onward, as if an invisible load were weighing down the clock's whole mechanism and holding it back. Madsen opened the top drawer of his desk and pulled out the magazine he kept there, an illustrated Christmas number of *All the World's Adventures* (he was fond of adventure stories). Appropriately, the first story was about a polar expedition: Sir John Franklin in the grip of the ice. Madsen stared at the text, but his mind refused to concentrate on what he was reading. Instead, the narrative and his thoughts ended up in some kind of dialogue with one another, like two men shouting from opposite sides of a field.

*

Grethe Mayer was dead. She'd fallen asleep a few days after New Year like the flame of a candle extinguished between finger and thumb. At the pinch of a moistened finger. One moment she'd been there, the next she'd been gone. Her son had taken it hard. Madsen hadn't seen him since; it was said he'd gone to Copenhagen to sort out papers connected with the family inheritance. Madsen couldn't imagine what this could be; the Mayers were destitute. He read how

Terror and *Erebus* vanished for ever into the pack ice, and he thought how Grethe Constance Mayer had now been laid on ice in the charnel house to wait for spring. A great beauty in her day, folk said. Scarcely more than forty kilos, Jup had confided in one of his more communicative moments. Not much to have to keep chilled. Madsen licked his finger and turned a page listlessly. There'd been a dog on board *Erebus* that belonged to Franklin himself, and it had played its part in the myths surrounding the expedition. In 1896 a passing ship forced off its course had heard a dog barking for hours on end on uninhabited King William Island, where Franklin had been buried in the permafrost in 1846. So the dog was still barking fifty years later. "In Franklin's journal the dog is described as a Ratcatcher," Madsen read, "a robust German breed with an unusually powerful bite, originally bred in Hamburg to catch rats and mice in the city's cellars and complicated system of sewers. This kind of dog is trained to bark to call for help. It is smooth-haired, muscular and supple so as to be able to work its way through narrow underground passages." Franklin had bought the dog in Portsmouth from a man who went from door to door selling animals. Lady Franklin refused to have anything to do with it so it followed Sir John on board. It was ugly but faithful, and Franklin called it simply "Dog". Dog slept in a specially made hammock in Franklin's cabin. Madsen put down the magazine and imagined the confectioner's dog snooping about the churchyard to Jup's impotent fury. Which is what the dog had done regularly until the weather got really cold. Were there rats down the churchyard well?

*

Tomas Rav had left his car at home. Usually the Ford whined and rattled along in all weathers, but that morning its engine was stone dead. He'd spent an hour fiddling with nuts and bolts and cables, but he couldn't coax the tiniest spark of life out of its oily sewing machine of a motor. In the end he closed the garage doors and set off on foot through the frosty white landscape. Jackdaws rose from the fields as he passed, strokes of black ink on a white world. Here and there smoking chimneys indicated that people were indoors taking refuge from the cold. The slippery ground slowed Rav down – he lived in a cottage a little way out of Grænsebyen – and it was after ten before he reached the main street; it took him another five minutes to get to the police station. He was met at the door by an overexcited Madsen, behind whom he caught a glimpse of the confectioner's submissive wife. She came no higher than Madsen's shoulder, and all Rav could see was her prematurely grey hair. This permanently waved head was convulsed with nervous sobs (the confectioner was a heavy-handed man, and his wife was usually on the receiving end, or so Tomas Rav had always suspected).

"The dog's down the well," said Madsen. "That bloody Jup took off the padlock, and the animal fell in. Apparently as long ago as yesterday evening." Behind him the confectioner's wife whimpered. The couple had no children, and this hideous cur was the apple of her eye. "I'll have to get Jup's ladder so we can investigate. We can't leave the creature down there. It could still be alive." The woman whimpered again.

Madsen didn't wait for Rav to answer but steamed out through the door and across the road with the confectioner's worried little woman at his heels. Emergencies always gave him unexpected energy. The sun had begun to melt the ice; the paving stones were wet but no longer slippery, and the two reached the other side safely. There they found the church caretaker perched like a crow under the cornice of the chemist's shop. Madsen had to shake the ladder hard to make Jup climb down. Rav could hear the two shouting at one another for some time before Madsen marched off with the ladder held tight under his arm and the confectioner's wife and a scarlet-faced Jup immediately behind him. Rav noticed the keen reporter J.U. Johansen from the local newspaper *Avisen* following them with his eyes as they vanished down the street. Madsen's face was shining with determination, the confectioner's wife's with anxiety and Ole Jup's with vague expectation. No-one said anything, but the three suddenly seemed to be of one mind. And there was nothing Rav could do about it. It was half-past ten, and soon it would all be over.

*

The dog was still barking. The confectioner's wife gave a little shriek and rushed to the well. The dog set up a heartbreaking whimper when it realised Mother was near. It was an old well; some believed it had been part of a large royal estate that had existed before the coming of Christianity. It had been built from even round stones which had settled with time and begun to lean inwards so that one couldn't see down to the bottom from the ground. Its lid was propped against the top layer of stones. The stone Jup had used to weigh the lid down lay a little way off. Madsen gently pushed the woman aside and lowered the ladder slowly into the dark hole. A sickening odour was coming out of the well, fumes he couldn't identify. Now that rescue was at hand, the dog had started howling. Madsen wished he hadn't been so insistent about being the one to carry the ladder, but it was too late now. A scraping sound announced that the foot of the ladder had reached the bottom. He drew a deep breath and climbed over the rim of the well. His trousers strained again but held once more. Jup took a firm grip of the top of the ladder while the police constable groped for the rungs with his feet. The last thing he saw as he went down was Jup's sneering smile, in itself a rare sight.

A certain amount of light filtered into the hole, and once Madsen had climbed down a little way he was able to make out a whitish sandy bottom. The dog had crawled onto something leaning against the wall, and Madsen could see its little eyes gleaming in the dim light. He and the dog clearly shared one desperate wish, to get back out again. The smell was worse now, rotten and pungent. He took out his handkerchief and covered his nose. As soon as he came near enough, the dog threw itself into his arms, and he climbed laboriously back to the surface under the struggling animal's wild manifestations of joy.

"I need a lamp," he said, once he had delivered the dog to the confectioner's wife. The dog was giving off the same indescribable smell, but the woman didn't seem to notice. After a while Jup returned with a carbide lamp which produced a cold white light. Madsen drew a deep breath and climbed down again.

*

At the bottom of the well, the body was standing to attention against the wall, wedged in its swollen condition between two blocks of stone. F.A. Nagler's eyes were closed as if in distaste for his surroundings; he looked like a diver deliberately holding his breath on his way back up to the surface. The cold had checked the process of putrefaction sufficiently for it to be easy to recognise him. He was neatly dressed in a buttoned-up khaki jacket and trousers – "Allan Quatermain on his way into the cave . . ." mumbled Madsen to himself, trying not to inhale the stench. The body continued to stand impassively where it was. The lamplight revealed a face chalk-white with frost, the mouth half-open as though Nagler had been on the point of saying something but had thought better of it. Madsen glanced quickly down. The German's hands hung shapeless and grotesquely swollen by his sides. His skin, stretched tight like a pink balloon, was beginning to split. A remarkable detail, to which the police constable's thoughts clung as firmly as if it had been a bobbing buoy, was that Nagler's shining boots still looked well polished. He lowered the lamp so that its sharp beam lit up the bottom of the well. There was nothing else except some pieces of Nagler's scalp complete with tufts of straw-blond hair which must have come loose in the night during the dog's desperate clawing. The ladder had nailed these scraps of flesh down firmly. Madsen was less than halfway back up to the surface again when he vomited over his uniform.

RESEARCHING THE SOURCES II

T HEY'D DUG UP the main street of Grænsebyen. The Chevy bumped over heaps of gravel, and it was only being so short that saved me from incessantly banging my head on the roof of the car. The mongrel was thrown about in the back seat like a football in a goal-mouth, and Mogensen swore passionately under his breath as he hugged the thin bakelite steering wheel with his hairy paws. The inhab-itants of Grænsebyen seemed to have moved out while their town was taken over by the diggers. The *Avisen* office also seemed locked up and deep in dust, and there was no sign of the old police station. My heart sank. Mogensen finally manoeuvred the car past the last crater and swung in to the kerb. I opened the door, and the mongrel shot out. He didn't go far but sat down and stared reproachfully at us from the fixed horizon of the paving stones. He certainly didn't have sea-legs. I followed stiffly, fitting my backpack firmly in place. Car jour-neys have always made me a bit lethargic. The street was like the desert in the opening scene of *Bad Day at Black Rock*. Here and there empty spaces gaped in the row of houses where some shack had been pulled down. Whirling sand made my eyes smart. The workmen had piled old paving-stones along the pavement in heaps like abandoned mole-hills. One side of each stone was smooth, the other rugged like a coarse lump of sugar.

The newspaper office seemed our only option, so, waving to Mogensen to follow me, I approached its cracked door, which opened with a high-pitched pling. Inside, behind an old-fashioned wooden counter, sat a short-haired blonde in her late thirties with a bored expression. She probably assumed this expression every time the door-bell went so as not to show surprise. Her face was sharp as a paperknife, her hair dry and lifeless. A large bulbous shiny gold heart hanging round her neck carried the inviting inscription *Popsie*. I doubted the bell had rung particularly often that day. Mogensen came in behind me, and at this she perked up a little. But only enough to become capable of looking directly at us. On a computer screen behind her a game of Patience was in progress, with the queen of hearts over the king of spades. Popsie must have needed an awful lot of patience in Grænsebyen; it had been an awfully long time since any kings had ridden past on this road. The office walls were papered with decom-posing pages from newspapers of the '30s and '40s, which in these dismal surroundings made an almost exhilarating impression. Daylight trickled grudgingly through a dusty window. The room smelt faintly of mould mixed with some kind of corrosive cleaning substance. The walls covered by the press clippings were saturated with several decades of greasy nicotine. Outside the window a CAT mechanical digger was returning to life after its lunch break. I hoped the Chevy was out of range of its steel teeth. Finally the blonde finished staring.

"Yes?" she said, as though we had interrupted her in full flight.

"We'd like to ask you a few questions," I said. "Has *Avisen* got an archive? We're looking for articles about the discovery of a body in 1938."

"Who wants to know?" asked the blonde, looking more awake now that she scented an opportunity to make difficulties. A Cerberus defending old news. The editorial staff had obviously moved elsewhere and left Popsie behind as gatekeeper.

"University of Copenhagen, Institute for Historical Studies," I said, and behind me Mogensen straightened up to his full height. I slapped down my ID card complete with the university logo on the counter. The blonde squinted, squirmed a bit in her chair, pushed together some papers, fluffed up her hair and finally rose with a heavy sigh and opened one side of the counter. The metal flap gave a screech. The duel was lost. Presumably we were unworthy opponents. A toss of her dry locks indicated permission for us to step into the inner sanctum.

"Go down the stairs," she said. "It's all in the cellar. Not in any particular order since the flood. Drains. More than seventy years ago," she added with a bleak smile. I was wrong; the first round had only just begun.

Mogensen lumbered out again to fetch the dog; Popsie had graciously granted permission for him to come in too. She was fond of ANIMALS she told us – as distinct, clearly, from other creatures she'd come across. I thought it safest to make no comment on this and made my way down the stairs without further fuss.

"And I shall just need a little signature later on," said Popsie. I made a mental note to write ESMÉ as large and coarsely as I possibly could.

*

The cellar had a low ceiling. It was a long narrow room with rough cement walls which presumably stretched the full length of the building. The floor was springy under my feet, and here and there the dirty grey linoleum had risen up in bumps, lying elsewhere in wrinkles like folds of ancient skin. Metal archive shelves stood out from the walls, all filled with old newspapers, some bound into large volumes, others rolled up in bundles tied with string. At some point a sense of purpose had apparently ebbed away. The whole lot was swollen and bulging with damp. It was as if the ancient library at Alexandria had gone to the bottom of the sea instead of being destroyed by fire. I hoped I wouldn't come across a mummified archivist among the shelves. Mogensen wheezed after me with Terror in his arms.

"Not much of a bird, that one," he said, looking a bit doubtful – after all, birds come in all shapes and sizes. He sniffed the air. "Bloody stink," he commented. He put Terror down on the floor, and the dog seemed to have his doubts too; if even he thought it was a horrible smell, we really were in a bad way.

We began by poking around without any real method. Mogensen took the left of the room and I took the right. In the middle there was a long table to which I carried my first cache of mouldering rolls of newspaper. The old copies of *Avisen* gave off a rich scent impossible to describe. Mildew, blotted printing ink and ripe history – as individual as the smell of Stilton or perhaps Gruyère. I could feel expectation beginning to throb in me like a current just switched on. The dog had climbed a little way up the stairs and was watching us with passive if respectful interest. Popsie brought down a bowl of water and a biscuit for him, after which he was content.

*

There's something special about paper. All that wood that starts in a little seed or pip which carries a germ and potentiality for development and holds in its soft pulp the image of a great tree as clearly and ineluctably as the image stamped on a coin. When the tree is transformed into something different like newsprint – a process which for some reason we call refining – the seed or pip returns in some sense to its origin, becoming once again the bearer of potential development. Those sour old rolls of newsprint, some of their sheets as brittle and tightly wrapped as dried rosebuds, were like layer on layer of the past, containing both what had actually happened and what might have happened – if history had taken a different turning. The origin or source of news is always alive and only becomes old when history moves on. Everything irrelevant to that new direction is forgotten, but its choosing survives in the texts of old dailies. And time after time the thought suggests itself that in precisely the same conditions the opposite could have happened, and then history would have been different. Not necessarily better, but different.

*

The first rolls were from the early 1950s, an era when mouthwash competed with Tuborg for advertising space on the page. In 1953 a travelling fair came to Grænsebyen. In July 1955 a Miss Grænsebyen was chosen, a certain Gitte Marcus from Bov. I tied the strings round these rolls again and moved to the next shelf. And so we went on, with Mogensen grunting from his corner. I wondered whether Popsie might consider offering us some coffee, but gave up on the idea. In the end she did come down the stairs, presumably tired of the evasive black king and his red queen. She'd put some chipped cups and an ancient pot on a tray. I wondered whether she'd used tap-water to make the coffee. If so, it was sure to be a powerful brew.

"The last person to poke about in those piles got polio," said Popsie. "What is it you're actually looking for?"

I wondered whether to entrust her with my theories about the archaeological excavation of texts but decided against it. What I wanted was a series of articles together with any other material, no matter how apparently irrelevant, published at the same time during 1938 and 1939, or perhaps over a longer period, depending on what direction history had taken. I wanted *names, pseudonyms, dates, information about places*. I wanted to see history *in situ*, to see the past walk round the corner with its collar turned up, to hear the sound of vanishing foot-steps, to hear voices no-one was capable of understanding. Tracks.

"Editions from the end of the 1930s," I said. The blonde was a good half-metre taller than me in her tapering heels, and that put me at a disadvantage (a simple question of tactics; I should have stood on the stairs).

"Sounds hopeless," said Popsie candidly, pouring coffee from the pot, a kind of thermos people used to use while watching TV. She reserved the only cup with a handle for herself. It looked as if she was planning to keep us company for a while.

"Where are the rest of the editorial staff?" I asked.

"He's moved up to the new pedestrianised area." She stared suspiciously at me again, clearly astonished at such a stupid question. Everyone knew that. She didn't enlighten me as to who "he" was. I tentatively tasted my coffee, which in fact was really good if not as hot as it might have been. Mogensen came lumbering up and picked up a cup with unusual shyness. Popsie smiled graciously, at the same time looking as if she was searching her brain for yet another disease likely to strike down anyone who disturbed the peace of the archive.

Scurvy possibly, or gangrene? It wasn't as if Lord Carnarvon and his gilded pharaoh Tut were down there! I took the arrival of Mogensen as a signal to go back to my researches and chose a shelf a bit further off. Behind me I could hear Popsie begin flirting again.

I pulled out a stack of bound volumes, easier to deal with than the rolls of newspaper, and saw something soft and nappy dimly visible behind the stack. Prepared for the worst, I cautiously inserted my hand and pulled out an old brown felt hat, battered, soft, soggy with damp, but a man's hat nonetheless. Its brim was drooping, but one could still detect traces of handmade silk-edged quality. I turned it over carefully. Inside were the name of the maker, A.K. Smirnoff, and the owner's name inscribed with old-fashioned care in ornate lettering: *Tomas Rav*. I put the hat down carefully and opened the top volume at the first page. Its dry spine creaked. *Avisen, July 30, 1938*.

*

"Hell, Esmé, you don't mean to tell me you took them." Peter Mogensen once again showed an astonishingly petty streak of bourgeois morality. He pouted in disapproval, his red lips framed by his wild beard. His brown eyes looked troubled. Maybe I'd spoiled his chances with Popsie.

"The occasion makes the researcher," I said. "There's no sense in them just lying there and mouldering away. These are primary sources, priceless facts in the case. Think of it as a rescue mission, like when they sawed up the temple at Abu Simbel." Images rose in my memory, parts of a face sailing through the air on thin steel wires – here an ear, there a nose, everything neatly divided up as if according to a plan. Mogensen still looked sceptical. The dog pulled at his lead in an attempt to reach a tree he wanted to piss on that had escaped the mechanical diggers. As always it paid to prioritise, to have an objective; even the dog understood that. I let go of the lead and followed, thus also escaping the watchman's reproachful gaze. *Carpo diarium*, I thought. It was my right. Anyway, who'd asked him for his opinion? With restraint so suddenly withdrawn, Terror almost fell flat.

In the car I took out my finds again and put the hat carefully into a thick plastic bag which I taped shut. The dog blew down my neck, once more ravenous with hunger. He was even prepared to consider a man's sixty-year-old hat as potential food if he couldn't do any better. I let the pleasant weight of the four volumes rest on my knees. They covered the period to the middle of February 1940. The 15th. Barely two months before the Germans moved in.

THE BOG

NEXT DAY AT dawn the sun was shining, and a fine morning was developing with the scent of early spring in the air. The sky was high and blue, with a nuance of Arctic ice. The sun warmed my hands. I decided to do what Mogensen wanted and go out to Frøslevs Mose, the place where they'd found the body in the peat bog in 1938. Mogensen planned to use this as a starting-point for a detour over the border, but he agreed to drop me and the dog and pick us up again at a suitable time. We reached the bog via a network of awkward narrow lanes marked with modest advertising boards. The final stretch took us through the plantation, a fragrant and densely planted fir forest which lined the rough road on either side. Only human beings are capable of creating such an impenetrable forest; you couldn't even see daylight between the trunks. At eleven in the morning Mogensen left us in the bog's parking area and zoomed off. The evening before I'd studied maps both old and new, and on the old ones the peat-digging patches were outlined like the quarters of mediaeval cities, narrow marked areas probably still visible from the air as shadows on the marshland. Everyone was meant to have a share of the sludge-coloured gold. Rights of usufruct had been allotted for centuries. Somewhere out there in the marsh lay the border with Germany, where Frøslevs Mose became Jardelunder Moor. Gabriel Mayer had written:

> The first definite evidence of the finding of bodies in the bog dates from the seventeenth century. In 1640 a prehistoric person was found in Shalkholz Moss in Holstein. Nothing more is

known of this body. Eight bog-people have come to light in the wetlands round the River Ems in Germany. On June 8, 1861, a farmworker and his family, father, mother, son and father-in-law, were cutting turf on a patch they had been using for at least twenty years. In the written history they have no names. That day their spades struck something other than turf, a dead sheep the farmer thought, but it turned out to be the body of a man lying on his stomach in the bog and with his face so well preserved that the farmer could still remember every feature of it years later. To the farmer the man seemed to breathe peace. He used to say that *if he'd ever met the man alive later on, he would have recognised him instantly*. The dead man was lying with his face turned down into the bog, his legs pulled up as though climbing. He was resting in what seemed to be the remains of an old turf-cutting patch, a black, tightly packed layer of earth to which he had been firmly fastened with sharp-pointed birch and fir stakes. Those who had owned the rights to the bog in prehistoric times had laid him there. Perhaps the bog functioned as the borderland between two worlds, between darkness and light, dry land and wetland, god and humans. Perhaps the man in the bog had agreed with his killers that they must kill him. The turf too had changed into something else – since what had once been dense opaque water was brought back to the homestead in the form of earth and transformed into fire and warmth, finally becoming air in the form of smoke which disappeared through a hole in the roof into the dark winter sky.

Soon the body began to smell in the summer warmth, with a strange sharp odour like moorland crowberries left on a tray to rot. This frightened the assembled public, so the remains were laid on a cart and buried later in a nearby churchyard. Perhaps the dead man had been a local – if so, by burying him in the churchyard they could protect themselves against any charge of not showing proper respect to one of their own.

In 1903 a naked woman was found in Hingst Moss, near Kreepen in the Hanover district. She too had been fastened to the ground, in her case by an intricate system involving osiers, ropes and a twisted iron ring. The ropes had been tied across her arms, breasts and legs. Nooses of osier bound her arms to the iron ring. Her hair was well preserved, her face gone. Too late to read in it the last thing she heard or saw in life.

The bog-people had all been killed: beheaded, hanged or strangled with running nooses. They had all been specially chosen, or excluded for one reason or another from acceptance, by the society they had lived in. This was not an unreasonable assumption: the farmer and his family thought they had found a sheep's body in the hole in the turf, and the man by the Ems and the woman from Hingst had been put to death as lightly as one might cut the throat of a ewe or break the neck of a cock behind an outhouse wall. Presumably then as now not everyone would have wanted to look on, though they would have willingly shared in the rewards of the sacrifice. This would have given the executioners a special status, based on fear. The identity of the rest was based on *being the same as everyone else*. The bonds linking human beings to one another would thus have been transformed into a game requiring three roles. An individual can hide behind the masks used in a game. What is too vast for us to comprehend can be transformed into everyday reality by a group of people who achieve *consensus*. They also agree on what reality looks like, seeing it as an image closely related to whatever they happen to be familiar with in their own time, a bronze axe perhaps, or the particular weight of a certain woven fabric.

In our day it is generally considered that these victims were sacrificed for some weighty reason. Something decisive at the time, some code or set of rules now forgotten. Law, religion, pleasure, profit, vanity, prejudice. Take your pick.

Our picture of them, our *consensus*, may be built up from completely erroneous assumptions. What is left is far too fragmentary; we lack the amplitude of written sources, their unambiguous ambiguity. Perhaps we should even find the motives of the prehistoric executioners valid, for what they did is something human beings have always done and presumably always will do. Such is human culture. The only difference is that some of those sacrificed are still physically here with us, travellers who have crossed an inconceivable distance in space and time. What separates us from them is that we can no longer remember why they were sacrificed.

Out on the bog a cutting wind was blowing from the west. The mongrel looked suspicious now we'd left civilisation behind us again. An embankment lined with dried yellow grass carried a road across the wide bog, a road as straight as if someone had laid a ruler on the map and drawn a thick line across the dunes. Maybe that was how it had been done. On either side of the embankment the bog displayed a rich vegetation of heather and coarse grass from the previous year. It wasn't possible to see what might lie beyond it. Even the wind seemed preoccupied, plucking at the dry brush and making a sound like bare feet clearing a way over the marshland. Birds of prey glided along high above us on cold air currents, warding off the wind with small jerky movements of their frayed wingtips, quills finely calibrated to suit the marsh's level surfaces, as they hunted their quarry, a rabbit perhaps, or a fieldmouse woken before its time by the spring sun. The ground started hard but gradually grew increasingly soft and springy, as if the bog had worked its way in under the embankment and was slowly undermining it. I walked carefully, thankful that I weighed no more than I did and had no height to speak of. The wind cooled and the sun warmed. My body felt sluggish and unused in the clear light. A bird cried out from west to east; I screwed up my eyes and looked straight into the sun, shut them and saw black spots dancing behind my eyelids. The heather gave off a warm, acerbic scent, a foretaste of summer. Birches and dense nooses of bog-myrtle huddled on the firmer islands, an archipelago of dwarf woodland performing a balancing act with roots huddled together. Here and there bulrushes clustered up to their ankles in black swamp-water, little fluffy grey-white tufts forgotten from the previous summer. I remembered stories I'd read long ago about how the down from the bogs was woven to make clothes for unfortunate boys who had been bewitched into birds. Human beings imprisoned in a condition halfway between human and animal, shy in their nakedness. I never understood what the problem was. For myself I'd have liked to be able to fly. My backpack chafed on my shoulders and reminded me of the heaviness of earthbound life.

To the left of the road lay a brown-painted shelter, and Terror struggled towards it. I let him have his head, and he whined in anticipation. Presumably he was hoping for food. Inside the hut were three tables screwed to the floor and generously spattered with birdlime and several information boards buckled with damp which gave a brief account of the bog's history. I went round and read a bit here and a bit there. The hut stank of sour timber, and dried birdshit crunched under my feet. Terror pulled and wanted to go out again, as inconstant as Kierkegaard's fiancée. An inventory entitled "Lepidoptera of Frøslevs Mose" had been drawn up as early as 1933. It included both butterflies and moths. One hundred and fifty-seven newly discovered species appeared in another inventory made in 1998, although seventy-two species had disappeared during the intervening years and so were missing from the 1998 list. I could see nothing about Lackey moths. But four photographs showed similar creatures with fat hairy bodies, prominent feelers and wings sparkling with colour. Blue and green, gold, grey and black. Only one of these had a paler hue as of yellow dust, its resplendent wings almost transparent.

There was no proper map. North, south, east, west. I had no idea which way to go if I ventured to leave the road. In the '30s they'd still been cutting turf on the bog, and a mass of paths had criss-crossed the wetland in all directions, each one used by a particular person, so

I imagined, and guarded by its *owner*. How deep underground does right of ownership extend? Five metres, ten, right to the centre of the earth? I wondered whether these various territories would ever meet at a common point where all the lines came together. Vertical lines, curved since the world is a globe, combining to form shapes like slices of cake. I wondered, if that were so, what one would pass on the way down: dark Hades, hot Hell or the icy underworld of Hel, the Nordic goddess? The thought was of course absurd, but so was humanity's claim to ownership rights in earth, air and water. We had turned airy blue emptiness into rooms and corridors. By doing this we were able to enclose our thoughts inside a comprehensible space, infinite but nonetheless demarcated by language. In the world of Jules Verne the central point of the earth was also the earth's prehistory, a boundless sea inhabited by plesiosaurs and gleaming primitive fish. A warm prehistoric sea which eventually belched out modern humanity with its learned encyclopaedias, magnifying glasses and unlimited grasping curiosity. I also thought of the traveller-explorers who had acted as the empire-builders' avant-garde. It was hard to understand Neil Armstrong's first tentative words on the moon except in relation to variety-performers and wordsmiths like Henry Morton Stanley. Think of him with Livingstone on the eastern shore of Lake Tanganyika in 1871. Their meeting framed under glass on the walls of countless geographical societies. Shaking each other by the hand with grateful savages in the background. Stanley had been brought up in extreme poverty in an orphanage; Livingstone was a Scottish Calvinist. The two white men are both as correctly dressed as if they were standing in front of a respectable audience at the Royal Society in London. It's the engraving that makes the event real.

Or think of Armstrong and Aldrin on the Sea of Tranquillity in 1969. I saw them a few minutes after they landed. The TV screen in our living-room at Tårnby was so grainy and reception so poor that for a moment you almost believed the moon really was made of cheese. Ownership is a state of mind, a fancy built on audacity and repetition. One wonders how urbanely the two astronauts would have reacted if they'd bumped into some native creature on the moon. A lawful owner of moon-gravel, darkness and weightlessness. When did it begin, this grubbing after boundaries and lines of demarcation? In Eden? Who can say?

The dog pulling at his lead brought me down to earth again. I took my compass out of my pocket and waited for its wiggling needle to settle. It reflected sunlight into my eyes. Mayer's *Four Illusions* had made me a bit pretentious.

*

The grassy road seemed to have a magic effect on Terror, and he was eager to move on. His little yellow eyes glittered in the sunshine. I ignored the compass and let him decide which way to go. Something out on the bog was attracting him.

At first our walk was very undramatic. He ran sneezing and snorting from right to left and back again, tracking some wonderful thing only he could see. I kept up at the other end of the lead. My arms ached. We must have rushed on in this manner for several kilometres. Then the road began curving, the ground became increasingly swampy, water slurped round my shoes, and I was beginning to think of turning back when Terror suddenly began to bark. Small nervous yelping barks. I too, struggle though I might, became ill at ease. Mogensen wasn't likely to be back for a few hours yet. Round about us lay the desolate bog, habitat of birds of prey, hibernating adders and other wild animals. Home to eccentrics of the borderlands. A head emerged from the ground only a few metres from us. I think I screamed.

"Well then," said the head. It belonged to a woman of about fifty in baggy clothes with copper-coloured hair streaked with grey and a fresh red outdoor face. "Just helping myself to a little turf to use at home," she said. "Nothing wrong in that." She stuck out her lower lip like a discontented child. "Nothing that matters here, anyway." She struggled out of the hole with long-drawn-out smacking sounds. The bog was never willing to let anything out of its clutches. Terror sat and stared at her brazenly. I looked away in embarrassment. The bog-woman came straight over to us. We could see, now she'd placed her big-booted feet on solid ground, that she was tall and well-built. Robust. Surrounded by a damp smell of sour swamp-water and bog-myrtle. Her camouflage-patterned green oilskin jacket was big enough to have contained both me and Kai, its wide folds like a tent for two.

"Jup's the name," she said, extending a big copper-brown fist. "Fire my own pottery," she went on, as if this bit of information clarified everything. Her eyes were speckled grey like a bird's egg and her gaze was as steady as a pebble. I offered her my hand with an uncharacteristic lack of hesitation.

Jup inspired confidence. Her grip was warm and firm; shaking hands with her was like grasping a happy piece of sun-warm wood. Her friendly smile revealed large, entirely regular teeth that looked a little unreal, as though carved out of some dense-growing material like ash or birch.

"Esmé," I said. Best keep things short and simple with this female giant.

"Uncommon name," said Jup, "but I like it."

I smiled happily. Terror thrashed the grass with his tail. Jup and I stood for a moment looking at one another. She narrowed her eyes thoughtfully, the speckled-egg effect thickening to muddy water.

Finally she said, "You're looking for something." I nodded.

"I want to know what it was like here a long time ago," I said. I must have sounded like an emissary from some local district association.

"I can show you what I know, which is quite a lot and at the same time not very much, I have to admit. I know this place as well as I know my own backyard." She flung out her arms, causing Terror to give a nervous yelp. "My workshop's not far from here, we can go there if you like." She was addressing the dog as much as me. He liked that.

She squelched off down a narrow path that to begin with ran parallel with the road. Like the dog, she seemed to prefer this quagmire, but I kept off it. We walked like this for about an hour, then she turned off towards an area I hadn't previously noticed where larger islands of dry ground were home to clumps of tall slender trees, mostly birches. The wind was ripping at their upper branches, making them creak and crack high above our heads. The landscape was also becoming more hilly, and after a while we were walking on firm ground in the shelter of a ridge. The air was cold and damp as in a river valley though no water could be seen. Dry grass rustled behind us, and we left no footprints. Jup kept turning to see if we were managing to keep up. She moved with surprising speed for such a large and apparently clumsy woman, her jacket billowing round her like a voluminous sail and her grey-streaked hair standing straight up on her head in wild straggling tufts. I could swear her clothes changed colour according to the changing colours of the landscape we were passing through. From having been dark green with black patches her oilskin had mutated to a delicate light green, and then to a yellowish hue to match the budding first leaves on the trees we were now walking under. The play of light over the cloth made her almost invisible. When the path descended her jacket darkened again, and I had to strain my eyes to make it out. The rugged path smelled strongly of earth and of the thick grey roots that crossed it in all directions. In the dim light it seemed to me as if snakes were tangling and twining round one another in a cold, rigid embrace. At the height of summer, walking here must be like entering a dense, almost impenetrable tunnel of leaves. My shoes chafed, I sweated, and the dog was beginning to lose heart. But eventually we arrived.

*

Jup's house was a long, low stone cottage with a grey turf roof and tall brick chimney. The roof seemed to be crouching under its own weight, and small blackened splinters of burnt stone had fallen out over the mouldering turf. Close by one gable stood an ancient and mighty ash-tree with a network of branches that seemed to reach right up to the sky. In front of the cottage, on a flat sanded area, stood an elderly and dusty dark-green Land Rover. On its roof was a searchlight, wedged at an angle by a bunch of fir-twigs that had been shoved under its stand. The whole thing reminded me of the feather in an Austrian hunting hat. Jup stopped and gently patted the coachwork much as one might stroke the hair of a fretful child.

"The Germans like my work. I have my own ways of crossing the border." She smiled again, showing her even wooden teeth. Terror gave a quiet whine. "I'll drive you back later. It'll be quicker."

The cottage was high up on the ridge with a view in all directions. A waterlogged road full of holes, leading from a different compass point to the one we'd come from, wound its way towards the cottage and the crown of the ridge. Up at the house the air was clear and fresh with none of the damp of the valley path. The only smell, a slightly unpleasant one, came from a large round kiln that stood a certain distance from the house in what looked like an ancient orchard. A sour sticky smell seemed to float out of the conical opening at the top. The kiln squatted among bushes and extremely old gnarled apple-trees that were clearly no longer pruned. Lower down, against the opposite slope, I could see the half-demolished foundations of several buildings sticking up from the vegetation. Jup followed my gaze but said nothing. Instead she unlocked the door of the cottage and motioned us to go in.

We entered a large room with a low ceiling, so saturated with smoke from greasy cooking that at first I couldn't see anything at all. It had the smell of a site where a house has been burnt down. The walls were lined with shelves full of pots and small figures, either black or burnt red, of fat and thin naked women of all sizes. For export to Germany. Some had huge bulging buttocks and bulbous limbs and some breasts like ripe pumpkins; a few were as thin as sticks of fire-wood. I'd seen nothing like it since the time I went to the sauna at the Central Baths in Copenhagen.

"Earth-goddesses, all of 'em," said Jup. "Or Mother Nerthus, as we say in these parts." She grabbed one of the smaller statuettes and held it up to me. The clay woman had a grimace on a small black face as crumpled as that of a guenon monkey, but the rest of her was contrast-ingly large, and the clay was polished, greasy and shining. Her eyes were mere holes, presumably poked in with a twig. Clearly the cult of Nerthus laid no emphasis on the mind. "The colour's determined by the chemical make-up, degree of acidity and basic quality of the turf combined with the heat of the kiln. And the availability of oxygen. The hotter and more tightly closed the kiln, the darker the end-product will be. The clay comes from up here on the ridge. Sometimes I thin it with turf."

So the little woman was black because she'd been stifled. Jup put the figure down and patted its hard little raisin of a head. A loved mother has many children.

"Tea?" she asked.

We left the home of the goddesses and went into Jup's kitchen. Here, in contrast, all was light and airy with an extensive view over green hills. Two wide windows at the corner. Cupboards high on the walls. Sideboard, table, grey-blue rag rug on the floor. I had time to detect a harsh smell, at once bitter and aromatic, before Jup quickly unfastened one of the windows and opened it wide. I looked round with curiosity. A large whitewashed range dominated the room, an old-fashioned double oven that extended into the long workroom and contained under its cover a wood-fired stove and a microwave. On the stove stood a black iron casserole with a lid. I wondered whether Jup was thinking of making us a snack. Frogs' legs or ancient grass-snake eggs? Or perhaps the monthly stew of root-vegetables from the kitchen garden? The dog sniffed the air suspiciously, then crept under the large kitchen table to bide his time. Jup shoved two mugs in the microwave and nodded to me to sit down.

"Please excuse me if I have a smoke first," she said. She took a rolling machine, Rizla paper and a packet of pipe tobacco and began to roll herself a cigarette. Her brown fingers pressed the tobacco into an even mass, moving quickly and nimbly in a manner that seemed to combine the dexterity of a conjuror with the skill and experience of a farmworker. On the packet were the words "Coromandel Strong Mixture". I rolled what was left of my prejudices up with Jup's cigarette-paper. She licked the cigarette to seal it and screwed it into a long amber holder. The smoke smelt of the tropics.

"What it was like here a long time ago . . ." she said, as if I'd just asked the question. "You saw the remains of the village?" I nodded. "I'm really a stranger here . . . in a way, even though my family, the Jups, have lived here for over three hundred years and made use of the turf for about the same length of time." She was silent again. The microwave pinged, and she brought the mugs to the table with two Tetley teabags. Jup alternately puffed Coromandel and sipped tea. "Surnames come down through the female line here . . . or at least they did in the village that used to be here once upon a time. My grandfather's grandfather didn't come from this area. Not even from Denmark, though in a sense he was from Denmark."

She got up, went over to the sideboard and opened it. From its top shelf she took a little wooden box with a silver pocket-watch in it.

"This watch belonged to Paul Natal," she said.

JUP'S STORY

PAUL NATAL WAS born in India in 1817 or maybe 1820, I'm not sure of the exact year, in the Danish colony of Tranquebar south of Madras. His father was a Danish naval officer whose name he never knew and his mother a domestic servant in the home of an engineer-officer and merchant called Mathias Jürgen Mühlendorf and his anaemic wife, Mette. The Mühlendorfs were childless, so Paul's status in the family was better than would usually have been the case with a half-caste child. They regarded him almost as a son. I know this because Paul told my grandfather about it. Paul possessed an unusual quality. He could only concentrate on one thought or desire at a time, and so long as this wasn't satisfied no other could take its place. This unsatisfied longing would fill him like water filling the shell of a fountain. He never made a fuss but moved calmly round the house whose dark rooms seemed to be waiting behind closed shutters and where the woodwork was so hot you could burn your palm on it. The place only became bearable during the evening hours, when a warm wind began to blow from the sea, bringing with it a slightly rotten smell like the breath of a sea monster.

Mathias Mühlendorf was said to be the son of a Danish king, Frederik V, I think. His luxurious house contained many strange and exotic objects, among them a small and exquisitely made wax figure, executed sometime after 1810 by a Chinese master from Canton who happened to be visiting the colony. This figurine or doll represented a Danish naval officer reproduced in the minutest detail and dressed in a uniform that was also accurate down to the last detail, with buttons and pockets that could be opened and closed. Its face was so lifelike that anyone would have recognised it if they'd seen the man it was modelled on. It also had real human hair, a light-brown lock said to have been cut from the naval officer's head. It was always kept on the shady side of the house, sheltered from tropical sun and melting heat on a mahogany shelf cooled by its proximity to the kitchen, which was itself cooled by running water – brackish like everything else on that coast. So Paul had plenty of time to study the figurine, which always stared back at him with an expression so blank that he could fill it with the contents of his own thoughts.

In the merchant's house in Tranquebar there was also a vault near the wine cellar in which a mysterious inscription could be found, a row of letters of unknown origin said to contain the secret of the engineer-officer's royal descent. D.E.M.E.P. This inscription gave the merchant a certain standing in the colony, a fleeting nimbus of distinguished ancestry. It could equally well have been mere nonsense, the graffiti of a local builder, but the row of letters and the little doll-figure put ideas into young Paul's head. He studied his own face in the cook's shiny copper pans and bowls in the hope of detecting a likeness. He began turning in the street to scrutinise every face he encountered in the colony's narrow crowded alleys and down by the harbour. He breathed in the sea smell of salt heat and rotting coral-creatures, listened to the breakers crash and hiss on the long shore and watched seabirds dive for scraps of fish thrown away unwanted by the fishermen of the Coromandel coast. He searched the dilapidated entrances to the warehouses and stores that had lined the coast ever since the heyday of the East India Company, their windows like blind eyes in a beggar's face. He noted every shadow, every unfamiliar voice, every anchor that splashed into the water in the estuary of the River Cauvery. He wandered on the outskirts of the town and searched its churchyard – God's acre – for leads. Paul Natal was looking for his father.

In 1838 he gave up trying to find him in Tranquebar and signed on for the Danish frigate *Vennerna*, home port Copenhagen. Mühlendorf gave him a rectangular packet wrapped in oilcloth, string and sealing-wax to deliver to an acquaintance in Copenhagen. The packet in fact contained ten cakes of pressed hashish – worth a fortune – but Paul knew nothing of this. In the end, it turned out to be water rather than blood that linked the merchant to his dusky young foster-son – the wide trading waters of the Indian Ocean. In 1840 Paul set foot for the first time on the stone-paved quays of Kongens By; he was then twenty, or twenty-three, years old.

*

Try to imagine Copenhagen at the time: half peasant village and half international city. Ships lay at anchor in the Sound waiting to unload their cargoes, their rigging an army of scarecrows with pointing fingers standing in a field whose surface was a choppy sea. The harbour was full of boats and barges being rowed or paddled backwards and forwards and loaded with whale blubber, rum, fat Greenland herring and who knew what else. On their way out to the ships' dark holds or in to the city. Carrying nails, lengths of cord, bolt-ropes, blocks and tackle. The bare feet of sailors with deformed toenails and black soles hard as pigskin thundered on wooden decks while packing-house winches creaked under loads of broadcloth, wine, meal and corn. Meanwhile farmers bringing in produce from the countryside mixed with the townspeople. Cocks crowed, pigs shrieked, sellers called their wares, street musicians wandered about playing ill-tuned instruments. Pedlars touted collections of ballads and "remarkable stories" from boxes carried on their bellies. Posters advertised a new production of Hans Christian Andersen's theatre piece *The Mulatto*. Humble carts and the carriages of gentlefolk met in the city's narrow streets, iron-rimmed wheels clattering on uneven setts. Beer tankards smashed. Church clocks struck the hour and half-hour. In Nyhavn ladies of easy virtue swung gaudy-skirted hips at sailors newly paid off. Flashes of white skin, dark bruises, red-painted mouths, rotting teeth, the odour of sweat and tar and the sour smell of lust. Black leather hats pushed back on heads. Coins changing hands in taverns, squeaking signboards swinging above doorways like ships on a sluggish swell.

*

Mathias Mühlendorf's business contact turned out to live in the old quarter of Copenhagen, the part of the city built in the seventeenth century by command of Christian IV. The man had a damp basement flat in a block next to the Round Tower in Købmagergade Street. It was late afternoon before Paul finally found his way there through the twisting labyrinth of the city. That's how long it took him to scrutinise all the people he passed.

The door was opened by a bent old man even shorter than Paul. (I inherited my height from my mother and grandmother.) The old fellow had on a soiled black jacket and a small blue velvet cap. He waved Paul into a dark little room filled with shelves stacked with boxes and bottles, a cubbyhole that resembled the inside of a beehive or the well-stowed hold of a ship. Highest up on the shelves were sealed glass jars containing ground rhinoceros horn and other rare powders and substances supposed to enhance a moment's worldly happiness or prolong life. Several rose-coloured seashells balanced on a glass cabinet made Paul think of the smell of the sea – the sort of shells that preserved the sound of the Indian Ocean deep inside their curves.

The old man was an apothecary, but he dabbled in other things as well. In his youth he'd been a ship's doctor with the Danish East India Company, which was how he'd come to cross Mühlendorf's path. He dealt in drugs, which he sold on in the form of finely ground powder to some of the city's variety theatres and to sorcerers and magicians anxious to persuade their public of the power of the paranormal. If you lit a few incense-sticks containing hashish or opium smoulder in the fires that burned in front of proscenium arches in those days, you could make people believe they were flying high above Copenhagen on threadbare Turkish carpets or levitating several feet above the stage. The condition induced in them was similar to sleep but did not bring rest or comfort. Those under the influence of such drugs could talk

– 183 –

and move about unhindered and afterwards imagined they could remember every detail of what they'd done with exceptional clarity. A larger dose would induce a sleep lasting several hours, a deep trance that could sometimes resemble death. The apothecary had a wide-ranging network of contacts throughout the city which he used to market his powders, drugs and decoctions, all prepared with a single purpose in mind – to create illusions. In his dirty black jacket and apron, he was a manufacturer of dreams.

*

Paul Natal lived with the old man in Købmagergade for several months. He was given an unheated attic and paid for his board and lodging by working as a messenger all over the city, up and down the streets and by rowing-boat as far as the bastions at Christianshavn, where soldiers who had become addicted to smoking hashish abroad would be waiting for him. After long periods of service overseas many of these suntanned men resembled exotic birds. Paul soon become acquainted with the guardians of the bastions known as Panther, Lion, Unicorn and Elephant. The apothecary regularly received new deliveries. He also prepared poisons for gardeners who worked for major landowners. Powder to be strewn finely over the earth or on leaves, dissolved in warm water or pumped in the form of smoke. If these treatments were applied in the evening, insects, whether spinners or flyers, would lie dead on the stone pavement next morning with their wings frozen close to their bodies. These poisons turned them grey like tin or sheet metal no matter how colourful they'd been in life. Their colour, which had sat on their wings like tiny grains of pigment, vanished in some remarkable way.

When the orders came, it was Paul's job to take horse and surrey out to the great estates with the sensitive merchandise in a cedarwood box, and on arrival to wait in some gardener's greenhouse, in a sun-warm scent of citrus, gardenias and camellias which reminded him of Madras. The poisons would have been put into blue paper cones and the drugs into white ones to prevent them getting mixed up. As time

passed, Paul learned nearly all there was to know about the preparation of these mixtures, about how much powder there was in a pinch
and about heating things in glass tubes over a naked flame, about
arsenic and the delicate art of pruning hashish plants. It was all a
matter of precision, weights and properly balanced scales. To this
knowledge he added things he remembered from his home in
Tranquebar, the round fist-measurements and careful pinches of the
woman who did the cooking and the black pots that simmered on the
stove and – the thing he remembered best of all – the gravity of her
dark face, an awareness of *knowledge*. He learned that substances could
be transformed by great heat, altered to something entirely different.
And that other substances could be preserved under pressure.

So the years passed. A letter came telling him that the two
Mühlendorfs had died of tropical fever, and that the house and all its
contents – among them his mother – had been auctioned off. He felt
no distress, sorrow or curiosity. It was as if he had used up the one
journey allotted to him in this life when he travelled from India to
Denmark. He never found his father, though he continued to scrutinise every face he saw, now more out of habit than anything else. The
old longing still filled him, but the feeling was so familiar that he
scarcely noticed it any more. It lived on like a tiny pain in his heart
and stomach, a little animal that now and then changed its position.
At Christmas 1847 he had to take something to the writer Andersen,
who was suffering severely from the neuralgic pain that had begun to
afflict him during his stay in London. The writer received Paul in slippers, a padded English morning-coat and a yellow silk cap with a
tassel. Andersen's apartment in Nyhavn was as full of strange objects
and keepsakes as Paul's foster-parents' house in India. His rooms
smelled strongly of the multifarious home remedies he constantly used.
Camphor and vinegar compresses. Extracts of various herbs for the
stomach. Valerian for restless nights. Foxglove for the heart. Belladonna
for . . .

The whole of the writer's past hung on his walls in the form of
miniatures, silhouettes and framed letters from female admirers. Over

his writing-table hung a dark red paper heart on a thread, something he'd conjured up with scissors . . . or was it perhaps a butterfly? It was hard to tell, it was so dark. All the curtains were tightly drawn because he was afraid of draughts. His large hands created the most delicate little objects, a paper world. Then there were framed photographs from Paris and Rome, and the harbour of Capri in stereoscopic images. On a little table, on a black cloth with a fringe, lay a dusty wax cast of the face of a drowned girl. Andersen had just happened to be passing when she was fished out of the harbour, and with the help of his well-filled purse he'd persuaded a man at the mortuary to let him take an impression. The temperature had been $-15°$ and they'd had to break the ice with poles before they'd been able to row out to the body, which had been frozen just under the surface at Nyhavn bridge. The girl had been wearing nothing but a thin shift. When the boat came near, the waves set the thin cloth in motion. Her skin had been cold as glass to the touch. Andersen had had to work fast because the staff at the mortuary didn't like having a stranger there. Someone alive. The girl's face was exquisite, pure and innocent. A snow-queen. An unknown street girl. Andersen carefully replaced the wax cast on the dark cloth. There was nothing incongruous about it, nothing at all.

He showed Paul everything, smiling, proud and talkative as a boy, his nervous pain seemingly dissipated for the moment, his arm round Paul's shoulders. In his free moments he was also working on a screen, a story of his travels, a collage of pictures from London. He'd included portraits of his colleagues Scott and Dickens, Tennyson and Byron, but also tall factory chimneys, gravel paths, excited crowds and a man with a dog. There was his glue pot with a brush beside it and a pungent smell. The picture was a fantasy, an *impression* compiled from a mass of small impressions, just as the little grains or dots in our memories can, taken together, re-create the past, and coarse daubs of colour seen from a certain distance in a painting resemble coast, sea or sky. Burnt umber or sienna for earth and mud, Verona green earth for the slopes of Lombardy. If the artist had the ability to remember *everything*, the picture would be overworked, ruined. The whole lot together was what vanished when a person died. A universe lost, a space extinguished. Andersen took his images from books and coloured magazines. When it came to completing his pictures, he was ruthless. In art he was a *plunderer* – he clipped the air with his scissors in front of Paul's nose. Snip, snip. But sometimes it disturbed him that fairy tales and stories he'd invented seemed in some way to become real. It had happened several times that his fantasies seemed to come true . . . Andersen found it creepy. Far down in the bottom right-hand corner of his screen HMS *Erebus* was sailing out of London in 1845 in search of the North-West Passage. Andersen hadn't actually seen this event, but he'd heard a lot about it. Finally he offered Paul mint tea in a sky-blue cup and forgot to say goodbye.

*

Then in 1848 came war, the first Schleswig war. The old apothecary died that year. Paul found him shrunk on his pallet in his dark little cubbyhole, his shabby jacket pulled round his shrivelled body like a pair of wings. Near the old man, surprisingly, stood a furled black umbrella; the object and the body were in some strange way alike, both conveying a sense of having been abandoned. The apothecary had received his last customer. Or had he perhaps left the house himself? That would have been unusual but not impossible. His face had lost all colour and was white as a paper cone. What was left was a shell, a heap of rags. The smell of medicaments, powder and herbs was being overtaken by the sweet smell of putrefaction. The old man left Paul nothing, and the building in Købmagergade was due to be pulled down. It was the only home Paul Natal had known in Denmark, so he enlisted. Apart from the old apothecary, he knew no-one in Copenhagen but the soldiers in the bastions, a tough bunch who mostly kept themselves to themselves. He was thirty now, perhaps thirty-three, his thick hair prematurely grizzled. When he left the house he took with him in his sealskin bag the old man's wooden box with a selection of blue, red and white bottles, all clearly marked with small handwritten labels.

The war was a sorry affair. People in Holstein rose against the Danish Crown, and the German Confederation, headed by Prussia, made common cause with the Holstein insurgents. To begin with, the Holsteiners fought in Danish uniforms, which led to confusion and casualties on both sides. Later the Prussians gave them pickelhaube helmets topped with sharp spikes so that friend and foe could finally tell each other apart. It was a war of misunderstandings, incompetent generals and bloody battles: Isted and Bov, Schleswig and Fredericia. Or, to put it another way, it was like most other wars. In 1849 Prussia pulled out, leaving the Holsteiners to fend for themselves. As best they could. And when it all came to an end in 1850, Schleswig, Holstein and Lauenburg still belonged to Denmark. All that had been achieved was a lot of work for the gravediggers. Paul Natal remained in the Crown's service.

*

You're probably wondering how he finished up here. Well, war broke out again fourteen years later. The same dissatisfaction lay at the heart of it, fermenting like a forgotten keg of beer in a cellar. The Duchy of Holstein again wanted to be free of Denmark, and again Schleswig and Lauenburg went along with it. You already know the story? Good. Paul Natal found himself in the thick of the final battle for the Dybbøl redoubts. In its last hours he thought he recognised his father in a Danish naval officer, but the moment passed before he could do anything about it. This brief instant of near-certainty was all he got in return for a lifetime of waiting. A new contingent of troops had been landed during the battle's final chaotic phase, and this officer was among them. The men were blinded by gunpowder smoke drifting to and fro, and the taste of sulphur on their tongues made them want to vomit. Their burning eyes smarted and ran with tears, and some soaked their neckerchiefs and wrapped them round their mouths and noses. The sun was lost to view; all was a grey mist, a ghost land-scape in constant surging motion as Prussian cannonballs bored into the ground, digging out new ditches. The hillside was transformed into a morass of blood, earth and mud. The fat rats had long ago left to take refuge underground, like an exhausted cannon-crew that had been relieved.

The last five hours were Hell. Young boys from Copenhagen wept and cried out for their mothers, though at least half of them were orphanage boys and forgotten sons of whores, but they longed to be back in the louse-ridden paupers' barracks of Nørrebro and Østerport as if these had been Paradise. Only the bullets whistling just above their heads stopped them running away like hares. Instead they lay pressed against mud walls, pissing themselves whenever a cannonball landed anywhere near them – if they survived it. The older men fired back and swigged the King's schnapps like water; when death came for them they were too drunk to notice. Palisades were blown to pieces without warning, showering white splinters and fragments of projectiles over the shattered redoubts. The relentless Prussian salvoes bored their way right into the earthworks. For the Danes it was like looking for safety behind rice-paper walls.

A team of Danish cavalry horses found itself in the Prussian line of fire by accident. The animals rushed here and there in panic, entrails hanging out and eyes staring in all directions with shock and pain. They ran on the stumps of shot-off legs with gaping red wounds in their sides. It was unbelievable that animals could shriek so much. At this shrieking the firing was intensified. The Prussians may have begun aiming at the horses, or at least at the fallen ones rolling down the hillside and the treacherous flashing of buttons and belts. The cannons were heavy and not easy to manoeuvre. Some of the horses stood still, twitching their ears as if paralysed by fear. A moment later they were gone. Then the Prussians began loading their cannons with rusty scrap iron. Only humanity can be so fiendish.

The naval officer was an elderly man with grey hair and features coarser than those of the slender-limbed figurine in Tranquebar. Weariness had made him more rigid than wax. But Paul was still able to recognise him. He passed in the trench less than a metre away, his uniform jacket unbuttoned and covered with mud. Paul remembered that the wax figurine's uniform could be buttoned and unbuttoned too. The man's face was grey so far as Paul could make out. But a common soldier is not permitted to address a superior, so he could not ask.

He survived and came to us in the village. A dark sorcerer with herbs and powders in his box. We were on the point of losing our orchards due to constant attacks by vermin. He was welcome.

THE WATCH

JUP'S FIFTH CIGARETTE lay stinking in the bowl. The kitchen was hazy with smoke, and her story was finished, her voice hoarse with the effort of telling it. She fished out the fag-end and took a last hungry pull, making the end glow just as Kai used to do. *To the last breath.* Several glowing flakes of tobacco zigzagged slowly down towards the table top. Jup seemed not to notice and reduced the remnants of the cigarette to pulp in the home-made clay pot. To me, the pot's edge looked like a string of pearls or budding women's breasts, but maybe that was just my imagination.

"And the pocket-watch was left here," I said.

"Of course," said Jup. "Ib's had a good look at it, and she says it's quite valuable."

Someone had come into the room without me or my watchdog noticing; Terror seemed to have dozed off under the table, no doubt lulled by Coromandel tobacco. Ib was a small pale woman, in every respect the opposite of Jup, slender and hardly taller than myself. Her hair grew round a little pointed face in airy light-grey tufts like clouds chasing across a windy summer sky. I guessed she must be in her fifties, perhaps not far short of sixty. A pair of unflattering if powerful spectacles made it difficult to get a proper look at her features, but I could see that her eyes were pale grey.

"Ib's a clockmaker. She restores old clocks at the other end of the house," said Jup, giving the pale little woman a loving smile. An odd couple. Ib's small white hand proved surprisingly strong and sinewy, but her handshake was as cold as Jup's was warm despite the fact that she was wearing a heavy grey woollen sweater in the warm kitchen, its cuffs turned back for extra warmth. I felt vaguely sympathetic.

Ib seemed unsurprised by our presence and wasted no time on small-talk.

"This watch was made in the early nineteenth century by the London watchmakers Brockbanks & Atkins" she said, her voice as pale and grey as she was. She stopped as if that should have told me everything I needed to know. My sympathy for her faded. Not only cold but a know-all. The dog emerged from under the table and sniffed inquisitively at her small grey woollen slippers. He didn't seem particularly charmed either. Her odour seemed to me a bit acid, like yoghurt perhaps, or a bowl of old-fashioned soured milk left standing too long. The little grey woman drew in her feet. Jup had got up noisily and motioned us to follow her, Ib bearing the wooden box with the watch in it before her like a royal Order.

*

We walked through the long building, past Jup's workshop with its ill-matched clay women and down a corridor panelled with dazzling white matchboards that resembled an airlock leading into Ib's domain. Several framed old photographs hung in the corridor above the boards, but I didn't have time to look closely at them.

I could hear the clocks before I went through the door, a deafening combination of ticking, whirring and metallic clicking in every key and at every speed, as if brass and steel insects were flying round the room and from time to time bumping into the walls. It was a cool, white-washed workshop presumably facing north. A convent cell. A clock glinted on every spare inch of wall-space.

Ib had rushed ahead of us in the corridor and now hurried to her place at the workbench. The lamp was already lit, and in a moment of confusion I wondered whether in fact she'd been sitting there all the time. The dog flatly refused to follow us into the room, squinting his yellow eyes as if asking to be excused. Clocks weren't his thing.

Ib had the pocket-watch open in her hand, seemingly unwilling to waste a moment. She held a magnifying glass over her little prize and let me look through it. On the outside the watch seemed a very modest object with several dents in its case. But inside it was a small miracle. Leaf-thin cogwheels of various sizes, narrow clamps and microscopic screws had all been combined in a universe of their own and screwed down as tightly as the contents of a submarine. Everything gleamed and moved with a precision measured out long ago, a tiny but definite step towards perpetual motion. A clock can make time concrete, or at least can come as near as possible to doing so. An ingenious plaything for human beings, something that can help us comprehend our own ageing. A faint smell of oil, grease and ancient silver floated above the watch. How many owners had this little thing outlived? Three, four generations? Its ticking was as light as the breathing of a child.

"Look there, on the inside of the cover," said Ib, pointing with a fine screwdriver at an inscription. Magnification made the text curve. *Sorrows pass, hope abides*, in writing as ornate as a Rococo scroll. A beautiful thought, if not always true. Under the words an anchor and a dove in flight were precisely etched.

"There's no date on it. Atkins the Younger worked as late as 1880, but I believe this watch to be considerably older than that, from between 1820 and '30. Look, the winding mechanism's at the back. There's no winder, so you need a key. Winders were first fitted in 1842. Amazingly, the original key has survived. I have skeleton keys and materials for every age and size of mechanism, but I didn't need them in this case." Ib pushed aside the magnifying glass. Inside the back of the watch was a finely chiselled little key in its holder. I reached out to touch it, but just at that moment an old wall-clock struck, and its deep heavy note made us all jump. Ib closed her hand over the little watch as if afraid it would fly away. I wondered what sort of time it could be that could only be reached via a back door and a tiny key.

*

In the late afternoon Jup drove us back to the bog. She drove exactly as she walked and talked – at full tilt all the time. She'd switched on the roof searchlight even though it was still daylight and she knew the bog roads like the back of her own hand. When she finally drove onto the sandy parking place and pulled on the handbrake with a snap, Terror shot out of the car like an arrow. He needed to rush round the place several times and piss out his territory before he could recover his balance. Mogensen was already there, dozing in the Chevy while the car radio sang "Lovely as a shooting star" in a shrill falsetto. He hurriedly turned off the radio when he saw Jup.

It was a difficult meeting, as always when two irreconcilable opposites are forced together. I finally managed to catch the dog and coax him onto the back seat again. He responded by glaring persistently and accusingly at me through the window. Meanwhile Jup and Mogensen said hello and made small-talk for a while about cars, the weather and bad roads, and a moment later she was gone, in a suffocating cloud of gravel, dust and oil-smoke. Men weren't Jup's thing.

On the way back to the cottage I thought over what I'd learnt. The village had survived till the 1950s in the persons of three dry-skinned single men each with his own decaying farm. Their names had been Ask, Dag and Puk, and they were not on speaking terms. Some serious offence connected with land ownership had been committed in the 1930s, and in the absence of the mediating qualities of a female memory nothing had been sorted out. Houses and outhouses were falling down round the three old men, a wall here and a roof there, as nature slowly but relentlessly reclaimed what she regarded as her property. Birches and alders shot up through rotting floors and lost roofs. Sharp water-loving grasses formed islands and small bridges and, eventually, a whole soft green mossy floor over what had once been ancient watering-holes for animals. The old men blathered on about the usufruct of the seven parcels of turf in which the large estate had held legal rights since ancient times (Puk had been a day-labourer at Viberød Manor). It was in this precise area that the body had been found in 1938. The old men kept their mutual hostility alive despite the fact that these rights no longer had any economic value whatever. Jup had shown me on a map that the area in question was a small one to the north-west too waterlogged to dry out in springtime, which implied that the soldier must originally have been submerged in a lake or at least buried in a piece of wetland. In the end only Puk was left of the quarrelsome old villagers, and he died in 1957 at an old people's home in Åbenrå to which his daughter had forcibly removed him. The ownership dispute was never settled.

Jup had returned to the village in the late '70s, after meeting Ib at a women's lib camp on the island of Sylt. They'd built their house together, Ib designing it and Jup taking care of heavy work like brick-laying and carpentry. They'd built it on the foundations of Jup's old family home, Jup Farm. Ib too had roots in the area, but her family had lost contact with its past and could no longer remember any details. As they worked to clear away trees and bushes from the site, both women had come across old objects and moving traces of their forebears' work. Paths that suddenly appeared in the grass after rain, flights of steps that no longer led anywhere, cultivated plants that forced their way up through the cleared ground, berry-bearing bushes and other, exotic plants with dark wax-like leaves, species neither Jup nor Ib could name. On warm summer evenings the cleared fields near the newly built house were as fragrant as a herb-garden, their scent so stifling that the two women had to keep their windows closed so as not to feel faint. At night they slept like stones.

The Jup family's apple-trees remained, too old and neglected to produce edible fruit, but little green leaves like mouse-ears would still miraculously burst from their grey branches as if no time had passed at all. Sometimes hard little greyish apples appeared too, incredibly bitter and harsh if you bit into them. It was as if the old trees could hardly remember what an apple looked like but were doing their best all the same.

*

On the way out of Jup's house I had had a closer look at the photographs in the "airlock". There were five. They all showed the battlefield at Dybbøl.

RESEARCHING THE SOURCES III

JENS MADSEN HADN'T slept properly for several nights. Every time he closed his eyes he saw Dr Nagler's rigid face before him, the dead mouth grimacing as if trying to get out some word or other. Perhaps "pyatt" or "piotr". Nagler's tongue moved laboriously in his mouth like a fat snail. It was impossible to understand what he was saying. In the dream Nagler pressed himself against the wall of the well just as he had done in reality, but the figure was somehow on its guard, as if preparing to jump. What Madsen dreaded most of all was that one night the doctor would open his burst eyes and look at him. So far this hadn't happened, but Madsen could feel his imagination bringing him closer and closer to it with every terrifying dream. Was F.A. Nagler by some chance trying to name his murderer? Sometimes Madsen woke with the vague impression that Nagler had indeed said something comprehensible, he just couldn't remember what it was . . .

*

Retrieving the body had taken hours. When Madsen had finally crawled out over the edge of the well, he'd been unable to say a word. It had taken three-quarters of a bottle of cognac in Aronius' drawing room before he could stop shaking. Everything he'd touched had the same revolting smell. Rotten, rancid, undescribable. He washed his hands and upper body in the pastor's wash-room, scouring himself with a hard brush and soapsuds till his red skin smarted, but the stench was still in his nostrils as if it had become part of himself. The smell of mortality. In the end Madsen stuck his head in the washbowl, but he still saw nothing but the doctor's pale moon-face, as inscrutable as a macaroon.

Eventually a sailcloth sack was lowered so the body could be hoisted up as discreetly as possible. (Johansen from *Avisen* was told it was the carcass of a sheep, but he wasn't going to let anyone pull the wool over his eyes and obstinately spent all day roaming about the church-yard. The church caretaker muttered something about scum on two legs.) Ole Jup fetched block, tackle and rope, which he fastened to a tree. To begin with, Tomas Rav directed the operation, and Jup the caretaker provided most of the muscle. But Rav still had to go down the well to tie the rope round the dead man and try to get the sack into place over the body. F.A. Nagler put up with everything without moving an inch. He was frozen fast, and if they wanted to get him up in one piece they were going to have to go very carefully. Jup, Rav and a pale grey Madsen fetched crowbars and spades to attack the frozen earth by the well wall and get it to relax its grip. When the rope tight-ened across the chest of the fat body, air squeezed out with an audible sigh that stank of the marsh and made the men scramble over one another back up to the surface.

By two in the afternoon Nagler was hanging free in the dark well, at a quarter past he was lying covered on a stretcher, and at twenty past Ole Jup locked him into the charnel house, where he joined the feather-light body of Grethe Mayer. Rav climbed down into the well again to make a proper investigation. He shook his head when he came out exhausted in the late afternoon, the lamp on a cord round his neck. He'd found nothing at all. So he said.

The doctor's death was a mystery from the very first. There were no marks on the body apart from those caused by putrefaction and his long stay in the well and of course the damage done by the dog's paws and teeth (the dog had been banned from the confectioner's until further notice, and his wife had gone to stay with her sister, taking the dog with her). The German's neck hadn't been broken, nor had he been strangled or suffocated, though at first his bluish colour was thought to indicate this. Had he frozen to death? Tripped and fallen into the well of his own accord? If so, how to explain the fact that Rav and Mayer had gone with him to the railway station on the last day of August? Rav didn't want to answer questions. For whatever reason, the simple fact was that the garrulous doctor had come back and now lay in the charnel house, dumb as a fish. Grænsebyen buzzed with rumours. The reporter Johansen – who'd caught a glimpse of Nagler's well-polished boots as he scraped over the edge of the well on his way up into the air like a sack of rotten potatoes – had rushed off to the *Avisen* office to write his piece. Soon the national papers would get wind of the story. And the Germans would have to be notified.

*

Next day Jens Madsen lay in bed till evening. The weather had broken and become milder, bringing fog which lay over the landscape damp, cold and almost impenetrable. The fog was lurking outside Madsen's bedroom windows like a grey body that had climbed up and laid itself on the window-ledge. His eyes turned yet again to the hasps to make sure they were properly closed. Despite the fog a wind had got up and was whining and rattling the windows in their frames. The putty was old, and at times the wind seemed to blow right through. He could feel a cold draught on his cheeks and nose and pulled the covers more tightly round himself. His feet were as cold as ice, and he drew them up to his body. He controlled an impulse to look under the bed. To save electricity he made do with the little reading lamp beside him, an island of light that merely intensified the darkness of the room, especially the corners. But Madsen couldn't bring himself to leave the warmth of his bed to turn on the ceiling light. He thought of Nagler out there in the charnel house. He'd barely even spoken to the man. It had been Rav who'd driven the car out to the bog. The walls of the charnel house were stone, but even so it must be warmer there than down the well though they wouldn't be able to keep him there long. Rav had already rung Åbenrå for a forensic specialist, who might arrive as soon as tomorrow if the roads were passable.

Madsen could hear cosy domestic sounds coming from the kitchen. His wife had been solicitous ever since he'd got home, so his terrifying experience in the well had had some advantages after all. The room smelled of sweetness and vanilla from the cakes his wife was baking. He could hear her clattering pans and bowls. But the wonderful smell wasn't quite enough to drive away his memory of the previous day. The last bit of the way up out of the well had been awkward; the swollen body had begun to swing between the walls like a pendulum, and the rope had got so tangled that the coarse sack had become twisted over Nagler's head. The doctor hung in this position with his full weight for a moment before Jup grabbed his legs and pulled him down to the ground. Madsen didn't see it himself but Jup told him later: the twistings of the rope had made Nagler's face come loose, so that the skin had slipped from his skull like a frozen rubber mask. At the thought Madsen threw his arms round his knees and slowly rocked backwards and forwards.

*

He read. The Franklin expedition wasn't the first encounter of the *Erebus* and *Terror* with polar ice. In 1839 James Clark Ross – nephew of the well-known polar researcher Sir John Ross, who had gone in search of the North-West Passage as early as 1818 – had set off for the area of mighty pack ice round the South Pole. What James Ross wanted to find out was whether there was any land mass at the South Pole or whether one passed through a great nothingness there. He sailed aboard *Erebus*, followed by *Terror* under Commander Francis Crozier. They reached Hobart, Tasmania, in 1840 at the beginning of the Antarctic summer. From there the two ships headed south through a sunlit dark-blue sea full of sperm and humpback whales, sealions, seals and other creatures, many so tame that the ships were able to sail right through flocks of them. The whales blew and dived without concern – they seemed to regard the two ships as floating islands or perhaps related species, as crusty with barnacles and other parasites as themselves. When the first great icebergs came drifting towards the ships, gleaming blue like mighty snow-lanterns, flocks of penguins emerged and followed them, playful and inquisitive, swimming from one iceberg to the next, in and out through the openings, corridors and ethereal vaults the waves had carved. Time and again these blue cathedrals of salt water submerged below the surface, forcing the penguins to leap into the sea from their smooth sides. When the sailors mimicked their cries with high-pitched sounds as if imitating women's voices, the penguins answered. Sometimes the sailors thought they heard the names of loved ones left at home on those desolate penguin voices that seemed to come from nowhere and echoed over the waves.

In January 1841 the two ships entered the pack ice in earnest, and several days later the lookout on *Erebus* signalled land, a black tooth of rock sticking up from the sea. Ross and Crozier had boats lowered and landed on a godforsaken, barren and mountainous island, inhabited by nothing but enormous flocks of breeding penguins which rattled their beaks angrily at the sailors. The shore crunched with the bones of dead sea-creatures, including some as thick as ancient royal oaks and still greasy with whale oil. The air was full of the sharp shrieking of birds. Ross had brought a Union Jack rolled tightly on a pole and, watched by penguins with eyes like bright pills, set it on a cairn where other seafarers would easily see it (*Erebus* had a dozen similar flags in her cargo, carefully mothballed in a chest). They named the land Possession Island and declared it British territory. It was the fifth year of Queen Victoria's reign. On the way back to the shore, one of the younger sailors was badly bitten by a frightened female seal, and the unmannerly beast was immediately killed with grappling irons and rifle-butts. After this the men quickly got back into their boats, though not without booty since some had found a nest with speckled eggs in it, the parent birds, unused to humans, being easily frightened off.

*

On January 27 they sighted land again, an island with a high, jagged coastline which Ross in his journal calls High Island. There was a storm of particles whirling through the air which the crews at first took for snow till it soon became clear that the island was dominated by a volcano, and that what was darkening the air and making it difficult to breathe were steam, fire and ash. Landing on the ships' frozen decks, the ash turned everything a silvery grey. It crunched between the men's teeth and under the officers' heels and gave their food a taste of fire. Ross named the volcano Mount Erebus. They tacked close to the sharp pinnacles that formed the coastline of this unfriendly place, and the sailors could smell the rank odour of sulphur and red-hot lava on the wind.

*

James Ross' silver pocket-watch told him that it took the two ships five hours to pass the island what with the currents and variable winds that constantly threatened to throw them off course, either onto the rocks or out into the dangerous pack ice. In 1847 he would give this same reliable watch to Lady Franklin as she worried night and day about what might have happened to her husband. Since it had been on board *Erebus* it might bring good fortune. "You must look on it as a talisman, an amulet that will bring good luck," Ross told her. In 1859, when she heard her husband had died long before and been buried on King William Island, Lady Franklin gave the watch to a sailor on the quayside at Portsmouth immediately after hearing the news from Captain Francis Leopold McClintock on board the steam yacht *Fox*. The sailor stood there and gazed after the vanishing carriage without fully understanding his luck, the metal a cold and meaningless weight in his hand. He in his turn lost it a few years later playing bezique with a dark-skinned Danish soldier in a Nyhavn tavern in Copenhagen. What happened to the watch after that is not known.

*

A cold route to Hell, thought Madsen, closing his magazine. A passage or narrow gap that opened by chance. Was that the way Nagler had died? If so, perhaps it wasn't so surprising that he couldn't say anything about it in Madsen's dreams.

The house had suddenly become still and silent, and Madsen wondered whether his wife might have gone out. The wind had died down, and the window had stopped rattling. All he could hear was the firm ticking of the alarm clock on his bedside table. Tick. Tick. Soon. Seven. The silence worried Madsen. Gingerly he set his feet on the icy floor and put on his dressing-gown over his nightshirt. He was freezing already. After a moment's hesitation he pulled on his wife's woollen stockings too. Then he rolled up his magazine tightly and with that in his hand left the room. The front room was icy, empty and silent. The light from a street-lamp fell on the floor, laying out on the darkness four pale squares like a simple game of patience. He took great care not to tread on them. His wife's dead parents stared wonderingly or perhaps reproachfully at him from their frames over the sideboard. It was impossible to be sure in the dark, but it had been no less impossible when they were alive. A floorboard creaked and he started, as if caught burgling his own home. He gripped the roll of paper more firmly and tiptoed over the cold floorboards towards the safety of the narrow strip of light in the kitchen doorway, moving more quickly as he got nearer just like when he was a boy and on his way to the comfort of his mother's bed, fleeing the bugbear under his own bed in a room full of bony groping fingers. He pushed open the kitchen door a few inches and stopped dead in amazement. His wife, a pale and exhausted Police Chief Rav and the shy wife of the confectioner were sitting there sipping coffee and nibbling cakes. A whole plate of these delicious little things was in front of them on the kitchen table. Two large shabby suitcases were standing by the door, and the confectioner's mongrel, freshly bathed and surly, was sitting under the table. Madsen could clearly see its small yellow eyes under the corner of the tablecloth.

"My love," said Fru Madsen, "so you've woken up again?"

*

I dedicated our final days in the cottage to a thorough study of the *Avisen* material. Mogensen was being sulky and difficult. He seemed to be brooding about something. He'd driven over to Grænsebyen a couple of times, but I'd no idea whether he'd seen Popsie. Now he was spending his time working on the Chevy's engine and gave off a sickening smell of lubricating oil. He was a puzzle, an irritatingly illogical and emotional creature, but at the moment I had other things to think about. The dog's sense of balance seemed somehow to have been disturbed by the drive with Jup, and he now spent most of his time sleeping at my feet, whimpering occasionally as if at some complication in the world of his dreams. He was the best company imaginable.

*

The body in the bog wasn't mentioned much in the newspapers. The first reference I found was a piece clearly written in haste on August 31, 1938. I counted four errors in six lines; the person who signed himself *JuJ* had obviously been in a great hurry. A body of unknown age and origin had been discovered out on Frøslevs Mose. Nothing was known about how it came to be there. "A German archaeologist on holiday in the area is helping police with their enquiries, since it seems likely that the body is extremely old."

A longer article was published on September 2. *JuJ* had been out on the bog and talked to the man who'd found the body. Puk Sørensen didn't know much. He was desperate to get on with his turf-cutting, but the police had cordoned off the area. "'F——in' pain in the -rs-,' said Sørensen, directing a gob of spit into a hole in the marsh." (*JuJ* had obviously enjoyed quoting the man verbatim.) "'They also 'ad a German f——er 'ere, a doctah.'" But the doctor had clearly gone home again, "'wiv his tail between 'is crooked bl—dy legs'." Sørensen hadn't been able to say as much about the body. "'S-dd-n' b-gg-r should be burnt. People wot put 'im there must've 'ad good reason to.'" And he had spat again.

I kept looking. The body in the bog had been taken to the charnel house in the churchyard. Questions began to be asked about Nagler. At the same time the choir was rehearsing for the Christmas concert. There was also speculation about the dead woman who'd disappeared so mysteriously. How could she have gone *straight through* a bolted door? Some said she must have merely seemed dead and have made off as soon as she'd come round; others whispered about earth-goddesses and stories they'd heard as children from parents and grand-parents before crackling winter fires. They said the sores under the woman's feet must have been caused by wandering up from the under-world. The old people had seen this before – but in the old days they'd been careful to bind such wanderers tightly to the underworld to make sure they stayed there . . . beings who otherwise would move between worlds. That's what the old people said. But there were lots of theo-ries. Some even whispered that the woman must have been a product of the pastor's overheated imagination. In any case, ghost stories were old superstitions "sensible people" paid no attention to.

Voices from 1938 jabbered on at each other in the columns of *Avisen*. I turned another page. Pastor Aronius ran a popular monthly column about his garden called "Sunlight over My Birdbath", which was accom-panied by a vignette featuring a spade and rake. Munch, the district medical officer, sawed into the soldier's body as if it had been a stump of juniper and stored bits of his leathery flesh in glass jars. After a while this flesh began to go mouldy, and Aronius' housekeeper buried it in the garden compost heap without telling Munch (but the writer of this anonymous contribution had seen her doing it . . . and headed his contribution "Ungodly!" – no spade or rake with this text). Autumn and its damp gloom sank slowly over Grænsebyen bringing violent storms and overflowing ditches. You could detect no boundary between earth and sky when you looked across the fields; everything was muddy, daubed with the same russet shade of wet earth. Two cows fell into an irrigation channel and drowned. Strange rumours circulated about the neighbouring country to the south. Those who tried to cross the border into Denmark were sent back, some many times. It was said whole lorry-loads of people were being buried or burnt in ovens – talk as crazy as the fairy tales about the earth-goddess. "No sensible modern person can possibly believe such stuff," wrote *JuJ*.

Preparations were made to bury the soldier – "An Unknown Young

Hero who Shed his Blood for his Country". An anonymous poetaster contributed a long poem on the theme, "So Broke a Young and Noble Heart", but I skipped that. There was a picture from the burial, a grainy photograph showing the pastor with a group of village bigwigs headed by the chairman of the South Jutland Antiquarian Association. These gentlemen looked as if they were freezing, but perhaps it was just that the printer's ink seemed to have given them red noses. Some were wearing what looked like medals covered with verdigris and odds and ends of military equipment they must have inherited from dead relatives, both Danish and German. I scrutinised the photo with my magnifying glass. All the inquisitive patriots of Grænsebyen seemed to have got together in a grey and black mass at the top of the picture. Several faces could be distinguished, pale grey roundels like seed pota-toes with potato-eyes as features. The caption told me what I'd already gathered from the picture – "Pastor Aronius lays a wreath for Denmark" – just what he'd said in his letter to Munch. If he wasn't Danish, this must have bewildered the soldier's unredeemed soul. I'd understood from Jup that at one time uniforms had been no more a proof of nationality than language, skin colour, hairstyle or any of the other devices we humans use to distinguish Jack from Joe. I looked at the photo again. There was a dark cur very like Terror in the foreground, but the similarity must have been mere coincidence unless this was some yellow-eyed ancestor of his with an equally thrusting personality. I put down my magnifying glass and concentrated on the picture as a whole. Did being related really unite people? I thought of Kai and was unsure. Common interest – surely that was all that mattered; there had to be some common gain or advantage if people were to keep together. Some reward or bonus. That must be why so many people developed long sulky faces; they were waiting for their bonus to arrive like a shower of gold after a lifetime of constant rain. But perhaps all we can really expect is a sort of retroactive inheritance, qualities that develop year by year like maturing bonds. Small splashing buckets of feeling. Courage, anxiety or meanness. Love, jealousy or indifference. I wouldn't call that a reward. Maybe that's why people take so much trouble to research their ancestry – they want to avoid surprises. I studied Terror's seedy-looking ancestor through the magnifying glass. Mogensen would probably have called me cynical if that had been a word he used, but I didn't know him well enough to know. Two hours later I closed the last volume of newspapers without being much the wiser. I still had no idea what had happened to F.A. Nagler.

THE JOURNEY HOME

THERE WAS STILL one thing to do before we drove back north: to research five different Madsens at five different addresses in Grænsebyen. It's a small place, so I decided to knock on doors. We loaded the car, locked up the cottage and sped off down the gravel track. The Chevy smelled of lubricant and dog and Mogensen's damp cigarette-ends. I breathed cautiously through my nose.

At the two first addresses I drew blanks. The people were "newcomers", families that had moved in only ten or twelve years previously. The third house was a white-tiled bungalow with bay windows fast shut and defended by decorative bars that looked like something designed for a cheap wedding-cake. It was at the far end of a cul-de-sac and contrasted with the wild and desolate bit of heath next to it where a flock of buzzards was circling with a purposefulness that suggested they'd found some carrion. Two swings squeaked shrilly in the cutting wind. Yet another building project nipped in the bud. The dog detached himself from me and sat a little way off on the paved path while I rang at the door. In the car Mogensen picked up a newspaper, wrinkled his brow and set about filling in a football pool.

T. Madsen turned out to be a short, fat, light-skinned man in his thirties. He opened the door just far enough to be able to squeeze himself out. Behind him I could hear shrill cries and random bumps, as if some hyperactive child was working on the furniture in anxious preparation for adult life. Presumably this was the case, for T. Madsen had a hunted look.

"Ye-es?" he said, when for an instant there was a brief hiatus in the youngster's yells.

"Esmé Olsen from the Institute for Historical Studies in Copenhagen. I'm looking for information about a certain Jens Madsen who lived in Grænsebyen in the 1930s." I tried to assume a friendly smile, but at the same time drove my hands deep into my pockets so as to avoid having to shake hands.

"My uncle," said T., pulling the door closed behind him to shut in the awful noise; the youngster had evidently moved on to throwing glass and china. T. Madsen rubbed his short blunt nose. "Jens Madsen was in the police here. What of it? You're actually the second person to come asking about him."

"A research project. I'm in the process of mapping out a little Danish border community during the period 1936 to '46. Your uncle's one of the people I want to research." This was nearly true. I smiled again. A better smile this time.

"Like the other one who came, right?" T. had no strength left for being inquisitive. The youngster produced yet another thunderous bang. "My two-year-old daughter," said T. apologetically. "She doesn't like being left on her own. Coming, Kri!" he shouted through the chink of the door. The youngster answered with another hair-raising shriek. T. Madsen hesitated, then anxiety got the upper hand. "Come in," he said, throwing the door open. Though we both had our doubts, the dog and I crossed the threshold.

Kri was a small robust blonde girl with a high colour and reddish hair. She was producing the hellish racket by hammering on various objects with a wooden ladle, something she did with enormous inventiveness; she'd already made a most impressive deep mark on the coffee table. When we came into the room she was enjoying a brief rest under a blanket-tent in the middle of the floor. Her round, blue, inquisitive eyes stared at us unblinking. She took an immediate interest in the dog, and oddly enough the dog seemed to like her. He trotted past me and sat down next to her on the floor. The two immediately started to communicate with one another in a low, gentle, murmuring language of whimpers and pats that neither T. Madsen nor I could interpret. I've read somewhere that, perhaps surprisingly, the most primitive human speech involves this kind of closeness. The exhausted father seemed relieved to have found a breathing space. The sun looked in through the barred windows, and suddenly the house radiated peace.

"My uncle died in 1975, and there's not a great deal I can say about him. That's what I told the other one too . . . He said he'd put my name in his report . . . when it's printed."

"That's what we like to do. What was his name?" I said. T. Madsen was clearly not without vanity, and that was usually something one could make use of.

"Can't remember . . . dark young man with a pony-tail. Said he was a doctoral student from Copenhagen. Worked for Rosen's historical something . . . hermit? Can that be possible? Gave me a phone number. Think I've got it somewhere." Madsen looked up enquiringly at the ceiling as though forgotten scraps of information and strips of life had been hung up there to dry like old-fashioned loaves. I swallowed my astonishment and took out a notebook.

"How old was your uncle when he died?"

"Jens was born in 1903 . . . so he must've been seventy-two. Quite a bit older than my dad, they were only half-brothers anyway." Madsen made the most of the blessed silence by sinking back into the sofa. He motioned me to sit beside him. It was the sort of sofa that swallows you up in a cushioned embrace, and I had to struggle to keep my balance. My feet didn't reach the floor. It was a moment before I felt secure enough to be able to go on speaking.

"Did he always work as a policeman?"

"Right up to retirement. Never liked to talk about the war years though. Said almost nothing about them. Odd really."

"Nothing at all?"

"Well, hardly anything. Just about his wife, the house they lived in, the sort of things she used to bake. Certain tasty things he still longed for. At the home they gave him vegetarian food, I'm sure about that.

The house has been pulled down now . . . But there was one really strange thing."

"What was that?"

"He wouldn't go near the churchyard. His wife was buried there, but he would never visit her grave. Not once . . . A *really* stubborn old man. He'd never say why either."

"So Fru Madsen died?"

"Much earlier, 1952. Jens never got over it. He really missed her. It was just that business of the grave . . . My dad looked after it instead. Put in plants and watered them and so on . . ."

"In Grænsebyen churchyard?"

"Yes, the older part, south of the church. It's still there. We try to keep an eye on it when we can." He shrugged his shoulders apologetically. "Not easy to find the time, what with the little girl and all . . . Jens himself is buried in the Garden of Remembrance in the new part. I've got some photos of him if you want to see them. One of them certainly dates from the '30s."

*

Kri had disappeared with the dog, to show him round the house or play Scissors Paper Stone with him. He was a dog who always landed on his feet. T. hurried off cheerfully to look out the photographs and Pony-tail's phone number. The silence had given him a new lease of life. I wondered if he'd ask me to take away the child as well as the dog when I left.

The '30s photo was a group taken in a yard, presumably the yard of the old police station. T. pointed out Jens, but I would have recognised him anyway. The same round fair type as his nephew. Beside Madsen stood the lanky figure of Police Chief Rav in a crumpled suit with his felt hat on his head, the brim shadowing his face. He had a serious, purposeful expression and a straight pipe. Gabriel Mayer was sitting on the steps of the veranda, a slim young man with a dark intense face in a well-cut light-coloured suit. Not quite how I imagined him. All three were smiling self-consciously. They were screwing up their eyes in the sun, but there were deep puddles on the gravel as if after heavy rain. The other photos were taken much later, faded yellow snapshots from the '60s which all showed a shrunken old man.

"In his later years he spent most of his time sorting papers," said T., seeing what I was thinking. There was Jens with little T. on his knee in a garden. Roses run wild and an apple-tree in the background.

"That was taken at the old house," said T. "I still remember it."

At the bottom of the pile was the Madsens' wedding photo: two round, gentle people, shyly arm in arm in another age. Someone had pencilled on the back *The 25th of May 1925*.

I asked a few general questions to reassure T. that I was a serious researcher. To avoid feeling obliged, I promised to send him a copy of my report. Eventually Kri and Terror came back into the room looking calm and collected, the dog still with his rat's tail up in the air. Time to say goodbye. Before we left, T. thrust a bit of paper with a hastily scrawled phone number into my hand. Rosen's doctoral students never seemed capable of writing legibly. An eight-digit Copenhagen number. Not one of the Institute's.

*

We drove through the centre of Grænsebyen on our way back to the motorway and stopped at the church; might as well do the job properly while we were about it. Grænsebyen church is a whitewashed structure that dates from several different periods. The tower's late nineteenth century, a tall thin wooden box that looks like nothing so much as the sort of cistern that used to hold water for cooling steam railway engines. The oldest part's the nave, with its narrow mediaeval windows and permanently cold stone walls. Infants who died from a few weeks to a couple of years old are buried nearest to its walls. The grief in the stone inscriptions seems not to have aged by a single day. The marble slabs, thin and brittle as the pages of an old book, give off an odour of damp and moss.

We wandered about a bit before we found the Madsen family grave. It was a simple rectangular stone flanked by tough juniper bushes and a single unpruned rose that no longer flowered. Jens' parents and wife were buried there together with a child not mentioned in the documents, a girl who had died in 1927 only a year old. There was nothing more to see. Perhaps Madsen had kept away from the grave because he couldn't cope with the feelings it raised in him. One can have worse reasons.

The dog and I took a walk round the churchyard, passing an old stone building used as a toolshed which now faced the church carpark. I wondered if this was the old charnel house. Set a little apart and shaded by tall lime-trees was the Bockmeister vault. Its green copper doors had lost their lock but were now welded together. The family had died out, so there was no longer any reason to enter it. Next to it lay the grave of the unknown soldier found in the bog; it announced in stiff narrow '30s lettering *He Gave his Life for Denmark*. The dog had caught sight of something or other and tried to drag me away before I'd had a proper look at the stone, but this time I won our battle of wills. I sat down and picked some birdlime off the stone. The names of members of the local branch of the South Jutland Antiquarian Association had been cut into the porphyry: late partakers in the bitter conflict between German and Dane as though the rumble of cannon over Dybbøl had never entirely died away. Now that every last defining buckle, clasp or button had long since rusted, the soldier had become *what they wanted him to be*. In any case it's much safer to use documents as weapons if you want to wage war. The soldier hadn't been given a name. Gabriel Mayer must have failed to discover his story.

I looked around; the churchyard was entirely deserted. A few graves away, wreaths were still in place on a new burial, a heap of rotting rubbish in garish colours. I took the unruly dog over and eventually chose a slender white flower whose name I didn't know, a hothouse flower, still beautiful even though it had begun to wither. Its scent was heavy and sweet. Lack of water had prevented it flowering properly, and its petals were carefully folded inwards as though hiding a secret. On another grave I found an empty glass jar. I filled it with water and left the white flower on the soldier's grave. I hoped he'd appreciate it.

DYBBØL,
APRIL 23, 1864

T HE THIRD MORNING he wakes with the taste of earth on his tongue.
How can he know what earth tastes like? He takes a quick breath
as if floating with arms outstretched in a calm woodland lake and
about to sink beneath the surface. The water's dark and opaque.
Bottomless? Could that be what his dream looks like? He can't
remember. He gasps for breath and feels he's regaining consciousness. That's how it often is when you wake up. Like being born. He
raises his hand and finds his face covered with sharp stubble and
rough dry skin. He passes his hand carefully over his features as
though they belong to someone else, as though they've been
exchanged while he was asleep. He tries to swallow but only gets a
dry reflex. His tongue feels stiff and sore; he must have slept with
his mouth open. Several seconds pass before he understands where
he is. His brain laboriously assembles the various bits, sorts them
and lays them out on a tray. Light, taste, smell, feeling. Like when
he takes great care to choose a suitable place, put up his work-tent
and set out his drop-leaf table on even ground with basins, tweezers
and fluids; then lifts the tent-cloth and looks out at the surrounding
landscape. Gently curving hills, a darker area of woodland, a light
blue sky, somewhere a stream. He can hear water again just as in
his dream. His mouth feels dry. He hopes to God the van hasn't
been disturbed.

Now he remembers. He's lying in a small room at a farm.
Someone's pouring water somewhere, from one container to another
it seems. His body smells of sour perspiration and ingrained fear.

And there's something else, something bitter: the herbal decoctions the girl rubbed into his chest. His shirt seems glued to his body. Someone's hung his waistcoat and jacket over the back of a chair. His buffalo-skin hat is enthroned on the seat. His trousers are missing, but his boots are leaning against the chair's legs, two black dusty leather servants without their master. Presumably his trousers had to be washed. This damned helplessness. His hand shakes when he holds it in front of his face. The room has only one small window, covered by an animal membrane that makes the light weak and yellowish. Never be any good for photography, this light. The room's in everlasting darkness, in permanent twilight, but these people move about as confidently as if it were the brightest sunshine. Like moles, they know every inch, curve and hollow in the poky little rooms in their simple dwellings with trampled-earth floors and tiny window-openings intended to keep out both heat and cold. The first afternoon he managed to look round a little. Their homes are so obviously their own it makes him feel afraid, a stranger. Yet they don't ill-treat him in any way. He's a guest in the village, free to go on his way as soon as he feels well enough again.

The fever has struck him down like an invasion of foreign troops, marching in as if with fire and brimstone to take possession of his body. But he uses clever stratagems and cunning to fight back. He's very careful about that. His body's still painful, but he's confident he's getting better. Yesterday he *demanded* they should never give him water to drink without boiling it first. Ib, the girl he prefers to talk to, nodded solemnly as though she understood. Now there's a clay mug by his bed, and he raises himself with difficulty on one elbow and tries to reach it. At the third attempt he succeeds. The water still has a sharp metallic undertone and tastes as if it came from a swamp. Is this how some poisons taste? He swallows it anyway, he has no damn choice after all. He's pleased to notice his thoughts are running more freely now. He's quite sure he's getting better and will soon be well enough to stand up. Käsemann has been more than two days and nights in the village now. So the girl Ib has told him. Today he's going to get up, wash, shave and have a good look round. Take his bearings. With this thought he dozes off again.

*

Next time he wakes it's evening and the little square of yellowish light has gone. He's seen that sort of thing through the bars at the Berlin Zoo, the eye of a beast of prey closing. For a moment panic gets the upper hand; he can't breathe in this darkness, it lies over his nose and mouth like a compact and evil-smelling pelt, the skin of an animal he can't see. He forces himself to calm down and thinks of his little flat in K——strasse and of all the things he'll need to do when he gets back. He goes through his two rooms mentally: the living-room with its walnut table and four curved chairs, the little writing alcove where he keeps paper and ink and his steel pens in their rack, his bookcase, and his bedroom with its beautiful green wallpaper and the fine bed he ordered from Paris. The sound of footsteps interrupts his line of thought. Someone's coming, an older woman this time, carrying a hissing tallow candle and a bowl of soup. She waddles slowly across the floor, and her shadow flutters unpredictably along the wall beside her. She feeds him patiently with a spoon, each unhurried movement precise and purposeful. The candlelight falls across her wrinkled face making it look like a painting from long ago, a canvas cracked into a hundred tiny fissures and edges. Afterwards she washes him like a child, working his sour shirt off him and wiping his body with a soft damp rag. Renewing him under her hard-worked hands. When she carried in the pail of warm water she spilled some on the floor, but the earth immediately soaked it up and it has disappeared. He is completely naked but feels no embarrassment, not even when she washes his sex. He can smell her odour, sweet with an undertone of smoke. In that moment he realises that he loves her as much as he loves his mother. She pulls a clean new shirt made of coarse home-woven cloth onto him. When she leaves him he again falls into an uneasy sleep. Like letting go.

*

He dreams he's walking down a path in the Tiergarten. Gravel crunches underfoot, but he's trying to walk carefully so as not to be heard; this is very important, but he doesn't know why. The park is lit by a strange bluish light. Is it night? People are strolling on the lawns; a well-dressed woman entirely in white squats over the silvery grass, pulls up her rustling skirts and empties her bladder right before his eyes. Her thighs are pale in the strange light. Her urine makes a dark pool. She looks him straight in the eye all the time and smiles with her mouth half open, he can see her tongue going in and out over smooth lips like the tongue of a snake. He can hear her breathing, short and fast as though she's been running. Her teeth are white and pointed like those of a dog or fox. Her pubic hair is black and fuzzy. He wants to touch her but is afraid she'll bite his hand. Embarrassed, he looks away; he's never seen anything like it before except perhaps in the army baggage train. The fully loaded rearmost wagons with their cargo of whores and kids. Women there who . . . He's seen them lie down with anyone at all behind a barn or in a ditch, dirty skirts pulled up to the waist, men humping them in a heavy loveless sexual rite with trousers round their ankles and white buttocks bared to wind and weather. The lust of the moment the only expression on empty faces. Pale masks with holes for mouths. He could never stop himself watching; the sight usually disgusted him but at the same time made him feel . . . more alive. Later he did the same thing. But never with a woman of this social class. Everything's topsy-turvy in this dream, high confused with low.

He goes on, his feet moving weightlessly as if in water, and when the path turns a corner he meets a dark-skinned man with a bright timeless face. The stranger comes face to face with him without a word, and his footsteps are inaudible. It's impossible to determine his age. In the dream this torments Käsemann, one more uncertainty, but the stranger just touches his brow lightly and holds out to him a little piece of white cloth on which incomprehensible signs are scribbled; he knows they're important, but he can't read them.

Now the dream takes on aspects of reality, and he suddenly remembers going to a meeting more than a year ago. Is he awake now? He can't be sure. The meeting is held in a shabby lecture hall in Kreuzberg. He's heard that the royal family's interested in the exotic and the occult, in spirits and tales of the fantastic. King Wilhelm himself is said to consult soothsayers to establish the nation's destiny and *the roots of the German people*. Käsemann wants to gain insight into what's new; it's important.

*

The meeting has been set for eight in the evening; he arrives early and is one of the very first to get there. It's a mixed gathering of people who make their way in among the simple wooden chairs in the hall. The place smells of burning coke and sweat and, faintly, cooking. Overcooked cabbage. A smell presumably oozing from people's clothes, from their dirty grey shawls and thick woollen waistcoats. Many are informally dressed in work clothes, as if they've just finished their shifts or are on their way to night-jobs. But there are also some better-class folk like himself in warm overcoats with fur collars. By eight the hall is full. Käsemann looks round curiously. Next to him is a woman in a threadbare coat. She could be any age between twenty and forty – it's impossible to say. Thin yellowish wrists stick out of over-short sleeves, and the joints of her fingers are red and swollen. She constantly licks her thin lips as if she is thirsty. A well-worn plain gold ring slips about on her ring-finger while her rough hands pick at loose threads on her coat like a diligent fisherman working at his nets. Her head is bare, her shining greasy hair drawn back severely from her face, which is as rough and unfinished-looking as the face of a badly made doll. Käsemann pulls his own coat round him and turns up his collar. The hall is raw and damp with an icy draught sweeping along the floor. The coke stove, just behind the platform, is unequal to its task. In any case it offers nothing but feeble embers smouldering behind a warped door, as Käsemann can see.

The evening's lecturer appears. Käsemann has forgotten his name, but he's a small bald man in a black suit, whom Käsemann would have taken anywhere else for a clerk or a bookkeeper. His suit's badly cut and his face pale and washed-out as if he spent all his life in dim rooms facing dusty ledgers filled with endless columns of figures. He moves uncertainly, mounts the speaker's platform carefully and at first doesn't even look over the edge. But when he begins to speak Käsemann is astonished. His voice is dark, powerful, almost guttural. He speaks in a broad south German dialect, and at first the photographer has difficulty following him, though his subject is the original home of the German people, that much is clear. Something about a forgotten empire or kingdom. The man tells his audience how to find their way back to it. His reasoning is very complicated and difficult to follow, but the doll-woman at Käsemann's side breathes faster and listens greedily with her mouth half open. Her face has taken on a little colour, sharp red patches over her cheekbones. She swallows every word greedily. Käsemann realises this is exactly how she looks – hungry.

*

Now without noticing he crosses the border between dream and waking. The first thing he sees is the face of the girl Ib. Pale and grey and slim as a reed. Her long matted hair is nearly white. She smiles at him, showing a row of bad teeth. She can't be more than thirteen. The nose in her little face is like a carelessly shaped lump of clay. Her eyes a clear green, her mouth wide and talkative. She's wearing what looks like a sack made from rough woollen cloth, despite the stifling heat in the room. Her bare feet are indescribably dirty. A little witch, no, a creature of the woods. He tries to sit up, but the girl shakes her head to discourage him. No, she says firmly, he's still too weak. As usual she's brought a clay bowl containing something with a sharp smell, a grey tallow-like paste that will help him get better.

"What's the time?" he asks, and to his astonishment the girl takes out a pocket-watch and holds it up to his face. The Roman numerals seem to flutter backwards and forwards as the light fidgets restlessly over its protective glass cover. It ticks drily. Amazingly, she has understood that it must be wound up. Eight in the evening. He no longer feels sleepy, but the fever has made him as feeble and helpless as a baby. When Ib has finished spreading the paste over his chest and back – it smells nauseating when it comes so near – she sits down full of expectation by his bed. As if from nowhere she conjures up Käsemann's sketchblock, wets her forefinger and turns its pages till she comes to a drawing he made of the landscape round Dybbøl.

"Teach me," she says.

Next day he's strong enough to sit up. He demonstrates the principles of perspective to the girl. She's extraordinarily keen to learn, a wonderful pupil. She in her turn shows the photographer how to extract simple colours from nature: black from a mixture of soot and fat from the pot, red from a scoop of earth laced with copper, oxblood is animal blood but the colour never lasts, cerise is a plant with powerful sap, and an altogether special yellowish colour can be extracted from the fat moth larvae she collects in the orchards. She shows him the contents of her dress pocket, a paste of crushed small creatures that will come in handy.

They sit like this till afternoon. Käsemann enjoys her alert and inventive mind. They use a combination of simple words and sign-language and the mixed German and Danish dialect that is spoken near the border. Ib fills his block with drawings; finally, fascinated by the possibilities of charcoal, she draws a boy or young man with features so individual that Käsemann realises it must be a portrait.

"Your sweetheart?" Käsemann wonders.

"The boy in the bog," says Ib.

Käsemann has no idea what she's talking about.

*

In the late spring afternoon they go for a walk. He's still weak, but the girl's drawing has woken a powerful curiosity in him. They go down a narrow path full of gnarled roots which Käsemann has difficulty not tripping over. Ib never once looks down, so familiar to her is this landscape with its winding path. Under the trees it's damp and dark even though the leaves haven't yet come out. Soon they'll reach the outskirts of the bog, and small clumps of birch and other water-loving trees will take over. A weak green shimmers over the branches. Now he can no longer make out the path; alone he'd never find the way back. Ib trots ahead, slapping a trunk here and a bush there with her strong little hands. The sun's low, but there are still a few hours of day to go. The air's as clear as glass in the spring light.

Soon they have to balance on tussocks, small islands in a swampy quagmire. The ground gasps with water at every step as if breathing. Käsemann sweats and feels giddy but is determined not to give up. They're almost there now, Ib indicates. When he stumbles and nearly falls, she grabs his shirtsleeve.

A little way out on the bog an ancient weathered wooden boat has been moored, a simple floating object hewn from a hollowed log, the old axe-strokes still visible but worn smooth by human fingertips. At this point the bog becomes a sludgy lake. At least that's what it's like in spring, says Ib. In late summer it turns to dry land. There's room for both of them in the boat even though it's so narrow, but Käsemann has to sit absolutely still or they could capsize. Ib smiles happily at him, her hair a white cloud round her head and her face red with effort as she skilfully poles them forward between islands of bog-myrtle and bulrushes while water babbles and clucks against the boat's smooth wooden sides. Now and then they hear the cries of birds they've scared, high shrill screams of warning that make Käsemann start. Eventually Ib makes the boat fast by pushing the pole hard down into the ooze and throwing a loop round it. The boat tugs at the line as if caught in a current, but of course this can't be possible.

"Here," says the girl, drying her hands on her coarse dress. To Käsemann this place looks exactly the same as every other clump or tuft they've passed in the lake, except that one end of a rope is floating on the surface, the rest of it disappearing down into the dark muddy sediment like a water-snake. Ib takes hold of the rope and starts pulling up something heavy as though it were an everyday bucket of water. The rope stretches, she struggles and sweats. A cloud of bubbles bursts through the sluggish mirror of the lake and fumes of putrefaction fill

Käsemann's nostrils. He sits in the boat as if paralysed, his gaze fixed on the surface, a taste of earth or iron on his tongue. Suddenly he feels an incomprehensible fear. His imagination has already told him what he will see at the end of the rope: the body of a young boy with his face and clothes covered in sludge.

"Here he is," says Ib, and at that moment the body floats to the surface.

*

On their way back, with the boy once again firmly anchored in the mud, he asks her again and again how it happened. This time before she let the boy go, Ib fastened a weight to the line, a round piece of greystone from the coast, to prevent the body ever coming to the surface again. The villagers have warned her. They don't always approve of her thirst for knowledge.

"Who was he?" persists Käsemann.

"Just a soldier. The village boys saw it happen. We did him no harm, just buried him in the right place." Ib's little green eyes narrow. His ungratefulness is making her cross. After what she's just shown him . . .

"I've got chalks and water-colours in my van . . ." he says. "I'll give you them if you tell me." The uphill path is taking away his breath.

Ib goes faster. Now they've reached the shadowed wood, and it's so dark that even she herself can't see what she's thinking. No-one else needs to know. Besides, she likes the big man. He teaches her things. She can hear him breathing heavily behind her.

"We can stop here," she says. She takes his hand and draws him into the undergrowth at the side of the path. A narrow path he hasn't previously noticed runs tortuously between the ancient trees like a wormhole. Sometimes it gets so narrow he has to set his feet precisely one before the other to avoid sharp reefs of blackberry on either side. Finally they come to a small round clearing, a little room with thick bushes for walls. The air's quite still and full of the fresh acidic odour of new vegetation. Light filters down through a network of slender branches. In here we're hidden from everything, even from the eye of God, thinks Käsemann.

"My place," says Ib.

*

She plays with small round stones while she speaks. She's brought lots of stones here, and the floor of her hideaway is covered with them. Afterwards Käsemann will always associate her story with the dry rattle of stones. Click, clack, a young soldier comes wandering through the woods, click, clack, or . . . not so much wandering as running, he runs through the undergrowth on the outskirts of the bog, stumbles and falls, gets up again and runs as if the Devil himself is after him. Some village children see him at a distance. He seems to be crying, calling for his mother. A young soldier in a uniform like the brightly coloured tin soldiers the cider-merchant sometimes brings home in his chest. The children can't understand why he's wailing. Soon they see men following him. It's the evening after the great battle at Dybbøl, and the countryside's full of soldiers, wounded or drunk, full of life or schnapps or grief, officers and other ranks. Horses exhausted by the endless cannonades are wandering here and there with white lather on their withers and hind quarters, their eyes still wild with fear, still impossible to catch or even touch. The smell of gunpowder and sulphur still floats in the air, reaching the village as a sharp, slightly rotten odour. The smoke rising from the armies' fires is turning the eastern sky grey.

The men hunting the boy are yelling and laughing, drunk; now and then one or another falls, swears loudly and has to be helped up again by his comrades. Germans or Danes, the village children can't tell the difference. The boy-soldier stumbles for the last time, and his pursuers catch up with him. Five full-grown men, big and powerful. They fell him with a blow to the jaw and turn him over on his stomach on the marshy ground. The children can't tell whether they're angry or happy, their faces are rigid like masks. Then they prepare themselves in a way familiar to experienced soldiers, and one by one each rapes the boy roughly and thoroughly while the others hold him down and egg their companion on, pressing the boy's head into the mud. The only sound is the grunting of the men and the clink of bottles. One moves aside to light his pipe and contemplate the peaceful landscape and the gleaming white moon that has risen in the spring evening and hangs in the vault of heaven like a ripe fruit, and reflects on how fantastic it is, after all that's happened, that he himself is still alive and breathing. He celebrates by taking several deep breaths. As for the boy, he's stopped crying and says nothing. Well hidden in their clump of trees, the children see everything.

When the five men have finished, they button their uniform trousers in silence, glance at one another and look away again. Then, taking a piece of rope from his pocket, one of them bends over the boy, makes a noose with a practised hand and strangles him quickly and silently like a rabbit. Then he too moves away. Clack. That's all.

*

"Afterwards Bue and one of the smaller boys went over to have a look," says Ib, holding up a stone in her short fingers. It's nearly dark now, but something inside the stone attracts what light there is, making it glitter weakly. Käsemann's face is an indistinct pale oval in the dusk.

"He was dead, they saw that at once." She puts the stone down. "They cut some heather and laid it over him to conceal him, then went home and told what they'd seen."

"How did he end up in the bog?"

"We put him there, so he'd find the way down rather than the way up. First we took off his legs so he'd go in mind and not in body. Sometimes they get lost." Ib falls silent as though what she's just said is self-evident. Something every child knows. She picks up another stone, entirely black this time, letting it rest in her dirty palm.

"And the rope?"

"I had to make sure he was still there . . . I only did it twice before. Though Mother says it doesn't work like that." She throws the little stone high in the air and catches it again with total confidence even though she can probably hardly see in the darkness.

"Just a soldier. But his friend knows exactly *who* he is." Her voice has an undertone of defiance. She throws the stone again but this time lets it vanish out into the darkness. Käsemann doesn't hear it fall.

COPENHAGEN,

APRIL 2000

I TURNED THE key and pushed open the outer door. The apartment felt like a place I didn't know; even its smell was unfamiliar – lifeless. It needed my well-trodden routine before it could be itself again. That's often how it is; I have to go round and sit and look at the rooms from various angles to reclaim them, waiting for them to recover their personalities like clothes I haven't worn for a long time. It's something to do with fit . . . I must have accidentally left the hall light on, because the bulb had gone and I had to grope my way to the kitchen. The drains smelt like drains. The kitchen smelt of abandonment and forgotten food. I could sense the spindly silhouette of the Russian tree down in the yard. Still there. It felt comforting.

Peter Mogensen and I had separated at the garage; I'd given him the keys to the Chevy and the garage door. I left him there in the oily gloom to check his new treasures, suddenly forgetting his weariness after the long drive. His red beard seemed to glow. I took the dog home with me. He was suspicious at first and, being unused to the clatter and racket of town, was careful to keep near the walls, but a bowl of food put him in better humour. Now he was sleeping calmly on the carpet in my bedroom.

I'd brought my books and documents home. I still had to put the material together and test the hypotheses properly against one another. I had no intention of writing anything, I never do that, it's enough to *know*. And I had that unknown telephone number to try. Rosen's doctoral student was waiting somewhere in Copenhagen's close-knit and chaotic labyrinth of houses. I unpacked my clothes, Mum's windcheater and several leftover tins of food and, last of all, nailed up the picture of Salinger over my desk. Esmé – named after a short story, not even a character in a proper novel, I never asked Dad about that.

*

What had he had in mind? To what size or dimensions had I been expected to grow? Esmé plays a minor part in Salinger's story, she's a child of about eleven. She never grows older than the story allows . . . In any case, I had no intention of going back to the ramshackle seaside bungalow again. It was getting to be time to close a few doors.

I made myself at home in my bedroom armchair. It has a steel spring missing underneath, so one immediately sinks back into the pose of a thinker. The upholstery smelt musty and homely. The room lay in a pleasant twilight, lit only by the lamp in the window. Above it, Frøken Jessen's prism twisted on its silken cord like a radar device sensitive to body-heat, reflecting an identical glass drop onto the dark window. I wound up the wall-clock and the mechanism ticked out its familiar rhythm, its pendulum a nimble silver tongue behind polished glass. I fetched myself a mug of coffee from the kitchen and began to feel a certain peace, but there was something that didn't fit – the photograph of Salinger disturbed my field of vision like a black blowfly on a white wall. It crept into the corner of my eye even when I looked away. In the end I'd had enough. I pulled it down and shoved it into a desk drawer; I could hear it crumpling as I slammed the drawer shut. It was beginning to be time to throw out some keys. When I went back to my reading-chair I suddenly became aware that my hair was brushing the reading lamp, which is normally a little way above my head. Maybe it was just that my hair had grown, but I had an idea I was on the right track.

Next morning I woke early, about seven, and took the dog for a turn round the block. On the landing I ran into my neighbour who quickly pulled back when she saw Terror. She didn't even pause long enough to ask any questions, though she'd already opened her mouth when the dog trotted over to greet her. She slammed her door making its glass rattle, and her sudden disappearance astonished the poor animal. He still had much to discover about Copenhagen. So much to learn about people who hastily judge dogs by their appearance. An hour later I was ready to try the phone number T. had given me. It rang seven times before anyone answered.

"Mayer." The voice was as thin and brittle as an antique fluted drinking-glass. I should have guessed.

*

Gabriel Mayer has his office in Gothesgade Street, exactly opposite the Botanical Museum. I've often crossed Gothesgade on my way to the gardens. It's an alarmingly busy thoroughfare, and you need winged feet to have any chance of reaching the other side at all. The build-ings date from the late nineteenth century; soot from old porcelain stoves and, more recently, exhaust fumes from cars have laid a dirty grey shell over what used to be light limestone façades, burying them like a sugar landscape inside a dusty Easter egg. I never normally needed to venture further from home than this, a few streets away from Lille Novicegade. Now my time was limited. I had a free day, but that evening I had to be back at work at the Institute. I wondered if Rosen had discovered something was missing. Probably not. He was bound to have assumed that the archival material he'd ordered had been delayed by some antiquated hibernating East European bureau-cracy. I planned to put everything back . . .

Gabriel Mayer spoke very slowly, with long pauses as though labo-riously struggling for breath. From time to time he fell silent. The line seemed to have been invaded by a strange noise, a rustling that rose and fell in the background, the sort of interference one associates with radio transmissions in the small hours over long distances and deso-late and inaccessible landscapes. It was as if the sound of Mayer's voice were rebounding from the tops of waves or perhaps sand-dunes. The silences came when the transmitted sound got stuck in the shadow of some barren massif or perhaps fell to the bottom of a ravine or *wadi*. I tried not to sound impatient. The interference came and went, and at times the line was completely clear. I talked about the report. Did he remember anything about it? I mentioned Nagler's name. Did he know anything about him? About what had happened? Gabriel Mayer merely said I was welcome to come and see him and that I'd find him at the very top of the building, entrance 7B. He was always there until six when a car called for him. It was like talking to history itself.

*

The entrance to 7B is framed with stone roses the size of fists, chiselled in an age when there was time for such things. The oak front door, as thick as your thumb, is adorned with a carved female face with a sullen expression and heavy wooden ringlets. Inside waits an early-twentieth-century cast-iron lift with ornate black wrought-iron gates and a shining brass plate that forbids you to spit on the floor. As I stepped into the lift's cool gloomy interior, I wondered how anyone would possibly want to do such a thing. The interior of the building gave off a weak smell of age, wax floor-polish and coin-operated washing-machines. Gabriel Mayer's name was indeed on the display-board opposite the lift. Under it in smaller letters were the words *Professor Emeritus* and, on the next line, *Cerberus Publishers*. Most of the others tenants in the building seemed to be lawyers, experts on one fine thing or another and consultants. Today's bloodsucking parasites. Hesitating slightly, I stepped into the lift, pulled its screeching wrought-iron corset shut and let the ancient Graham Brothers motor crank me slowly and jerkily up to the top of its shaft. The mechanism stopped with a final parachute-like tug at the sixth floor. I made a mental note to use the stairs on my way down. Mayer's door was ajar, so he must have heard me coming. The only other doorway on the landing had a second iron gate which I assumed must lead to the attic. I knocked lightly on Mayer's door and went in.

If, not knowing his background, I'd expected a conventional office, I'd probably have been astonished. A massive coal-black monster of a

German cupboard dominated the entrance hall and to all intents and purposes occupied the whole floor-space. Close beside this wooden monstrosity stood a little old man. His full head of grey hair was combed back from his brow, and the skin of his face was a shade or two darker than is usual in the Nordic countries. We were about the same height. I would never have recognised him from the old photograph, but now as then he was wearing an elegant, well-cut suit.

"Come in," said Mayer, smiling. His smile was like a little rent in his wrinkled face, and his eyes were friendly and not at all old.

"Esmé Olsen," I said, offering my hand.

"Esmé. An unusual name . . . but beautiful."

It was like shaking hands with a bird's wing.

*

We sat on a sofa in what had once been the apartment's drawing room and was now stacked from floor to ceiling with books and documents. The rich smell of quietly mouldering paper immediately made me feel good. From somewhere came the brittle silver chime of a pendulum-clock. From the old man came a good smell of expensive aftershave. I was suddenly reminded that Rav's hat had smelt of pomade, a strong floral smell like a woman's perfume. This smell had been captured in the carrier bag and was very powerful when I opened it. Rav had looked macho in the picture. His smell hadn't at all been what one might have expected.

Mayer's sofa was of the old-fashioned well-stuffed variety. Its cushions were hard so I was able to lean back with confidence. I'd already said most of what I had to say on the phone so we skipped introductory pleasantries. I just hoped he was old enough to dare to tell the story.

"I know Professor Torkel Rosen very well," said Mayer in his dry tight voice. "In fact he was once one of my doctoral post-graduates . . . decidedly mediocre so far as I can remember, but a capable summariser. He would take the *spirit* of what others said and make it his own – in some respects a good quality in a researcher, in my opinion. Ambitious and envious and rather stupid. And with a good memory. Not a bad combination for university life." Mayer laughed and had to struggle for breath. It took him several minutes to recover. "There's a boy who does a little work for me these days and keeps me in touch. Gossip. He's one of Rosen's doctoral students. Like yourself, I believe?" Mayer's sharp bird-like eyes watched me. I nodded almost imperceptibly. In a way that's what I really was; in any case I did all my research at the Institute. After hours.

"I haven't been back there since I finished . . ." Mayer went on. "To tell the truth, the work that went on at the Institute never interested me. Too many forms to fill in about grants and conferences." He smiled again. Smiling made his face look younger, more alive.

"You asked me about Dr Nagler . . . a strange coincidence since I've taken a new interest in the case in recent years." And Gabriel Mayer started telling his story.

*

"Leaving Berlin meant leaving most of my life behind me. My mother was determined to return to her birthplace in Denmark; she thought things would be better there, but it soon became clear that she'd made a mistake. My father died in uncertain circumstances in the autumn of 1935, and we were left on our own in a small and very narrow-minded community. They weren't openly antisemitic, just very suspicious of all strangers. Paradoxically, it was their nearness to the border that made the people of Grænsebyen so unwelcoming to outsiders. So many bad things had happened there. Well, I expect you know all this . . . Mother fell ill and I became assistant to Pastor Aronius and Tomas Rav, two jobs in two different offices – the church in the mornings and the police station in the afternoons. But I was young, and the work wasn't particularly onerous. It was thanks to Aronius that we had somewhere to live. And it was thanks to my mother's contacts from her youth that I found any work at all.

"I don't really know what happened to F.A. Nagler . . . or rather, I know only what Tomas Rav chose to tell me. He didn't tell it all at once, but in short instalments like the serial films that were so popular in those days – a new instalment once a week. I had to piece it together myself. The fact is, we really did go with Nagler to the train that late August afternoon in 1938. He climbed into the carriage with his luggage and vanished. A stout disagreeable figure in riding breeches and leather military belt, a ridiculous caricature of a German. But I bore him no ill-will. I was indifferent to him. That's what I remember: a thick-necked figure disappearing into the train for Hamburg-Altona. It was a warm afternoon, with thunder in the air yet again. The dusty coaches smelled of hot metal and lubricating grease. You could hardly see through the windows. There was nobody else on the platform; Fårhus is a little station, nothing more than a halt. Rav's Ford was parked not far away on the gravel road. The moment fixed itself in my young memory.

"We didn't wait till the train left, there was no reason to. Nagler wasn't seen again till January 1939, when his body was fished out of the well behind the church. How had he come to end up there? Only Rav knew the answer to that question. Maybe you know he organised an escape route across the border for refugees?"

*

"Late on the evening of August 31, 1938, when Nagler should have been well on his way back to his work in Berlin, there was a knock on Rav's door. Outside stood Nagler with his shirt-collar unbuttoned and his face red with excitement. It must have been past eleven. The dampness of night must already have laid itself like a grey veil over the fields and meadows. Owls and other night-creatures had begun hunting their prey in the darkness. Rav lived in a cottage a little outside the town; Nagler claimed he'd got there by borrowing a car from a member of the Antiquarian Association (later Rav came to know that he'd taken it from outside the station, which turned out to be lucky). Nagler insisted Rav should come back with him to Grænsebyen. There was something about the body they'd found in the bog that he wanted to look at, he said. Something he'd forgotten to check. It wouldn't take long, the police chief would soon be able to get home to his bed. Rav eventually gave in, and the two men set off in the dark. Nagler wasn't sober, according to Rav, and several times narrowly missed steering the car – a heavy green Hubmobile – off the winding road and into the ditch, but finally they reached the church. The night air was cold and damp, and the tall trees shading the churchyard were full of sleeping starlings which rose terrified when the car swung into the gravel parking space. The sound of a hundred fluttering pattering pairs of wings took the two men unawares, and the chilly night air sobered Nagler up. Rav had brought lanterns, and the two men entered the charnel house; Rav had the key. The stillness of the place put them both in a gloomy mood. The German swore and hissed about this and that. Rav, tired and annoyed that he'd had to come along at all, waited outside. The starlings flocked back and once more blended into the shadows of the leaves. Soon the churchyard was totally silent except for the natural rustling and creeping sounds night-creatures always make.

"We shall never know what Nagler was after. Perhaps he thought he'd found new evidence that the body from the bog was indeed ancient, something that would put his name in the prehistory books. He was ambitious and stupid enough for that. Or perhaps he wanted to alter the evidence, to remove and destroy whatever didn't fit into his plans. To rewrite history. Or perhaps he was a hunter who wanted to take his prey home. An anonymous dead body can become whatever you make of it."

*

"In Berlin, F.A. Nagler was notorious for his theory that the Roman Empire had stretched considerably further north than material evidence suggested. He imagined he'd found links between the Graeco-Roman Demeter-Ceres myth and the Nordic myth of Nerthus. He also had extensive theories about the possibility of passing from one world to another. How in the classical myths you find animals or other beings capable of crossing between what we wrongly describe as life and death, like the mischievous squirrel Ratatosk who scampers up and down the grey trunk of the Nordic World Tree Yggdrasil. Nagler called such creatures 'go-betweens'.

"In 1927 he published a paper in which he launched his theory that in the year AD 9 one of Varus' Rhine legions survived the massacre in the forest known to the Romans as *Teutoburgiensis saltus* and fled northwards. Perhaps their descendants were still there . . . Utter rubbish of course, but the idea attracted a certain amount of attention at the time and was not only discussed in certain circles but cited in several established professional journals. The whole thing became a question of legitimate claims to territory. If this theory was accepted, it meant the Romans could be made to serve as precursors for a new Western-German world supremacy. It made the Romans important forerunners. Prototypes. What attracted attention was that Nagler traced contemporary Germans back not to the early Germanic peoples and their wild if hardy chieftain Arminius but to the cultivated Roman Publius Quinctilius Varus. History can be used to serve whatever purpose you like, don't you agree? And it isn't always logical."

*

"Outside the charnel house it was now as black as a coal-sack. Nagler was still rummaging about in the inner room, and no light was escaping from there. It was nearly one in the morning. Waiting outside, Tomas Rav decided to light his pipe. He struck a match and by the fluttering light of its flame saw an extraordinary sight. Scarcely two paces away from him stood a woman. He recognised her at once. She was the ice-wanderer, the woman found dead in an outhouse the previous winter. Her pale oval face seemed suspended in the darkness. She was exactly as he remembered her, with the same white shift-like dress, pale flesh and thick fiery red hair; Rav had time to establish this before the match went out or was perhaps blown out. She also seemed to be smiling at him. He dropped his pipe on the ground, then just stood there in the darkness.

"It's not clear what happened next . . . Rav came to his senses, ran into the charnel house and found Nagler dead. Frightened to death? Apparently nothing else in the room had been disturbed; the oil lamp was still burning with a clear flame, the doctor's instruments lay spread over the bench, and his suitcases stood by the door, but Nagler himself was stretched out in the middle of the earth floor, pale and dead as a landed fish. There wasn't a mark on his body. His blue eyes were wide open, but Rav couldn't stand their relentless stare and closed them.

"What he'd seen made the police chief stop and think. Who was going to believe him if he said Nagler had been carried off at midnight by one of Nerthus' handmaidens? Though this was what he did believe at that moment – after all, he was a native of the district himself. Absolutely no-one else would though. Besides, there were rumours in the village about Rav's providing an escape-route for refugees. That gave him a motive for the murder. In addition the doctor was known to have left earlier in the day. So no-one in Grænsebyen was going to ask after him. The church clock struck one. The police chief left the charnel house, shut the door securely behind himself, crossed the open space and fetched Ole Jup's wheelbarrow from its place against the churchyard wall. His first thought was to hide Nagler in the Bockmeister vault. He fetched Jup's little sledge-hammer and struck off the rusty padlock. The clock struck half-past one as he was working the barrow with its heavy contents over the open space and onto the churchyard's twisting gravel paths. Somewhere in the darkness an owl hooted. The wind rustled among the branches. He'd covered the doctor with a used potato-sack, and all that could be distinguished in the night apart from an irregular grey lump were Nagler's boots sticking out from under the rough cloth. Rav didn't dare keep his lantern lit. Occasionally when the wheel bumped over a tree-root in the darkness, the doctor's body shifted and Rav had to rebalance his load. It had the weight of lead shot, and Rav was sweating despite the night chill. If anyone should see him now . . . At twenty-five to two he reached the vault only to remember that Aronius and the Antiquarian Association opened its copper doors in early September each year to lay a wreath in memory of Justus Bockmeister. There was nowhere to hide a body on the floor inside. And he'd never manage to lift any of the coffin-lids on his own, even if Henriette Honorine Bockmeister's coffin was made of lighter material than the sarcophagi of the rest of the family. The only safe place was the well. So that was where Rav put Nagler."

*

Gabriel Mayer leaned back on the sofa. He seemed to be smiling. Hardly surprising after such a story.

"Didn't you hear anything yourself that night, Professor Mayer?"

"Not a sound. But in those days I used to sleep the deep healing sleep of youth." Laboriously, the old man began to get up. "It's been nice talking to you, my dear. I wish you every success with your researches."

"When did you move to Copenhagen, Professor Mayer?"

The old man sank back into the sofa again with a sigh. My company was beginning to weary him.

"It must have been a few months later, I think January 1939. It's such a long time ago now. I'd promised Pastor Aronius to try and find out the dead soldier's regiment and if possible select a suitable name for him. I had a look at Cohen's standard work from 1865, but found nothing there. Cohen lists all those who fell in both Schleswig wars and has a note of where they were buried. The 1864 war ended in chaos and mass graves. Before the defeat at Dybbøl, men were recruited en masse, including some who normally would never have been accepted as soldiers. But they were good enough to serve as cannon-fodder, as in all wars before and since. I searched the lists at the National Archive for information but found nothing. The boy was unknown or maybe simply too insignificant to be remembered. Not everybody finds a place in the written sources. From what I heard they put no name on the stone, is that right? It was only because he was unknown that he could become a hero. For the rest, I sent my notes to Aronius, and he passed the information on to the Antiquarian Association. Have you found them? A notebook and one or two other things . . .

"Then for various reasons I was able to move to Sweden in 1940. One can say that I exchanged information, that eventually I did find out about the events surrounding my father's death. My knowledge could be exchanged for theirs. I was also able to get a small remnant of my inheritance out of the country. There isn't much more to tell. I spent the war years in Malmö. Things didn't go so well for Tomas Rav. He was seized together with Johansen of *Avisen*, and they were shot by a German firing squad on April 12, 1940, in the churchyard I think."

EREBUS

A FTER THAT THE story is enveloped in silence. That's often how
it is; hunting the past is like venturing out over the trenches
of the bottomless deep, feeling your boat meander over invisible
furrows of current while you cast a net or lead-and-line and in your
innermost self feel confident that you will be able to bring something back to the surface. Something you can still identify. This
must be how Captain McClintock's crew, searching for any trace of
Sir John Franklin, must have felt as their boats slowly neared King
William Island in 1859 – a place that would reveal itself to them as
an island of death. Their steam yacht Fox was anchored somewhere
behind them in the fine falling snow, invisible to their eyes in a
world without sky or horizon as they slowly rowed towards the
pebbled shore through a sea the consistency of inert grey slush.
After Franklin had died, the 129 survivors of his two crews had
struggled on to the island under Crozier's command. They'd
achieved the expedition's declared aim and found the North-West
Passage but one after another had died of privation with no chance
to make their discovery known. Maybe they hadn't even realised
themselves what they'd achieved. All they'd left behind were bones
and buttons, combs and portraits of their sweethearts frozen into
the ice for ever. Now the Fox's boats were nearing the shore; soon
the men would have to jump in and wade through the icy waves,
all that could be heard was . . .

*

From his place on the living-room sofa, Terror yaps in his sleep. Sometimes his stomach rumbles. Beer-sausage in all its forms. He's already made the acquaintance of two waiters at The Blue Grape, and they understand his appetite.

It's five months now since I first read the documents in Rosen's box. Of course I've put them back now, what did you think I'd do? Once I've decided on a particular course of action, I nearly always stick to it. *Vitam impendere vero.* Now butterflies are swarming in the Rosenborg Gardens, crowding lightly with their pale yellow or mottled dark red and black angular wings over the heavy greenery of high summer according to nature's apparently illogical way of organising things. My fieldwork's finished; now it's time for evaluation. I've no plans to write down my thoughts, at least not yet. The other day I tried to find Jup's ceramic workshop and the site of the old village on an extremely detailed map, but oddly enough I couldn't. The map showed marshes, ridges and valleys but no house, either old or new, where I expected to find one. I searched with a magnifying glass under a strong reading-lamp for over an hour but eventually gave up.

During the last few weeks, I've wondered whether to stop my night work and enter the world of knowledge by day instead. To begin to study "properly". Peter Mogensen natters away at me. He came to see me at home the day I came back from the Botanical Gardens. I'd been sitting there for more than an hour looking at the winding sandy paths, lawns and small greenhouses where foreign plants learn to adapt themselves and live a good life in the middle of Copenhagen, while I thought over what Mayer had told me. The sun was really hot that afternoon and the air full of the sweet aromatic scent of budding trees and bushes. It was only the thought of the dog that made me return home to Lille Novicegade. Mogensen and I took him out for a walk together, and that wasn't too bad. You get used to things. Mogensen understands there are times when I'd rather he didn't talk. He's worried about accommodation: the couple whose home he rents and who he looks after "this and that for, yeh" are planning to come back to Copenhagen after several years in Spain. A shipowner and his wife.

When they do come back Mogensen will be homeless. I've told him he can stay with me *for a while* so long as I'm not too aware of his presence.

The same evening I went down to the yard and burned the bundle of letters Kai wrote to J.D. Salinger. In one of The Blue Grape's dustbins. "To Esmé, to do what she likes with." They burned quickly with a clear hot flame as if there was something flammable inside them. I never opened them; they were never intended for me but had been written by my father to someone else. There were also several letters to Lara P. in the pile (and to a dozen other women whose names I didn't recognise). In the late '70s Lara had lived in Århus, evidently in perfect health . . . By then Bitte from the Social Services with her short-clipped hair had already placed me in my second foster-home, with the Jeppsens in Roskilde. Bitte said I'd "seen things children shouldn't see" (they always fall for that kind of crap). Bitte also said that I lacked any "basic social adjustment and needed to be seen and empowered", but that was only because she too was incapable of seeing me. It was something she'd read that sounded good. In fact I was stronger than I'd ever been. I sat down on the stone border in the yard while the fire fizzled out. Seen at close quarters, the larch looked in better shape with clusters of small fine bristles on its dry branches and needles as soft as Mogensen's beard. Perhaps it had been able to sense the coming of spring even in that cramped, narrow place. Bitte was wrong. You can never see inside another person, can you? No-one should ever be allowed to be so presumptuous as to think they can.

*

Gabriel Mayer hadn't been at all what I'd expected. Before I left he showed me a gloomy grey painting of a road and a forest. The colours ranged from a washed-out grey to a shade of sickly pea-green. A mediocre canvas by a naive untrained hand, but someone had bought an expensive broad gilt frame for it. "I've lived with this all my life, but it still feels alien to me," said Mayer. "That's why I keep it. Maybe

I shall see this road when I die and finally discover where it leads."
What could I say to that? Sorrows pass, hope abides.

He was lying about Rav of course. Either the two of them killed the German together, or Rav did it on his own. I only had Mayer's word that there were no wounds on Nagler's body. What is most remarkable is the silence of history, how the little border community closed ranks round what happened like an obstinate fist hiding a scrap of paper. There wasn't a word in *Avisen* about Nagler's fate. I've no idea what happened to the body, whether it was buried with Grethe Constance Mayer or perhaps in the Madsen family grave – which would explain Madsen's reluctance to go there later. Perhaps all those involved simply agreed one evening to keep their mouths shut and rebury the doctor somewhere where no-one would find him. Then a few months later the Germans crossed the border, and people had other things to think about. Perhaps Mayer had informed on Rav to the Germans; it was Rav who'd been in charge of the aborted investigation into his father's death.

Mayer told me that the soldier's body ended up in a little wooden box; by this time eager amateur researchers had probed and investigated the body from the bog so thoroughly that there were only a few bits of it left. Ole Jup had an old box that was considered suitable, a little cedarwood apothecary's casket old enough to have existed in the 1860s. It still had an unusual smell when one opened the lid, bitter but with overtones of citrus and stale seawater. So that's where he lies.

*

I too went looking for a name in the National Archive, the War Archive and the Royal Library. Sat there many afternoons searching registers and winding microfilm: regiments, dates, names – it could have been any or all of them. Kristian or Poul, Moritz, Gad or Frederik. Coins worn smooth in an old purse. Some of the documents were kept in folders marked in pencil F for *fidus*, which meant that some archivist at some time had suspected tricks and falsification. Now even this was part of history.

I did eventually find Paul Natal in a special auxiliary regiment that had been moved to Dybbøl a few months before the battle. A regiment made up of boys and old men, which suffered severe casualties. Their place of burial was given as "mass grave on the battlefield. Danish and German". Perhaps they all marched on from there to the same place, to Erebus, where souls live and are able to exchange all the confidences they can never share in life. A place to come together and make history whole again.

I came out of the paper-dry peace of the reading-rooms to see the old bronze Lion of Isted sitting staring on his plinth, still as haughty and vigilant as when he watched over the graves of the Danish war dead in Flensburg churchyard, before Flensburg was lost to the Prussians after Dybbøl. On the steps below, a boy with fair hair was sitting reading a book. He leaned back against the plinth and closed his eyes. The afternoon sun shone on the Lion's verdigris-green mane and the boy's coarse blue shirt, and gleamed on his book as its pages slowly blew backwards and forwards in a light wind coming from the harbour. A flock of pigeons rose with a sharp clatter and took a wide swing out over the sea. Somewhere a clock struck five. The boy didn't move; perhaps he'd fallen asleep. The sunlight sharpened every detail of the scene.

Søren Kierkegaard Square is an austere area of greystone and steel-bright water, yet as I passed the boy I was aware of a faint sweet scent of flowers.

AFTERWORD

T HIS IS AN invented story constructed from fragments of reality. A priceless collection of photographs of the battlefield at Dybbøl is preserved in The Black Diamond (as Copenhagen's big new Royal Library is called due to its dark glass façade). These pictures were taken a few days after the battle by someone signing himself *K-mann* and were mounted on cardboard by the Imago Studio in Berlin. The photographs, and the able photographer who took them, were awarded an honorary mention by the Comité Nadar in Paris in 1867.

The Royal Library also has a note mentioning a manuscript found among Hans Christian Andersen's papers in a trunk that contained a rope, one of the writer's large black umbrellas, a sketchblock, a morocco album of silhouettes, a pair of sharp pocket-scissors and a sprig of dried heather whose flowers lost their honeyed scent long ago. The manuscript of Hugo von Hoffroder's *Transformations* can be ordered in the reading-room by anyone with an interest in turgid German Romanticism and tales of the supernatural.

It has been said that at the bottom of Andersen's trunk there was once a single sticky cake of East Indian hashish too, but this claim has never been officially confirmed. It's probably nothing but gossip.

Both Schleswig wars (1848–50 and 1864) had complicated preludes with many twists and turns. As Erik Kjersgaard writes in his *History of Denmark*, "The British statesman Lord Palmerston maintained that only three people ever understood the Schleswig question – a German professor who had since gone mad, Queen Victoria's consort, Prince Albert, who was dead, and Palmerston himself, who had forgotten it."

It has not been my ambition to surpass these gentlemen.

The story of Sir John Franklin and his fateful polar expedition of 1845 has been stretched a little here and there to suit my purposes. But in most respects it is accurate.

The three quotes at the beginning of the book are taken, respectively, from *Cassell's Latin Dictionary*, *The New Oxford Dictionary of English* and *Nordisk Familjebok*. The text about Dybbøl is an edited and translated version of the original.